Finding Griffin

Finding Griffin

Barbara Delaney

Cover artwork "Morning Mist" by Elfriede Abbe
Book and cover design by Melissa Mykal Batalin

Printed in the United States of America

The Troy Book Makers • Troy, New York • thetroybookmakers.com

To order additional copies of this title, contact your favorite local bookstore or visit www.tbmbooks.com

ISBN: 978-1-61468-061-1

To Russell Dunn,
my husband, collaborator, and best friend;
whose ongoing encouragement and support
made the words appear on paper.

Acknowledgements

Finding Griffin is the result of the goodwill and generous contributions of many erudite and thoughtful readers including: Thomas Delaney, Russell Dunn, Talaya Delaney, Mike Canavan, Christine Canavan, Persis Granger, and Steve Hoare. Their thoughtful comments about structure, characters, and plot, greatly enhanced the story. And a special thanks to Richard Delaney and Deborah Allen, whose careful final edits ensured there would be an excellent manuscript presented for publication.

The image used on the cover of *Finding Griffin* is thanks to the gracious permission of highly regarded artist, Elfriede Abbe, for use of her lovely print "Morning Mist." The final cover design is the beautiful work of Melissa Batalin at The Troy Book Makers.

I also thank my esteemed reviewer, Persis Granger, for finding in *Finding Griffin* the story I meant to tell.

And finally, I thank my husband and sometimes co-author and editor, Russell Dunn, for his constant unwavering support through thick and thin—even on those darkest, most discouraging days when completing the story seemed a foolhardy mission.

I also thank those unknown, eavesdropped snippets and unbidden memories that inevitably are bound to find their way into a story.

The griffin is a legendary creature usually depicted with the body of a lion combined with the head and wings of an eagle. Griffin is also the name of a lost village in the Adirondacks. It is a family name of some earlier settlers in the Adirondacks.

one

CONNECTING

Time is an elusive friend, she thought. It was not so late in the day, but Anna felt rushed and prickly. The day had started leisurely at mellow sunrise with fresh steamy coffee; now she was bolting the cold, bitter afternoon dregs.

Angling and squinting at the photo, she paused. Yes, it definitely was a water stain. Why hadn't she noted it last night while compiling the folio? Still, the rosy darkening sky behind the monarch butterfly perched on goldenrod was exceptional, a lucky catch. She could remount it. No, no time for that. She had said she'd be at the gallery 7:30 p.m. sharp.

Of course, what she should have done was come straight home after closing her shop, instead of stopping for a *quick* vino with Cara, her friend and colleague. Well, late was not an option. She gingerly fluffed her short blond hair, buttoned her black suede jacket, gathered the folio and closed her front door. Guido had said 7:30 p.m. It was only 7:15 – and she was a fast walker. Time was always measured so precisely – to be early, to be late, or to be 'on time.' To Anna's thinking, 'on time' was best.

When Anna caught her own reflection in the Stewart's convenience store window, she saw a slightly scowling, middle-aged blond. She reflexively arched her brows, picking up her pace.

Nevertheless, once seated across from Guido at his gallery, Anna relaxed, admiring the bright renovated space, its track lighting and clean, bone-colored walls. Perhaps the earthy shade would have bearing on selecting new mounts. Guido had a tinge of old world courtly manner and effusively praised her photos.

"Very, very nice," he nodded, scrolling through his calendar. "I was thinking June for the show. Is that possible?" he said.

"Yes … mid-June? I plan to round out the show with some new shots. I'd like to call the whole thing 'Adirondack Sessions'.

"Yes, yes—I like the title."

They decided to leave the details about the prospective show until later, but shook hands on the June date at the doorway.

Since home was now the only destination, Anna thought to amble through the park. Actually, her brownstone bordered the park; it was directly across on the other side. The tree branches were spare and dark, backlit by the illumined street lights. The occasional benches along the path made spongy, angular shadows. She felt good to be having a show, the first in about twenty years, really. It was appealing to probe at the edges of her period in Italy too. Those had been great times – the best.

The park was very quiet on a chill spring night. Then she heard steps behind her—running. At first she willed them away. Yes, she had once been confronted in this very park, years ago. She'd been knocked down and robbed.

Anna picked-up her pace, her throat tightened. When his hand tapped her shoulder she screamed … and screamed.

"Please, please, wait, stop!" he stammered. "You dropped this." He held one of the mounted photos. She took it; could have explained. Instead, she yelled "Thanks", but he turned with a dismissive wave and ran the other way.

Once back in her kitchen with a cup of tea she tried to sort it out. Tears came to the brim. But, damn it all to hell, she wasn't going to cry. Okay, she had *felt* threatened. Apparently, she had over-reacted—this time. She sat awhile and pondered without reaching any conclusions. Truthfully, at this point, she was more embarrassed than frightened by the park incident. And, after all, it was a good thing that the stranger had found her photo. The ups and downs of the evening left her feeling weary.

Anna brought the blue teapot and cup on a tray upstairs to her bedroom. She checked her phone messages before settling under the poufy, cream coverlet. The message from her son, Jack, asked if she would mind if he dropped Emma with her for spring break while he and Dee went to what sounded like some kind of relationship workshop—whatever that might be. Well, she liked spending time with Em. Tomorrow she'd return Jack's call and say 'yes' to that. Maybe she'd find out what was what with Jack and Dee too.

Readied for bed, Anna took a Kate Atkinson book from her night stand, hoping a half-hour or so of a good read would settle her down.

What a kaleidoscope of a day! It may be awhile before that guy in the park attempts another good deed, she thought, before dozing off.

Good to her word, Anna was pleased to have Emma visit.

The afternoon sky was cool blue with pale yellow sun threading through the spidery branches—April in the Northeast.

"What the heck, Emma, it wouldn't hurt for us to take a trip to see it—and don't give me one of those looks, either."

"Yeah, yeah, when I was your age and so on … Okay, *okay*, I'll go with you tomorrow, Gram."

They were in the process of clearing out the attic of the family home, the Bleeker estate, a brownstone on Washington Park that had been built in the 1870s. True it was a little down at the heels, but these days it might still bring a nice price … once they cleared it out and spruced it up. Besides, sorting through the old stuff in the attic had seemed a perfect task to do with a nearly fourteen–year-old granddaughter on her spring break. However, after two days at it, it appeared *more* than boring. That is, until they found the stained packet of letters, letters written to a possible earlier relative named Theresa and who was nicknamed Tess.

Emma's thick blond eyebrows furrowed as she sat in the dusty shaft of light coming through the arched attic window. The letter she was reading seemed stilted and quaint in its loopy faded script, yet at the same time intensely immediate in its importunity. She could feel her cheeks warm, partially because of the sun on her fair skin.

It was hard to say how old the letter recipient, Tess, was or the letter writer, Luke. But it was clear that Luke lived in a town named Griffin and that Tess had visited the town in the summer of 1872. Apparently, Luke was hoping she would visit again or invite him to visit Albany. Emma and Gram had only read two out of the neatly stacked and tied packet of letters. They agreed that the description of the woods and waterfalls sounded beautiful: … "It is spring, again, and the waters leap over the rocks under the falls to rejoice … Tess, I wish you could see it." Then Luke went on to talk about school in Wells and his hopes of working in the tannery that summer. He mentioned having just seen a cartoon by Thomas Nast in *Harper's Weekly* that depicted an elephant as symbol of the Republican Party, calling it a curious choice.

"So, Gram, how long a drive is it to Griffin?"

"Well, we'll look on a map. But, it must be pretty close to Wells, and that'd be a couple of hours from here, at the most. I'll pack a lunch and we'll start out early. If you'll just help me sort through that old trunk, we'll call it a day."

"Alright," Emma sighed, "I'm kinda tired. Can we bring the letters downstairs?"

"Emma, just focus on this trunk and we'll be done in less than twenty minutes," Anna said, a bit sharply.

Anna always regretted when she lost patience with Emma. After all, the kid probably felt a little left out and lost, being dumped in Albany with her Gram while her parents were at some kind of touchy-feely, improve-your-marriage workshop. Anna was skeptical of that kind of thing in general, and of Dee in particular—whom she considered a bit of a whine-ass. Anyway, a jaunt in the country and maybe a hike in the woods could be just the thing for Emma. Refreshing.

Later that evening as they sat in the library, Anna with a martini in an etched Fostoria sherry glass and Emma with a chai in a blue-and gold-rimmed china cup, they continued to read the letters. The library's warm oak walls and burgundy upholstered furniture reflected in soft light the room's decorous earlier age. It was Anna's favorite room.

"Wow, Gram, did you read the part about the beautiful flowering apple orchards in the spring and the baby lambs?"

"Yeah, well, sounds like old Lukey was quite a catch," said Anna, tilting the glass to catch the last dram. "Tell you what, Em, let's hit the hay so's we can get an early start tomorrow." Anna stood and placed two folded sweaters, one tan and one navy, on a chair by the back door—ready for the morrow.

The morning sky had changed to the color of the outer skin of a hard-boiled yolk—grey with just a hint of yellow underneath. A storm might be lurking ... but still. After a quick coffee, they headed north, Emma with the map acting as navigator. They took comfort in knowing that Griffin, the tiny hamlet they sought, was near Wells, a town that was noted on the map.

About an hour and a half into the trip, they were passing a town called Northville.

"Gram, there's something called Griffin Falls on the map, or here's the town of Wells—which should we go to?"

"I wouldn't mind another cup of coffee, and I'm pretty sure there's a place in Wells. Besides, somebody there might know something about Griffin."

Anna thought, *So far this is going well. Em seems to be enjoying the trip, and the sun is out. This is definitely better than poking around the attic.* Jack had called her late last night to ask if he and Dee could take a few more days—not necessarily a good sign. Anna didn't feel the news was going to put Em any more at ease. Somehow it seemed prudent to broach that news to Em later—best for now to proceed with the daily distractions.

"Gram, there's a place—park here."

Emma was hoping Gram wouldn't take long in the diner or, worse yet, decide to look in store windows. Just for good measure, she kicked a clump of dirt before following Gram through the door of June's Place.

"Sit here, Emma—at the counter. Let's see, one coffee … um, on the light side and … What for you, Em?"

"Coke, please."

The welcome coffee was served in the ubiquitous green glazed mug. It was about 9:30 and most of the customers were those not rushing off to work or wherever. Anna thought the older gentleman in scruffed blue jeans and a red cap looked like a native, someone who might know something about Griffin. She was puzzled when he laughed and said, "Well, I can tell you how to get there … but there's not much to see."

"Thanks again for the map," Anna called back as the door swung shut behind them. Anna was tempted to look about, but sensed Em was getting squirmy. Maybe they'd look around later. There was an interesting-looking antique shop up the street.

On the map it looked like Griffin was about five miles from Wells. Anna and Emma sat in the front seat comparing the hand-drawn map to the gazetteer before Anna turned the ignition. In no time they were on Route 8 heading north.

"Gram, left … turn left on that dirt road!" Emma exclaimed. *Finally,* she thought.

The road was dirt and rutted, winding and steep in places, bordered by heavy brush and tall pines. They came to an old iron bridge that crossed tumbling rapids set in a granite gorge. You could see the top of a waterfall downstream to the left—grey granite, green conifers.

After they crossed the iron bridge, Anna was perplexed. Obviously, even with the trusty Subaru, they couldn't go any farther. A sidelong glance showed Em scowling with a jutting bottom lip. The sky was turning grey, mauve and gold, still overcast, but promising.

"This isn't the place. We must have turned wrong," Emma challenged.

"Well, Em, let's get out and explore. There is a road—just not drivable," she said gently. *It is confusing,* Anna thought. *Clearly we are in the right place—the bridge, the east branch of the river, the waterfalls.* It seemed best to just plunge forward until they found some sign of a town. Though disconsolate, Emma followed her.

"Emma. Here! … Over here! I found something interesting … seems to be an old foundation … and here are pieces of rusty machinery." Emma's curiosity kicked in. Pretty soon they were finding other stone foundations and rusting implements. For a while Emma skipped and jumped through the underbrush with excitement. She saw a pine-needle-covered path by the river and urged Anna to follow her, which she did. Finally, at a smooth rock, Emma plopped down and put her elbows to her knees. When she looked up at Anna, her eyes were moist.

"Where is it Gram?" she sighed. "The apple trees … the swing … the big porch … the corner store. I mean … shouldn't *something* be left?"

"To tell the truth, I would've thought …" Anna's voiced trailed off. "Look, I say we walk a bit further on this path and then head back to that waterfall and have lunch. Deal?"

"Deal," Emma sighed. "Could we ask that guy fishing if he knows anything?"

"What guy?" Anna said, always wary of strange men in the woods. To her dismay, Emma was already sprinting his way.

"I don't mind, they're not bitin' anyway," the man said, presuming Anna was chastening the girl for interrupting him. "Besides, I only live a pace or two from here—fish 'bout every day."

"Wow! Then you must know, I mean, know where Griffin is!"

"Sure do," he said. "I live there."

"So, can we walk there from here?" said Emma.

The man gave a little laugh and said, "Why, it's right here! You're standin' smack in the middle of it." Then, seeing the confusion on their faces, he went on to explain that a little over a hundred years ago Griffin was a town with three hundred or so people in it. But once the tannery and mills closed, people drifted off and the woods took over. "Yep, now it's just me who lives here." After a pause he said, "I've got some pictures; my dad and Uncle James passed 'em on to me. You look like okay people. Wanna see 'em?"

"Sure!" said Em enthusiastically, ignoring Gram glaring daggers at her. "Oh, we wouldn't want to put you out … " said Anna. The sky had turned a worrisome shade of grey.

"The name's Miles … No problem, no problem," he said, gathering up his fishing tackle. "Just follow me."

In spite of Anna being ill at ease and the darkened sky, they walked forward, following the stranger in the green plaid shirt and tan work pants.

Miles explained that he had first come to the Griffin area as a kid to hunt with his dad and uncle. After the Vietnam War he decided to live in a nearby hunting cabin. Anna felt herself relax a bit when she saw it. She was struck by how neat the yard looked. There was a plot for a garden and a picnic table under a tarp shelter. It all had a tidy, if sparse, feel.

"You all set at the table while I get the pictures. Care for a coke or a beer?" he said, apparently to them both.

"Uh, uh—no thanks," they said in unison.

In a jiffy he bounded out, beer in hand, with a folder of pictures. Anna was intrigued, and she could see that Em was positively fascinated. Some of the pictures were faded, but still discernible. There were photos of people, the tannery, some houses, a horse with a carriage full of young people, the river and what looked like a waterwheel and some people sitting by the falls. Miles told them that Griffin had been a boomtown when logging and tanning hides were important North Country industries. The workers lived in company houses on the hill, and there were stores and a hotel where dances were held on weekends. The pictures backed his stories. The stories had been handed down to him and to his father before him. He only knew the name of one of the boys in the pictures, however … and it wasn't Luke.

Later, he walked them to a place where there was a gigantic conifer that he said had probably been there when the town was a "happening" place. When it came time to leave, Anna sincerely thanked him for his time, and he seemed to genuinely appreciate their interest. Em smiled at him and startled him by touching his hardened hand.

Anna and Emma walked the pine-covered mile to the bridge in silence. Anna got the sandwiches and juice from the car, and they headed for a rocky area they'd spotted below the falls.

"Gram, do you think Luke and Tess ever got together? Will we ever find out what happened?"

"Well, it's hard to say," Anna said, skipping a stone on the lucid pool below. Ripples. Clear. "*My* grandmother always said, 'Seek and you shall find'—though what it might be when I found it was never elaborated on."

"I guess … and sometimes it's more fun to skip stones, right, Gram?" said Em, smiling to herself.

"Right." But Anna knew that the puzzle was likely to linger and call again.

There was a light breeze. The weather looked like it was going to hold.

Miles watched Anna and Emma walk the path to the bridge until they vanished in the trees. He hardly ever encountered visitors. They seemed curious and nice. Would this be something he'd tell "Bumble," Dr. Bumby, his counselor at the VA? He walked back to the bench by the cabin and sat, running his fingers through his grey-brown hair. He had mentioned to Mary Lou that he might stop by, but decided he'd had enough conversation for one day. Once more he thumbed through the folder of pale images … always made him think a bit.

Jack and Dee arrived at Anna's late Sunday morning, just in time for the blueberry pancakes that Emma and Anna were mixing.

"Hey, Mom, look what Gram is teaching me! You and Dad are just in time!"

Anna could see the fleeting indecision on Dee's face swept away by Jack's enthusiastic grin.

"Well, can't say as we don't have room for a pancake or two," said Jack, breaking off a corner to dip in maple syrup. "Mmmmm … *molto delizioso*," he said, comically rolling his eyes—much to Emma's delight.

Anna enjoyed watching the father-and-daughter antics. She thought of Jack as a young boy with her and Nick, the years they lived in San Quirico—the sunny, young, healthy years. She could still clearly see them standing by the farmhouse sink washing ripe red tomatoes and dark green peppers for an evening meal.

Anna sighed and then smiled. "It's great you all saved your appetites. Plenty of coffee in the pot, and Em insisted on fresh-squeezing the orange juice too."

"Like in olden times," said Emma, giving Anna a conspiratorial glance.

Anna set out two more of the old cobalt-rimmed white plates and napkins with blue irises. She moved the blue glass vase full of daisies and sprigs of hyacinth to the counter, and dutifully listened to Dee's newest challenges as VP of Arrow Insurance, reminding herself that she was glad they seemed settled in Barnfield; after all, the Berkshires were only a stone's throw from Albany.

"Honey," Dee said to Emma, "did you practice your violin this weekend?"

"Um, a little—and Gram took me to this *way* cool music club on Lark Street last night! They had a fiddler in the band that was really awesome—blues, jazz stuff. I talked to Pete, that's the guy who plays the fiddle, during break."

"Well, sounds like fun," Jack quickly interjected.

They all lingered over a second cup of coffee, and then Jack, Dee, and Emma took their leave.

"Bye, Gram—I'm going to search the Web for some of those names. Oh," she said airily, addressing her parents, "Gram and I are doing a family research project."

Anna waved as they pulled from the curb, and then walked back to the kitchen. Glancing at the sink full of dishes, she picked up the Sunday *Times* and walked to the library.

After a long, satisfying perusal of the news, Anna decided she'd walk over to Bella Fiore, the shop on Wren Street that she and Nick had started years ago. It was closed on Sundays, except for the major flower holidays—Valentine's Day, Easter, and Christmas. She often went there on Sundays under the guise of prepping for Monday. Truth be told, it was a comfort to be surrounded by flowers in the long shadows of a Sunday afternoon. She knew that Cara, store clerk and friend, had probably tidied and dead-headed blooms after Saturday closing.

Tossing on her cream-colored Irish knit sweater and sneaks, she clicked the lock and bounded down the stone steps. Since it was still sunny, if crisp, she determinedly decided on a walk through the park on her way to the shop. Walking usually had the effect of elevating her mood and sorting her thoughts.

Anna skirted the park once, and then decided to walk around the lake. The spring light was shallow and cool, the sky anemic. Yet, thought Anna, the contours of the park showed best in the early months of the year. The park had been designed by Frederick Law Olmsted, the designer of New York City's famous Central Park, and Anna enjoyed the casual yet deliberate design created from Olmsted's nineteenth-century sensibilities. In later spring, when trees and shrubbery bloomed, the romance of it all would appear; now, it was a palette of minimal colors, a sketch.

As she walked, Anna mused about the weekend with Em and reflected on her son Jack—and, of course, on Nick and their early lives together. She liked calling to mind the images of their small Italian vineyard near San Quirico, Nick and she clipping vines or picking grapes, Jack toddling or sitting in the dirt. She sometimes wondered how long they might have lived there if Nick hadn't got sick, or whether they would still be running the flower shop here if he had gotten better. After twenty-five years she was comfortable just looking back at the happy, sunny images. She had learned through the years to wall out the pain and disappointment. All in all, her life was comfortable and pleasant.

As Anna approached the shuttered door of the shop, she was surprised to hear music from within. Clicking open, she saw Cara energetically wiping down the cooler to the beat of "Sergeant Pepper's Lonely Hearts Club Band." The afternoon shadows bouncing to the beat highlighted a vision of an earlier version of Cara Morgenstern, a transplant from Manhattan via Vermont. This afternoon she wore tight jeans and an oversized black cashmere sweater. It was easy to imagine her years past living on a commune outside Burlington with her then-professor husband, teaching piano to local children and matrons.

When Anna and Cara met at a women's studies book group some twenty years ago, Cara was a resolute iconoclast given to flamboyant bursts of antiwar and antimale sentiments. She was equally determined to remember the tragedy of Vietnam and to forget her philandering ex-husband. Over time Anna and Cara had developed a strong bond, somewhat inexplicable given Cara's exuberant risk-taking and Anna's natural reserve.

"Hey!" Anna called, gently tapping Cara's arm.

"Hey yourself!" said Cara, turning and grinning. "Had to close a little early yesterday—came in today 'cause I didn't want us to be too rushed tomorrow morning. Had a bit of a date last night," she said, with a gleeful toss of her reddish mane.

Anna laughed before she even heard the story—and she knew there'd be one. Cara was a good worker and a great friend, infinitely amusing but wise according to her years. Cara liked to refer to herself as a scandalous fifty-five-year-old.

After straightening up shop together, they decided to stop for a quick bite at Justin's, an old neighborhood bar with charm and good food. Anna was in the mood for a glass of wine and some girl talk.

It was pleasantly dim and noisy as they walked the steps down to the basement bar. "Hey Lena!" waved Cara to the bartender. They took a seat in a secluded booth at the back, away from the hubbub. After the waiter had poured two glasses of the mellow 2001 amarone and they had thoughtfully swirled and sipped, they settled in.

"Ummm ... delicious," purred Cara. "This was a little extravagant of us, yes?"

"Well, I surely hope so," laughed Anna "We're supposed to be too old to drink the cheap stuff!"

Cara related her story about her amorous escapade with the thirty-year-old guitar player, while Anna predictably admonished her about health and safety issues. Then Anna began to talk about her weekend with Em and their adventures reading the old letters and searching for Griffin. She described the overgrown woods, the moss-covered ruins and the clear, tumbling mountain stream. She talked of Emma's youthful hopes to find something tangible at Griffin, and her strong but fleeting disappointment before deciding they should forge ahead with family research. She also mentioned the hermit, Miles, and her initial uneasiness with the encounter. She pondered aloud about Em's exuberance and resilience, and wondered aloud about her own attitudes. Was she becoming cautious and rigid?

Cara took a long sip and looked at Anna attentively. "Are you asking or telling me?" she remarked, before brushing aside Anna's attempt to respond and adding, "You know, we all get a tad cautious as we age—or we should," she grinned. "However, you, in my opinion, are accelerating towards fuddy-duddyism. I mean, you're just getting closed in. I'm not saying you don't have a great life, 'cause you do. But, you know, it's … well, *too safe*. And when have you last had a date, for gods sakes?" she gestured expansively with her wine glass. After a pause she added, with mock innocence, "You did ask … "

"Sure, what are friends for—I just hate it when you agree with me!"

They had another glass of wine and talked of sundry things, including Anna's upcoming photo show, then parted at the restaurant door with their usual hugs and air kisses and went their separate ways.

It was a short walk in the cool breezy night to Anna's house on the park. She liked the bite of chill on a late spring evening, causing her to accelerate her pace for warmth. She knew there was more than a gram of truth to Cara's bantering assessment of her current situation, too. But hadn't she endured enough upheaval in her life? Comfortable was good, right? Also she'd forgotten to mention the dropped photo encounter.…

Anna turned the lock and clicked the hall light in unison, seeing her image in the large, gilt-framed mirror. Her grey-blond, windblown bob and rosy cheeks were still attractive, she thought—simultaneously acknowledging that the mirror was old and murky. Nevertheless, she smiled and fluffed her hair. She restlessly walked the ground floor rooms, tidying as she went, lighting the kettle for tea. It was too early for bed, but a little late for beginning a project. She carried the tea tray to the library and lit the stove. Sipping and mulling, her eyes lit on the tidy packet of letters that had set their adventure in motion, she and Em.

Carefully untying the packet, neatly organized by Emma, she started to read wondering, *who were these people? What link might they have to me and Em?* The first letter appeared to have been written in the fall of 1872. It was penned in a neat hand by Luke to Tess. Apparently, General Grant had just been reelected president.

She read, "I was wondering what you thought of General Grant getting reelected, seeing as you were keen on Mr. Greeley ..."

TESS 1872

Tess took quite a bit of teasing when the postman arrived at the door of the family brownstone on the park with a letter postmarked Griffin. Her sister, Isabella—Belle—and her brother, Henry, crowded behind her and pretended to read over her shoulder. They were teasing, but also genuinely curious. Belle, at eighteen, was two years Tess's senior, but often acted more childish, or lighthearted, than Tess. Henry, at fourteen, seemed to specialize in pranks to bedevil them all. Tess thought, *one thing's for sure—they're not going to get my goat this time.* She smiled demurely and tucked the unopened letter deep into her apron pocket, deciding to wait until bedtime before reading the much-anticipated letter, though the suspense was killing her.

"If I was you, Henry, I'd get my algebra finished before dinner time," she said. "Papa will be joining us, and he's sure to quiz you."

Tess and Belle headed to the kitchen. Pa had made it clear that they were to start helping Maggie, the cook, now that Maggie was getting along in years and had a touch of arthritis. In truth, however, they both enjoyed being in the kitchen. Maggie was a fabulous cook—plus she knew all the downtown Albany gossip. Tess and Belle helped Maggie peel potatoes and season the chops. They all sat in the parlor after dinner discussing the day. It seemed forever before she could say her good-nights.

Finally, at last, alone in her bedroom she could read Luke's letter in peace.

Dearest Tess,

I miss the wonderful walks and talks we had in August. As you can imagine, it is pretty quiet around here after harvest, though I did get to Gloversville by way of Northville train last week. They have built a roller skating rink there that cousin Joe and I got to try. By the end of Saturday afternoon we'd got pretty good at it, though you might have laughed to see us taking spills!

I was wondering what you thought of General Grant probably getting reelected, seeing as you are keen on Mr. Greeley. My Pa thinks Grant is doing good work with the Civil Service Commission, as there sure are a lot of crooks in the government.

Some of the fellows out this way are joining a new group called the National Rifle Association. Pa and I are going to a meeting about it in Wells.

I sat by the falls on our favorite rock this morning. It felt cold and lonely.

> Yours Truly,
> Luke

Tess sighed and neatly folded the letter, tucking it back in its envelope. She then carefully put it at the bottom of her linen trunk, supposing that Belle could hardly be bold enough to search there. She thought of how pleasant it had been in Griffin in August, how much fun it had been riding horses to Wells—she and Belle with cousins Helen and Cynthia and, of course, Luke. She thought about the times that she and Luke managed to elude Belle and the cousins ... and the kisses, losing innocence as the summer heat crested. Thank goodness Belle wasn't one for tattling! As for Helen and Cynthia, they would spill the beans to Gram—providing they knew anything—which she was sure they didn't.

Tess put on a flannel nightgown, got into bed and pulled the pink-and-white-patterned quilt up to her ears. She thought about Luke ... and smiled as she drifted off to sleep.

The next morning Mama—also named Isabella—announced that Tess and Belle were going with her to a lecture by Mrs. Stanton and Miss Anthony at the First Reformed Church at the bottom of the hill.

"How exciting!" said Tess, grinning at Belle. "I hope they wear their bloomer outfits!"

Mama smiled. "Well, *you* two are wearing your new flannel suits. We can think what we choose, but it is important to look like ladies. After all, Belle is at an age to be receiving suitors. In fact, Mrs. Cantwell has asked if her son Peter might call next week."

Tess was so excited about the prospect of wearing her new green suit with the black soutache trim that she almost missed the pale furrowed brow of her sister. Clearly Belle was not looking forward to Peter's visit. In fact, her eyes were becoming moist.

"Mama, I don't think I'm ready for that kind of visit," she stammered.

"Well, honey, you just think about it," said Mama, not unkindly, patting Belle's hand.

Though Tess was two years Belle's junior, at this moment she felt very protective of her older sister. Belle loved nothing better than to stay in her studio and paint or draw. This past summer she'd taken to *plein air* painting and gotten praise for her landscapes, too. Tess knew that in her heart of hearts, Belle didn't fancy having a husband and children—not now, anyway. As for her own future, well, Tess was certainly glad to have two more years at the Emma Willard School for Girls in Troy. Actually, she thought, sixteen was probably the perfect age.

First Church was already filling when their carriage pulled up to the curb, although they were at least an hour early for the lecture. As they climbed the stone steps to the open doorway of the church, Tess knew they made an attractive picture—she in her dark green and Belle in a light grey flannel. Mama looked elegant in her aubergine outfit. Belle, with her almost black hair, was beginning to look like Mama, Tess mused, whereas she, with the darkening blond, was more like Papa's family. Maggie had rinsed her hair that morning with a lemon and egg mixture to bring out the blonde highlights, though Mama laughed and said the ingredients might be better used in a pie.

There was an electric air of expectancy in the usually staid house of worship. After too-long introductions by two local ministers, Mrs. Stanton and Miss Anthony took to the lectern. There was a wave of hushed murmurs—they were both wearing bloomers under rather sedate knee-length dresses! Mrs. Stanton had bouncy gold ringlets and spoke with animation. Miss Anthony had pulled back her dark hair into a chignon, in keeping with her serious demeanor. She was the taller and leaner of the two, but they were both attractive in person and manner. Tess was so captivated by the appearance of the women that she missed some of their initial words.

Miss Anthony's talk focused on the evils of drink; she was a Methodist and an ardent supporter of temperance. Tess knew that Mama and Papa drank wine, as did Maggie if she was cooking with it, so she figured this part of the talk might not apply to her family. However, she was mesmerized by Mrs. Stanton's talk on bloomers. Mrs. Stanton contended that bloomers were sensible dress. She said it freed a woman's hands while she was carrying children or bundles up and down stairs. Tess thought this made good sense and made note to discuss it later with Mama.

After the stimulating talk there was a reception held in the downstairs gathering room. Tess and Belle were enjoying the punch and cookies when Mama motioned them to join her. Of all things, she was smiling and talking with Mrs. Stanton!

"Elizabeth, I'd like you to meet my daughters, Tess and Belle," she said, as pleasantries were exchanged.

"Yes," said Elizabeth Stanton to Mama, "I heard your girls were attending our old alma mater, Emma Willard. I would have sent our girls there, if we were not living in New York most of the school season. Tell me, are you enjoying your studies there?"

Tess answered in the affirmative and then blurted, "I think what you said about bloomers being practical made sense." Mama's eyebrows raised a hair.

"Well," said Mrs. Stanton, smoothing any ruffled feathers as she spoke, "I trust you enjoy wearing bloomers during gymnasium activities at school."

Turning from her and Belle, Mrs. Stanton invited Mama to visit her in New York during the winter holidays. Though Mrs. Stanton was older than Mama, it seems her cousin Grace attended Emma Willard when Mama did.

Later that evening, still keyed up by the lectures and meeting Mrs. Stanton, Tess lit the lamp by her bed and started a letter to Luke.

> Dear Luke,
>
> Today was especially exciting. You'd never guess—we heard a lecture by Mrs. Stanton and Miss Anthony! They were well spoken and interesting, though you might have been taken aback by their bloomer outfits.... Belle and I are helping the cook plan Papa's birthday dinner. I'm enjoying studying Botany at school this year.
>
> > Cordially,
> > Tess

There! she thought, quickly sealing the letter, *now I'm tired enough to sleep.*

As she drifted to dreaming, she thought about Mrs. Stanton and Miss Anthony. Probably she and Belle would someday get to vote.

ANNA

Anna refreshed her tea and continued reading the letters from Luke to Tess, once again wishing she knew what responses might have gone from Tess to Luke. Who knows? With some research, they probably could figure out who Tess was at least—that is, if she and Emma really felt up to doing the research. The period that Luke and Tess were writing to each other, the 1870s, must have been very interesting—post–Civil War, suffragists, abolitionists. *Really*, she thought, *a lot of parallels to the 1970s—my own revolutionary heyday.*

Do current governments and the wars in the Middle East only seem worse, because my perspective is up close and my views more informed and wiser with age? At her age she was, after all, post-idealistic.

Thinking again about Luke and the letter she had just read, she supposed that Luke, or his Pa at any rate, were supporters of President Grant. It seemed Tess's family was probably in the Horace Greeley camp—maybe "liberals." And Tess . . . would they ever know more about her?

Anna rose from her chair and stretched, put her mug and teapot in the kitchen sink, then climbed the stairs to her room.

The work week at Bella Fiore was especially busy. Just the mere hint of spring boosted the sales of bouquets. Also, this was the time of year that Anna surveyed yearly costs and made decisions about potential flower outlets, marketing resources and the like. It was another kind of pruning and weeding, she always thought. *Thank God, last year's decision to expand the greenhouses had been a sound investment—or so the tax man said.* She enjoyed being surrounded by colorful flowers in her upscale, tasteful shop, and she turned a tidy profit, too. Having Cara on board was a nice bonus, she thought, listening to Cara's merry, contralto laugh as she, no doubt, made a large sale to the handsome restaurateur out front.

When Anna finally arrived home, the red light on the answering machine was rapidly blinking. She briefly considered ignoring it. After all, it was 8:00 p.m. Friday evening and she had planned on a quick shower before a late dinner with Cara at Ambrosia—the restaurant that would be displaying this morning's lavish floral purchase and graciously hosting them gratis, according to Cara. Then again, you never know which call might be important.

"Hi, Em, you called?" said Anna. "What's up?"

"Hi Gram, I was just wondering if it'd be okay to come visit Sunday and stay over Monday to go to the State Library. Monday is a teacher's conference and the library will be open then. I was thinking, you know, we could do some family research. I already found out some awesome stuff at the Pittsfield genealogy center—about a possible relative named Abigail Bush who could have been in the suffrage movement. Anyway, what do you think? And ... "

"Whoa! Em, give me a second here to catch up. Hmmm ... well, Sunday is fine, of course. Looks like we could do the library after lunch Monday—though I'll have to make sure Cara is willing to cover. Sure—sounds like a plan."

"Great, Gram, I told pop you'd be cool with this—he says he'll drive me over. Um, I said maybe you'd drive me back?"

"Anything for the budding scholar," Anna chuckled. "See you Sunday."

Anna smiled to herself, thinking about Em's enthusiasm as she quickly showered. She hoped that this venture of theirs would yield some interesting information about the mysterious Tess and Luke.

For the moment, however, her task was to find a suitable Friday-evening-at-a-posh-restaurant outfit. Navy sweater and suede skirt with pearls? Lime-green knit dress and black jacket? She sighed and dabbed some mascara and blue shadow, thinking she looked alright. Besides, this was going to be Cara's opportunity to continue the morning's flirtation with the restaurateur. *Let's face it*, she thought, *I'm merely a prop.* And then, less sourly, she decided a spring evening on the town wasn't half bad an idea.

When she returned home, with a bit of a glow on, she felt cheerful and relaxed. Actually, the evening had been fun—and Tony, the restaurateur, had heaped praise on the lush flowers he had purchased that morning. The arrangements were, if she did say so herself, lovely—huge bouquets of white and blue hydrangea, dark purplish-lavender larkspur, and some showy shoots of golden loose-strife. Max, the restaurant's architect, had done a wonderful job of redesigning the space formerly called L' Auberge with deep mustard walls, black lacquered furniture, a few nice paintings, and soft lighting. *Probably it was a good business decision to show for dinner. Really, I sometimes forget to do the obvious,* she thought while brushing her teeth in front of the lavatory mirror. She padded barefoot down the hallway, pulled back the puffy, crocheted comforter and slipped between the creamy satin sheets. Sleep came easily.

Sunday, after a long walk, she arrived back at the house to find Emma and Jack sitting on the stoop sharing the Sunday *Times*.

"Hey there!" she said. "You're a bit early—but very welcome."

"It was just too nice to stay cooped up—so here we are. Dee took an early plane for D. C."

"Well, I say we shouldn't waste a warm April afternoon in a dark old house. Let's take a march around the park. I heard at the garden club that they're trying some new kinds of tulips over by the Moses Statue and some shoots are up."

"Gram, should I bring my camera? If I get something good, I can print it on your computer."

"Sure. We can take our time—sauce and meatballs are in the crock pot," Anna said, smiling at Jack.

In just a week the park had changed from bare limbs to fledgling light green. Wooden sticks and branches were unfurling lime-green buds. Once again it all felt new. No one minded the occasional squishy mud in the pathway.

"Dad, Gram, over here—by the boathouse—ducks! I'm getting some good pictures. After I'm done, I'll get you two on the bench—the one under the crooked tree."

Anna was happy to sit quietly with Jack, just drinking in the sounds and sights of the city on a Sunday afternoon. They decided to circumnavigate the whole park before returning to State Street.

"You know, Emma, this park was built around the same period that those letters were written—the ones you and your grandma are sleuthing."

"Dad, "sleuthing"—I like that word—makes Gram and me not sound so weird and nerdy. And I think you told me once before about Olmsted—like *every time* we come here," she giggled. "You know, I *do* like to think about Tess—that's the girl in the letters—walking in this park. Maybe her foot stepped right here!" she said, stomping in the mud.

Jack looked at Anna and made a mock raised hands gesture as they laughed together.

Anna directed Em to set the table and Jack to make salad, while she journeyed to the basement for a nice wine. *Ummm … yes, a brunello, 2000 vintage*, she thought. When she got to the top of the stairs, she heard the melodic aria from *La Traviata*—her favorite, apparently Jack's selection. Em had rummaged around in the sideboard and found a blue tablecloth imprinted with lemons—one from the old days. Anna had almost forgotten it. It looked lovely, if a bit nostalgic.

The dinner was simple and magnificent: rocket greens, fresh mozzarella and tomatoes drizzled with balsamic vinegar and olive oil for starters; next, capellini with meatballs and sauce, with warm artisan bread; and finally, homemade almond cake and Strega (chai for Em). Afterward they adjourned to the library, its cozy burgundy furniture illuminated by old Tiffany lamps.

"I think you're right, Mom. No sense driving over the mountains tonight. I can call Dee from here—and the *Banner* can live without me until tomorrow morning—late morning."

"So how's the promotion to assistant editor going? I heard on public radio that the *Barrington Banner* was in contention for the Paley Prize—Nice," said Anna, swirling her Strega.

"Well, the job's going great. Basically I'm a reporter at heart. Being top assistant means I can slough off the boring stuff to the newbies and still do features, if I want. It's true we might win the Paley, but our circulation is kind of low. If it wasn't for tourism inflating the numbers, I doubt we'd even be in the running." After a slight pause, he continued, "So, Mom, am I happy yet? You bet! Super daughter, mom, and wife! Great wine, fantastic meal, nice fire in the fireplace (albeit gas)—doesn't get better than this. *Molto bene!*"

Anna found herself laughing at his good-natured enthusiasm—and wondering if the super wife was destined to remain "super." Why did she worry so much about that?

"Will you continue teaching Italian in the fall?" she asked.

"I think so—keeps me from getting rusty."

They stared together into the fireplace, drifting to past or future places, thinking about their earlier lives in Italy.

"Dad, Gram, may I use the computer? Actually, I wanted to show Gram some interesting genealogy websites that Ms. Taylor at the Pittsfield archives showed me. Dad, you can look, too. It is *so* way cool, you won't believe it!"

Em's ebullience hit them like a splash of cold water, lifting them from their reveries. It was hard to remain dozing by the fire when faced by a fourteen-year-old on a mission—and, fair's fair. It *was* a stated mission. So they skipped or trudged, depending on age, to Anna's rather smart, modern study.

This was one room in which Anna eschewed the Eastlake furniture and rampant Victoriana. The oak table, bookcases, and computer station were blonde modern. The lights were burnished steel, matching the elegant flat-screen computer. There was a black leather settee facing a curious Adirondack coffee table, two oak armchairs with black-and-mustard-striped cushions and a tasteful blue-and-gold oriental rug. This was the office, the one room Anna had refurbished before the market had become so uncertain.

"Look here at all the cool sites! … So, we put in Tess and Luke's full names, other family names, roughly when they were born, then check counties and town. Some of it we could do here on the computer, but since our ancestors, the Bleekers and Bushes, are known old Albany families, we might get some clues at the State Library—anyways, that's what Ms. Taylor said. Also, after we find more or get stuck, they'll maybe help us in Pittsfield."

Em spent a good half hour clicking on sites and scrolling to pertinent information. They all agreed it was pretty interesting. Anna, as usual, was very impressed with Em's abilities and was actually looking forward to their library trip.

"Uh oh, Gram—you got mail!"

"Junk, no doubt—though I cleared messages earlier. Scoot over, Em, so I can read. Don't recognize the sender ID … hmm … appears to be from that fellow in the Griffin woods. Seems to be using a friend's PC—somebody named Ned who runs an antique store. They think they have some more interesting Griffin pictures."

"Gram! You clicked it before I finished!"

Anna laughed, "Well, it *is* my mail."

Jack smiled and said teasingly, "I think Gram's blushing. Maybe this guy Miles has designs."

"You should see him, Papa—kinda rumpled and backwoodsy, with an accent—*definitely* not Gram's type—though not bad looking for an old guy. Are we gonna go see the pictures, Gram?"

"Whoa, Em, one step at a time." said Anna.

"And you, missy, are in the midst of the school year—tomorrow's library foray is your special treat. If your mom were around you'd be using the time for homework and violin practice."

"The *library* is a special treat?" Emma pouted, then laughed in spite of herself.

Anna bid them good-night and decided to straighten her desk before retiring. The computer was still on and beckoned for another read of Miles' e-mail.

> Dear Anna,
>
> Hoping that you are the Anna Novelli that I met near Griffin Falls. Just wanted you to know that I located some more interesting pictures of Griffin in the old days. My friend Ned at Owl's Nest Antiques, whose computer I'm using, says he knows the names of some of the people in the pictures. If you are interested, you can leave a message at 862–2410, Ned's store. Perhaps we could meet at June's Place, the diner in Wells. Anyway, I enjoyed the visit with you and Emma.
>
> Yours truly,
> Miles Duffney

Anna reread the note and sighed. It all seemed straightforward and aboveboard—so why the prickle of discomfort? She felt like she was being pulled by a hidden current. What had started as a day's amusement on the East Branch for her and Emma was rapidly getting out of control, she feared. She thought of the beautiful, strong flow of the clear, rocky river … and the whirling eddy below Griffin Falls.

Well, tomorrow is soon enough for a response, she decided. *I can sleep on it.* She shut down the computer and climbed the wooden staircase. As she pulled the silky sheets over her, images of swift, foamy rapids spent in deep clear pools played the part of a dozing dream-saver as she drifted towards sleep.… There was someone on the shore.…

The next morning after quick bowls of Rice Krispies, they waved good-bye to Jack as they headed to Bella Fiore—just to check in before going on to the library. The morning was briskly chilling, the sky overcast grey-blue. Birdsong was competing with traffic noise as they crossed Lark Street. Cara assured them that she could handle the day by herself, so they continued on their way.

They enjoyed researching on the 7th floor of the Cultural Education building, and they found plenty of history about Anna's family, the Bleekers, dating back to the early 1800s. It looked like Colonel Edward Bleeker, a possible relative, may have been the surgeon who attended General Richard Montgomery in Canada during the early battles of the American Revolution, though they agreed that the information was pretty sketchy. Of much greater interest to them was the fact that Abigail Bush, a likely ancestor living in the mid-1800s, had presided over a meeting of suffragists in Rochester in 1848. Apparently, the fiery women's rights meeting in Seneca Falls had been so successful that another meeting was convened in Rochester two weeks later.

They were so engrossed in reading, note-taking and making copies that they lost track of time. Nevertheless, Anna made good on her promise to Em that they'd stop by the Institute of History and Art for a short visit.

The two open, curving, light-grey marbled staircases led to the 3rd-floor galleries. The rose-colored plaster walls in the entrance room lent a rococo feel to a space dedicated to delicate neoclassical sculpture. There was a good collection of nineteenth century landscape paintings in the American gallery, which fit thematically with the day's library browse.

"Gram, here's a nice one. Is Tivoli Falls in Albany? What a super place for a picnic!"

"A reminder of summer days, eh? *Tivoli Falls* by William Hart. Can't say I've heard of a falls by that name ... but, it could have been on one of those streams long since erased by urban development."

It was certainly a pretty scene. Two young couples were seated on a picnic blanket at the foot of a waterfall in a verdant setting. A path to the right of the falls led to the top. As was typical of the time, the couples were somewhat formally attired. Cutoffs and t-shirts were way in the future. With a glance at her watch, Anna hurried them along. They could visit again on another day.

Walking back uphill to the house on State Street, their backpacks were full of paper and their minds crammed with a broad range of information—most of it probably irrelevant to the task at hand. They had found nothing but a possible date of birth for a Theresa Bleeker, 1856, and a sister, Belle, born in 1854. But it was a start.

The wind was picking up as they neared the brownstone. Ghostly eddies of last year's leaves circled in whorls through Washington Park. Jack was due to pick Em up at 4:00 p.m., and it was already nearly 3:00.

"Gosh, Em, I'm not going to get high marks as a grandma for neglecting your lunch," huffed Anna, running up the stone steps and clicking open the door. "We just about have time for a quick cup of tea before your papa arrives."

"No problem, Gram. Teenagers are supposed to have anorexic phases—and I'm a teen," said Em, patting her concave tummy.

Anna gave her the raised eyebrow as she opened the fridge and plunked down cheese, grapes, peanut butter and jam, pouring a tumbler of whole milk in a cobalt-blue glass.

"Gram, *honestly!*" Emma exclaimed. "You *know* I don't drink milk in blue glasses—looks icky!" She stood on her tiptoes, reached for an old clear glass with Donald Duck printed on it and poured in the milk from the blue glass. "So, when are we going back to see that guy Miles with the Griffin pictures?"

"Well, it depends," said Anna, stirring some honey into her blue mug of Constant Comment tea. She paused. "There's your school, my job, the long ride … maybe not much in the way of pictures anyway."

"Gram, you know we've *got* to go there," wheedled Em. "You can write or call Miles to find out, *at least.*"

The door chimed, saving Anna by the bell.

BELLE and TESS 1872

It was a rainy September afternoon, the kind of day that was designed for indoor activities. Tess thought about the benefit a good soaking would have on the young trees as she gazed out the library window at Washington Park. She turned to see Belle smiling mischievously, a sheaf of drawing papers in her arms.

"What have we here?" Tess said, as Belle plopped the drawings on the library table. Belle had completed a fanciful drawing of a woman in bloomers! Tess laughed and complimented Belle on the graceful lines and pretty design of the costume.

"Well, Miss Moody," joked Belle, "I brought down plenty of paper and pencils. You may as well draw as look out the window—probably mooning over Luke."

"Belle Bleeker! I am *not* mooning. Furthermore, I can't draw as well as you."

Belle put on her mock Miss Murty—a teacher at Emma Willard— look. "Girls! Girls! This is not a competition! We all have *taaa*lents." she said, making an exaggeratedly prim face and tapping the library table.

After a few tentative sketches, Tess found her enthusiasm rise. She, too, began to draw unselfconsciously, absorbed in the fun of it. Some of their drawings were of smartly dressed women in elegant outfits;

others featured comical ladies in outlandish garb. They all, however, sported bloomers in common. Belle had just completed an exquisitely drawn design of a wedding outfit with lacy flowing veils decorated with flowers, elegant pointed shoes and below-the-knee-length, poufy, ribbon-tied bloomers!

"Hmmm … I think she's wearing white silk stockings under the bloomers," Belle said.

By this time they were both laughing heartily.

"Maybe Miss Anthony could wear it—that is, if she ever decides to marry," laughed Tess.

"I wonder what," Belle paused for dramatic effect, "Luke might say to this outfit."

"Don't forget, the groom doesn't get to see you as a bride until you walk down the aisle," laughed Tess. "Of course, Mama would see." They both giggled. "Besides, you are probably going to marry before I am."

Belle sighed, "Well, so far there's nobody I'm the tiniest bit interested in. Mama says I should meet Mrs. Ross's grandson, another stuffed-shirt lawyer, I presume. I think you are avoiding the Luke question" she said, tapping Tess with her pencil.

"You know, I do have feelings for Luke. He's smart and I like it when we, um … spoon. But when I hear women like Miss Anthony and Mrs. Stanton, I feel excited in a different way—like I could make a difference, be part of changing the world for the better," she said animatedly, color rising in her cheeks. "Belle, do you know what I mean."

"Not exactly, but I know there are times when I'm outdoors drawing—like this summer in Griffin—when I wished I could be on my own, studying and drawing. I think I'm not immodest to say that cultured people find my paintings pleasing. If I were to marry, I would probably have children and household responsibilities, not have much time to paint," she said tentatively.

Belle clearly did not relish the prospect of meeting potential suitors. Mama, not unkindly, fancied the girls marrying well and had begun arranging social opportunities for them, particularly Belle, the oldest. Marriage was a reasonable option, even for talented and educated women of the period.

Tess rose and walked to the window. She watched a man and woman walking companionably under a large black umbrella. Belle had returned to her drawings, adding deft touches of color to the graceful bloomer costumes. Tess smiled to see how perfect Belle's drawings were.

Maggie knocked lightly before entering the library with a tea tray. A rose-patterned chintz tea cozy covered the everyday blue-delft teapot. There were scones wrapped in matching chintz, blue-delft plates and silver accoutrements.

"Oooo, you little divils," she said, chuckling with amusement as she saw the drawings. "Oh my, *my*! I've niver seen the likes … such good imaginings. "

"Please sit and rest a moment," said Tess. "You can see better if you sit near the lamp," she said kindly.

"The doctor doesn't pay me to be idle," Maggie feebly protested.

"No matter," said Belle. "Remember, we get to peel the vegetables tonight."

They all spent an enjoyable few minutes enjoying the afternoon's fanciful endeavors.

Sunday afternoon found the girls anticipating a social visit. It was another grey, chill autumn day. Though the rain had stopped, wet leaves were plastered to the sidewalks, and the trees in the park cast no shadows. Time was muted, negated without the passing sun.

Belle and Tess were vigorously brushing hair and buttoning garments in preparation for the expected guests. Mrs. Charles Cantwell—Rose—and her son Peter would be paying a visit. Belle was fretful, as this might be preliminary to Peter calling to court her in the future.

"Oh, my hair is just impossible!" Tess said, turning to Belle. "It's this damp weather! I can hardly get a comb through it!" she cried while attempting to untangle her blonde curls.

"Well, that's a problem I don't have," Belle said, carefully arranging pins to hold back her dark locks. "Besides, I strive not to overwhelm with beauty," she said, making a comical face.

The parlor was at the front of the house to the right of the spacious hallway, across from the library. It was the formal room for entertaining visitors, resplendent with a corner white marble fireplace and subtle white and green fern-patterned wallpaper. There were two long windows overlooking the park that were covered with lace curtains overlaid with heavy green velvet drapes to hold the heat in during winter. Most of the furniture was stuffed and covered with green and rose fleur-de-lis pattern upholstery. An elegant green and rose oriental carpet dressed the hardwood floor, and lovely gilt-framed woodland scenes adorned the walls. Isabella was especially proud of the Thomas Cole painting, which she said was bought for a pittance by her father some thirty years ago. She found the room pretty, though staid, so she had cushions in a riot of patterns and color scattered about, as well as pots of tall ferns. A small piano sat along the inside wall. The sofa and chairs usually curved facing the fireplace, but today were faced expectantly towards the piano.

"Oh, gracious, Mother! Surely you don't think one of us will play this afternoon!" exclaimed Belle upon entering the room.

"Now girls, a little music is very cheering on a cloudy day—and a nice break if the conversation lags," she said in her practical voice.

At exactly 3:00 p.m. the doorbell chimed.

"Rose, Peter, how delightful to see you," exclaimed Isabella, ushering them into the parlor where Tess and Belle were seated.

A rosy glow from the fireplace gave off a false cheer to the room of faltering conversationalists. It was the season when gardens had been put to rest and talk of holiday plans premature. Politics, an oasis of conversation for the like-minded, was a likely bog when in the company of someone as apolitical as Rose Cantwell. *Nevertheless*, thought Tess, *mother is a champion at cheerful chatter*. Tess was looking forward to the treats she had seen in the kitchen, which were going to be served with tea. She fervently hoped mother had put aside the idea of a piano performance, but was not surprised when she heard …

"Tess and Belle have been learning a very pretty duet—Mozart piano sonata in C major. Perhaps we could prevail on them. Mind, they are both modest."

"Oh, one of my very favorite pieces!" exclaimed Mrs. Cantwell with genuine enthusiasm.

"I think Mother means we're modest in talent," said Tess *sotto voce* to Belle. She caught a look of amusement at her comment in Peter's deep grey eyes.

Actually, however, Tess and Belle began to warm to the duet once their fingers touched the keys. Belle played the melody, and Tess wove the complex chords around the tune.

It seemed a winning moment for the social occasion until the door, discreetly opened by Maggie wheeling the teacart, was intercepted by Smokey the cat lunging underfoot, perhaps seeing a mouse (though no one made mention of such). Maggie managed to right herself without falling. But horrors! The teacart was rolling on its own toward the fern stand and the front window. Peter nimbly jumped to action. It was a long reach, even for a tall fellow. He stretched and grabbed, stopped the cart—unfortunately landing up to his sleeves in cream puffs. There were maybe five seconds of bewildered silence, then a light ripple of suppressed giggles finally rising to a crescendo of eye-watering laughter. Even dainty Rose Cantwell had to reach for her hankie. Meanwhile, Maggie efficiently returned from the kitchen with a second tray of luscious pastries.

"Mr. Cantwell, may I take your jacket—best to get right on a spot," she said, whisking it away with her. Brother Henry used the incident as an occasion to absent himself to the kitchen with Maggie, first tossing a wicked grin at the sisters.

The mishap and resultant amusement had brightened the stilted atmosphere. They sat back in their chairs and relaxed in the cheery glow. Tess thought the cream puffs were the most delicious she'd ever eaten—and said so, helping herself to seconds.

Peter told Belle and Tess that he very much enjoyed the piece they were playing. His mother, now loosened up a bit, let it be known that Peter had studied the piano for eight years and coaxed him to play for the group. He played effortlessly and very well.

Tess noted the muscles of his back and shoulders, evident once he took off his jacket to play, and his long graceful fingers. He seemed lost in the music, gently swaying as he plied the keys. His playing far outshone theirs. Tess wondered what impression he was making on Belle.

Later that evening as they readied for bedtime, Belle said Peter was nice enough, but seemed unenthused. Tess had hoped they might talk more, but Belle abruptly stood and went to her room, softly bidding good night.

Tess decided to respond to Luke's latest letter before retiring. She thought he would find her account of the day's mishap at afternoon tea with the Cantwells amusing. She also needed to respond to his request to pay a call when he came to Albany on business with his uncle James. She began:

> Dear Luke,
>
> I enjoyed your last letter—especially about your adventure roller skating, which I've never tried. However, Belle and I both enjoy ice skating.
>
> We had a very interesting and funny afternoon.... Imagine how comical ...
>
> As for the political situation, it is true that father would prefer Mr. Greeley run for office. I guess the new organization you speak of, the National Rifle Association, would appeal to persons depending on hunting. Father says he is not familiar with it.
>
> Mother says you are welcome to visit us for tea when you come to Albany on business with your uncle James. Our Grandmother Gifford, in Griffin, speaks highly of Mr. James Girard.
>
> I, too, liked our times sitting by the falls.
>
> > Best Regards,
> > Tess

Tess thought about the day's events and her conversations with Luke that past July. Summer sometimes seemed a distant memory, yet when she put pen to paper it all returned vividly—the splashing falls, the huge pine trees, the gentle breeze and the times picking ripe red strawberries, which Grandma Gifford turned to luscious shortcakes or fragrant jams.

As she drifted off to sleep she dreamed of lying with Luke in the meadow of berries and finding bright red stains on her shirtwaist that she'd have to somehow conceal from Gram. Awaking briefly with a start, she was thankful it was only a dream.

Three days later, an invitation from Peter arrived in the mail. It was addressed to Misses Belle and Theresa Bleeker. They were cordially invited to go horseback riding on the Sunday afternoon two weeks hence. Maybe they'd ride in the country near Tivoli.

Tess wondered what the near and far future held for her. What possibilities?

two

EXPLORING

ANNA

Anna went to her office and opened her e-mail, studiously ignoring yesterday's previously opened mail from Miles, which was already casting a shadow over her shoulder. As she prepared for bed, however, she resolved to take the bull by the horns and respond to the e-mail. *I've always prided myself on good follow-through*, she thought. *Tomorrow . . .*

The next afternoon Anna sat at her computer trying to respond to Miles' e-mail. She had left the flower shop early in hopes of tackling house chores. *Damn!* she thought, *this shouldn't be so hard.* Nevertheless, she once again hit the delete button. In the end, the gist of her note said that she and Emma had enjoyed finding Griffin and were interested in seeing the newly found photos—perhaps some weekend later that spring.

"There!" she said aloud, "one task out of the way." She felt relieved, and started to carry a box of winter clothes toward the attic door when the phone rang. Setting the parcel down, she reached for the receiver.

"Hello, may I speak to Anna?" It was Miles! His voice sounded warm and friendly.

"This is she."

"It's Miles Duffney. I happened to be at Ned's store and saw your e-mail. Thought we might get something on our calendars—that is, if it's convenient. Hope I'm not intruding."

"No, not at all," she said. "Lucky you reached me—I'm usually at work this time of day."

Miles sounded slightly uneasy when he said, "Well, since I don't have a phone or computer, I've come to rely on luck. You know, there's a lot of luck in life. Anyways, you and your granddaughter seemed so interested in Griffin that I hoped you could see these pictures I found." There was a pause as they each consulted calendars.

"Okay," she said later, "I'll check the weekend of the 10th with Emma and send you a note."

Anna sat with the disconnected phone in her hand, wondering why setting up this meeting with a stranger—after all, that was what he was—seemed so natural. For all she knew, he could be pathological. She smiled, however, and thought of the parable that she and Cara often humorously elaborated on, called "It could be a good thing—it could be a bad thing."

Miles, for his part, felt pleased he'd be able to share the long forgotten album, though he noted his hand felt damp as he hung-up the phone.

Jeezus, he had a hard time dealing with strangers—even nice ones, he thought.

Later, Anna called Emma, who was delighted at the prospect of another trip to Griffin. However, she seemed even more excited about some additional information she had found out about Abigail Bush— that she was probably an aunt or cousin of Tess Bleeker.

"Gram, I found this way cool book in the library. It says here that Abigail Bush was the person who led a meeting of suffragists in Rochester two weeks after the famous 1848 meeting in Seneca Falls. That's a pretty interesting fact—and remember how in one of Luke's letters he says something about Tess's Cousin Abigail? I dunno exactly what he said—but I remember thinking it sounded kinda strange. Can you look it up tonight?" Emma was rushing her words in excitement.

"Whoa, Em, slow down a moment. I'm not sure I'll be thumbing through that pack of letters tonight, but I'll find it by Friday—promise. In fact, there'll be copies of all the letters for you when you get here. Bye-bye, honey," she said as they hung up.

The rest of the work week was busy but uneventful. Friday evening she and Cara stopped at Justin's for their usual glass of wine to start the weekend.

"I'm afraid I'll have to make it a short night," she said to Cara. "Em and Jack will be at the house by nine. Em and I are doing another trek to Wells in the morning—to see more old photos. You would not believe how Em has taken to researching family history, and I must admit I'm getting pulled in myself."

"So you're going out in the woods to meet up with that strange hermit? I'll tell ya, even I might hesitate at that! Though I'm all for adventure."

"Oh, it's nothing like you're thinking. We're meeting in Wells at a diner called June's Place—not much chance we'll get abducted from there. Besides, while I'm up that way I thought I'd try to get some photos to finish up the Adirondack series I'm working on. Em likely won't mind. I gave her one of my old Canons—she has a good eye for composition." *There, it all sounded normal and plausible.*

Cara fidgeted with the stem of her glass. "I hope I don't sound like a pesky kid or something—but could I come?"

"Sure, but why? I thought Saturday was date night," Anna teased.

Cara sighed, "Even *I* need a breather. Tony's ex-wife is in town; best I don't seem the whiny, jealous girlfriend—new girlfriend. Stan's watching the shop tomorrow. Also, I really do like jaunting around with you and Em. We haven't done a girls' day in the longest," she grinned.

"Okay—just remember, you're on Novelli time tomorrow. And you should bring a camera or magazine or something—and some bug spray. Could be some black flies out by now. Also, don't come if it's just some silly notion that we're in danger."

They parted ways in front of Justin's. Anna had some mixed feelings about including Cara, but Em always liked Cara and what she called "adult conversation."

The day started in a wavering grey and was crisp for the 10th of May. As they headed north, Anna thought about taking photos. Sometimes the lighting was fine on an overcast day—especially if she were to take any pictures of the West Branch.

Predictably, Em and Cara were talking animatedly. As a former music teacher with still the occasional piano student, Cara was genuinely interested in Em's progress on the violin. Just now, Em was putting on a country western CD that supposedly had an interesting fiddle solo. At least, thank goodness, they had stopped singing that song with the line "I've got high friends in low places."

It seemed that they reached Northville and the Great Sacandaga in no time. The next part of the ride would be especially pretty. The birch leaves were a fresh light green highlighted against the dark, sturdy conifers. The cold, bony look of the woods had passed. There were no borders of ice on the lake shore, and the streams were swollen and rushing. Had the last visit been only four weeks ago? Everything looked and felt so different. *Of course*, she thought, *it is different, because this time I know where we're going.* That is, she knew what Wells and June's Place looked like . . . and she'd met Miles. Yet, there was definitely a quickened sense of expectation.

"Hey, you guys," she said, turning to Emma, "turn down the music and read me your notes about the Bleekers and Giffords—might as well get our thoughts perking before we get there, which is in about ten minutes."

Surprisingly, Em eagerly obliged, saying that Cara should have some background.

"Cara, Gram and I just might be about to discover a hidden love story. It's sorta like this big mystery about a girl who lived in Gram's house, a relative—an aunt or cousin from way back, like 1870!"

Then she rattled off the sketchy details in her notes—sparse but compelling, akin to completing the outer edges of a thousand-piece jigsaw puzzle. Catching a glimpse of Cara in the rearview mirror, Anna had to say that she seemed attentive, or at the very least a really good sport.

"Alright, my worthy sleuths, there's June's Place," Anna said, pulling into the small asphalt parking lot. The day had warmed considerably. Haze lay on the mountains. Briefly checking her mirror, Anna fluffed her hair and swiped on fresh lip gloss, which caused a chain reaction of fluffing and glossing in the car. *We are a peculiar gender*, she thought.

The diner door creaked and slammed, just like last time. At first they didn't see him and stood three abreast scanning the room. Then they heard, "Hey" from the round corner booth. Miles smiled and waved. He was not alone.

"This here's my pal Ned—the fella runs the antique store, Owl's Nest, just up the street."

After introductions they sat on the red vinyl banquette around the chipped, round, grey, Formica table. Miles sat in the middle with a worn photo album on the table in front of him. Anna sat to his right, next to Em. Cara sat to Miles' left with Ned next to her at the other end—all a bit too cozy for Anna's taste. Anna could see that Cara was quite delighted to be the proverbial "rose." Personally, Anna was not drawn to Ned's dark intensity.

They all ordered raspberry crumb muffins and coffee, and a milk for Em. The waitress, buxom and cheery, was definitely giving the two older gals the once-over. Anna could imagine the buzz after they left … and probably before they arrived. The cook, presumably "June," was craning her neck around the kitchen door.

Surprisingly, it didn't take them long to settle into comfortable conversation.

"Yeah, we were both in Nam," said Ned, "though we didn't meet up 'til we moved here. Me, I was originally from Brooklyn. My folks ran a used furniture store/antique shop. Summers we'd bring up a pickup truck to the Warrensburg village garage sale—buy piles of junk and haul it back to the city. Pop had an eye for the good stuff, and I liked to tag along and learn what I could. I always liked it up north and later decided to settle here. Exceptin' for the war, Miles' always been here—right?"

"Right."

"So, does your family like it here?" said Cara unabashedly.

"No such—another story another day," laughed Ned, throwing Cara a flirting glance.

Anna was doing a mental version of rolling her eyes. She never found heavy gold jewelry attractive on a man. Em was jiggling one foot under the table. Miles fingered the worn leather album in front of him and cleared his throat.

"This here's the pictures I was mentioning," said Miles, addressing Emma. "There's an old house up on Route 10, which I sorta caretake. I say 'sorta', because it's pretty ramshackle. Use ta belong to the Girard's, but seems like none of them's real interested—heard they live out Buffalo way. I remember some of them from when I was a kid—before my papa passed. But it's the historical group that's interested in it, because it's the only building standing from the old town of Griffin. They're trying to buy it. Meanwhile, I keep my eye on it. A few years ago it was slightly vandalized. Nuthin' serious—maybe hunters. Luckily, it's off the beaten path. So, after Emma and Anna here came to visit Griffin (He smiled at Em)—I thought I'd take a quick look-see. That's when I found this book in a box of old junk tucked in a kitchen cupboard." Miles patted the cover, looking satisfied with himself.

Emma, who had been straining to remain quiet while the adult was speaking, couldn't hold back any more.

"Girard!" she burst out. "Girard was a name mentioned in the old letters! Remember when we saw you by the river fishing and I told you about how we found letters in Gram's attic? You know, ones from a boy named Luke to a girl named Tess? Well, in one of the letters he talks about going to Albany with his uncle, *Mr. James Girard!* This is so totally amazing!"

Miles sat up and beamed, then furrowed his brows a bit. "Ya know, Em, could be somethin' of interest here, but maybe not. Just so's we don't get our hopes too high up."

Clearly this was Emma's moment, so it seemed only right that she switch places to sit next to Miles. In changing seats, Miles' right thigh brushed hard against Anna. The jolt of sexual electricity was sharp enough to cause an involuntary intake of her breath. Safely seated now with Em as a wedge between, she thought, *how unexpected!* Once again the subterranean currents of sexuality were running on separate circuits that had no connection to the wires that carried her thoughts and intentions. Or did they?

The activity of turning the album pages was riveting for Em, if not for all. The pictures of Griffin were very old and the details in some had lightened to the point of being elusive. The inked names in loopy script were also a challenge. Miles had listed in a separate notebook all of the titles and names he could decipher. There were Giffords, Clarkes and Carsons, and other names they couldn't quite make out. There were scenes of the tanneries, the hotel, the schoolhouse with pupils lined in front, formal family poses and some tintypes. Was there a palimpsest of meaning here? Obviously, Miles had put some effort in cataloguing the lot.

"Did you find anyone named Luke?" asked Em, squinting intently at the photos.

"No, but there is a fella in the school picture labeled 'L. Girard.'"

"Wow! It could be him. Hmmm … wish it were a clearer picture. It's kinda whited-out. Still, he looks nice, maybe handsome." Emma glanced at Miles and took a deep breath. "Thanks, Miles, this is really super. Gram, isn't there a way to fix old photos?"

"Sometimes, honey—but these aren't ours to fiddle with."

"Tell you what, Em," interjected Miles, "you can bring these back to Albany, entrusted to your Gram—though I'd appreciate them back in a few weeks. What d'ya say, Anna? Sound okay to you?"

"Hmmm … well, I could make some decent copies—maybe take them to Shutter Speed—good photo restorers. But I don't want to cause you any worry, with them being in your care and all."

Ned mentioned that he, too, knew some antique photo restorers, if Anna's source didn't pan out. His hirsute but manicured hand briefly reached across to rub Emma's hand. Though Em quickly flicked her arm away, she did not seem distressed. Anna, however, felt uneasy. She thought Ned looked at Em in a too-familiar way. She had earlier observed him, left hand under the table, patting Cara's knee. *Well,* she thought, *it could just be one of those Mediterranean male mannerisms. Still . . .*

After a bit more back-and-forth, Anna carefully tucked the smaller album in her large purse. Glancing up, she saw the waitress flip the dog-eared sign on the door to "closed".

"No hurry for you folks," the waitress said, tossing a look at the men.

They chatted amiably for a while about the old towns in the Adirondacks, the beautiful hiking areas, the bountiful lakes, swapping tales of their favorite outdoor adventures.

"I guess it's time we moseyed on," Anna finally said, immediately regretting her choice of words, which seemed to mimic Miles' style of speaking. She was amazed to think the time had flown by so gracefully, *like a red hawk on the wing,* she thought.

In the parking lot they all shook hands. Miles' friendly, appreciating eyes held her for a moment, and then they were on their way.

Once on the road, Emma and Cara exploded into a barrage of full-throttle chatter. At first the theme was how amazing and interesting it was that there were so many people living in Griffin some 125 years ago, and that there were so many pictures of those long-gone. At some point the talk began to focus on Miles and Ned, the flesh-and-blood quarry.

"Well, they both seem nice, interesting men in my book. Ned gave me his business card and I, of course, reciprocated," exclaimed Cara.

"Gram, isn't it good luck and pretty terrific that Miles lent us the album? I mean, it's so old it's got to be valuable. I can't wait to see if you can fix some of the pictures. Will it take long?"

Anna smiled and gave Em's blue-jeaned knee a reassuring pat, telling her that she'd drop the album at Shutter Speed first thing on Monday.

Although it was getting a little late in the afternoon, Anna decided they'd take a quick hike into Tenant Creek Falls; the light might still be okay for some good shots. It was a pretty place that could yield some good photos. Em was enthusiastic, and Cara was agreeable enough.

The creek was high and frothy from recent snowmelt in the mountains. The worn trail to the falls was spongy with pine needles under a canopy of tall conifers. The roar of the falls heralded its presence to them long before it could be seen. Em was delighted to be taking pictures, jumping from rock to rock for good vantages. Anna was pleased to see her interest—this could be a blossoming hobby, yes? Cara took a few shots and then lay back on a rock to catch some rays. Anna set her tripod and tried for some interesting exposures, hoping she'd get one or two good compositions. Unfortunately, the light wouldn't cooperate … and her concentration was a bit off. Nevertheless, it was a good place, she thought, as they sat on a large flat rock contentedly chomping on apples and being mesmerized by the dancing light on the waters. For a while they just listened to the water without talking.

On their way back Emma spotted a clump of trout lilies and some yellow violets. Anna told them how Native Americans had revered waterfalls and used them as sacred sites for ceremonies. They talked together about the sounds of nature and how sounds must have been different for people living in the wilderness hundreds of years ago when ears stood ready to interpret every sound as dangerous warning or friendly greeting. Cara ventured that today one of the functions of music was to remind our ears of primordial sounds that we would otherwise ignore.

As they neared the car, Emma said, "You know, Cara, when I'm playing my violin and shut my eyes, I'm sometimes so full of sound that I *am* sound. You know what I mean?"

Cara gave her a hug and smiled. She knew *exactly* what Em meant. As they drove back to Albany, the rain started, providing background music to the Mozart CD and the sounds of the road. Cara asked to hear the spring part of Vivaldi's 'Four Seasons'.

Emma, listening to the music, smiled to herself, thinking about the pictures. She wondered if they would ever find a picture of Tess. It would be way cool if they found more pictures. Maybe she would write an essay about Griffin for English class.

Monday morning, on the way to Bella Fiore, Anna dropped the CDs, rolls of film and the old photo album at Shutter Speed. On her return after work, her photos were done but Sam told her that he would need a few more days, maybe a week, to assess the pictures in the album. He assured her, however, that some were probably salvageable.

She clicked open the door lock, walked to the kitchen, poured a full glass of Nero D'Avalo and sat at the table, then eagerly opened the packets of photos. "Damn!" she said aloud. There were only three, maybe four, shots of exhibition quality. She tossed the photos aside, and sat back, absently sliding her glass back and forth on the white enamel top, watching the sun making wavering rose patterns on the table.

TESS and BELLE

Tess and Belle knew this would be an exciting week. Luke was going to come for tea, and they were going to go horseback riding with Peter. As luck would have it, these events would converge; Luke would be in Albany the very weekend they were to go riding, so Tess and Belle decided it would be fun to include him in the outing, that is, if Peter agreed and Luke wished to join them. So, a hasty RSVP to that effect was posted to Peter.

Tuesday evening, after completing their studies early, Tess and Belle found themselves alone in the room they shared weekdays at Emma Willard. They were good students, and the school found it agreeable that they only board at the residence hall Tuesdays through Thursdays except, of course, in winter months, when they hunkered in with the rest of the girls. Their room was simple, with two small feather beds, two desks and chairs, and the family's old stuffed settee that papa had insisted be carted over last spring. The green damask settee, where they now sat, was under the two joined windows overlooking the sloping green behind Van Rensselaer Hall, a stately three-story stone building.

"Do you think Luke and Peter will get on?" queried Tess. "Luke's an excellent horseman, and I assume Peter must be as well."

"Well, we hardly know Peter—though Papa and Mama certainly approve of his family. Of course, there's the fact that he is attending Columbia. I'm not sure what they think about Luke, other than that they know we like him and Grandma has high regards for the Girard's. But, to answer your question, it probably depends on how graceful Peter will turn out to be."

"You really mean, whether or not Peter's a snob, don't you," Tess responded heatedly. Then she sighed, "I guess it's a town versus country thing. Here in the city a good, formal education means more than it does in the country. We're lucky Mama and Papa are so liberal."

"You might find Papa pretty resistive, if he concludes Luke is too ordinary." Belle looked up from her pastel drawing and met Tess's eyes. She had said what needed to be said.

"You needn't look so concerned, Belle. I know these things. It's just so complicated. I mean, there are so many thoughts and feelings to contend with. I mostly like to explore and experience. Truth is, I'm not feeling settled on Luke nor anyone else," she said conspiratorially. Tess felt relieved to tell this to Belle.

"But you can't go through life flitting from flower to flower like a butterfly. Men begin to take you seriously, expect you to stay." Belle held up her drawing of two monarch butterflies on a shaft of goldenrod.

"Belle … how beautiful!" exclaimed Tess, happy to leave the train of conversation. "They are so lifelike—no, better than life. The goldenrod bends so gracefully, like in a light breeze. The monarchs appear to be floating, ready to soar. Where did you sketch them?"

"It was late August. I was walking out that road at the end of State Street where the fields begin, planning to sketch a landscape, when they appeared … hundreds of them, maybe thousands. There were so many that for a while I couldn't even concentrate. I was sitting on a rock when one landed right on my yellow gingham skirt! Anyway, I did a bunch of pretty good sketches." She paused. "Actually, I think I went right by the stables from where we will go riding with Peter."

At Tess's urging, Belle brought forth a stack of her latest sketches, many of which were of flowers and butterflies. Belle on a Saturday or

Sunday afternoon could be found in fields or woods on the outskirts of town sketching or painting. She had wholeheartedly adopted the *plein air* concept of creating drafts directly from nature.

"You know, Belle, that new art of photography will never capture sights like these."

They had both sat for photograph portraits earlier in the year. It had been tiring to sit so long while the photographer arranged the scene, but it was intriguing to look at their pale images in dress-up clothes. Tess thought her looks had already changed, that she was taller and more womanly. But now, with the photographs, when they grow old and look back at their portraits they will remember being young.

"You're right, Tess, photographs will never be able to capture the color of life. We look like ghosts in those frames on the wall. Still, I hope one day to try a camera. Photographs are interesting."

Later, after lights-out, Tess thought of butterfly catchers with nets trying to snare and pin the colorful creatures to black cloth. In her sleep, she dreamed of a field of bright green-gold tilting against a lapis sky. There were swallowtails, monarchs and dots of blue karner's, swooping to an unknown cadence, held earthward by a meniscus of gravity. They arced in graceful expanding circles. The awkward beings in dark trousers lumbered kitty-corner across the field, swinging nets on poles. Occasionally they caught one of the daring creatures, interrupting its silent melody and placing it in a screened box. Suddenly the sky grew a dark black-orange. There was a *whoosh* and the inverted vortex of color whisked from sight. The men sat on the ground quizzically considering their plunder.

A residue of her dream hung like a damp spider web in the brightness of dawn when she awoke.

Friday afternoon Luke and his uncle, James Girard, arrived for tea. Tess was pleasantly surprised to see Luke in a suit—not the latest fashion, but a proper suit nonetheless. Though his uncle carried the weight of the conversation, Luke responded confidently and directly when Dr. Bleeker, Stephen, asked him about his experiences at the Port of Albany.

James Girard owned the largest tannery in Griffin. He and Luke had come to town to assess a cargo of hides that had arrived at the port before they were loaded on the freight train for Northville. They were making a jaunt of it, however, according to James. He said they found their accommodations at the Wellington just fine and the food at Keeler's Restaurant first-rate.

"I'll tell you, Stephen," James said, "I could get used to the city life."

They spent another hour or so pleasantly discussing new developments in Albany and Northville. Stephen promised he'd seriously consider joining James and his crew on a hunting trip next fall, and James agreed to join Stephen at The Fort Orange Club the following evening.

James told Isabella that her mother, Sara Gifford, had just taken in the new young lady schoolteacher as a boarder, which by all accounts was going agreeably well. They all chimed in with comments about Washington Park, the green across the street. Since it was fall and the flower beds had been put to rest, Isabella prevailed on Belle to show James and Luke her summer drawings of the park in full bloom. They were attentive, clearly impressed. Luke used the opportunity to smile and look directly into Tess's eyes. Tess smiled back demurely.

"If the park is half as pretty as Belle's pictures, I'll have to bring the missus here next summer," James said.

After cakes and tea, Luke left with his uncle. It was agreed that he would join Tess, Belle and Peter for riding the following day.

As luck would have it, the following day was accommodatingly warm, with a blue sky and only a faint rustle of a breeze in the burnished foliage. Once at the stables, Luke, Tess and Belle took some time looking at the horses and assessing which would be the best rides. Peter had his own, a spirited roan-colored horse that boarded at Samuel's Livery and Stables. They decided to ride west of Albany to Tivoli Falls, then picnic.

At the start the path was broad, allowing Tess to pair with Luke and Belle to ride with Peter. However, a few miles east of Albany the terrain was wide open, good for a brisk gallop. Luke and Peter were in the mood for a challenge, promising to wait for the girls at the top of the ravine. Tess offered to take the picnic pack, which was bulky and quite heavy.

Tess and Belle nudged their horses toward the perimeter of the apple orchard, where there was a good vantage—though they agreed that this was an unexpected turn of events. At the wave of Belle's handkerchief, the race was on. Both boys were experienced horsemen, though Peter was at an advantage with his own pony. The pace was fast and even. First, Luke held the lead and looked like he'd maneuvered to keep it. But, as they turned and headed up the knoll that led to the ridge, Peter kicked hard and his horse, Buttermilk, flattened his ears while lengthening his stride. Still, in the end, Peter won by a length.

By the time Tess and Belle trotted up to the top of the ridge, Luke and Peter were laughing and in high spirits. When they were within earshot, Peter gallantly told Luke he was an excellent rider.

Tess wondered if there wasn't a hint of condescension in Peter's voice—but, no, maybe not.

It was another three miles to their picnic destination. Instinctively, they all picked up the pace, eager for lunch.

At Tivoli Falls they dismounted and tethered the ponies. In summer this was a popular spot for walking and picnicking. The centerpiece was the thirty-foot-high waterfall with trails to the top and along the streambed at the bottom. There was a grassy, park-like area on the south bank, where Peter was diligently spreading blankets. The sky was blue and the water glinted white and silver. A stand of garnet-orange maples completed the scene.

"Why, this is pretty as a picture," said Luke, glancing at Tess. "Remember the picnics we had at Griffin Falls?"

"They both make lovely scenes, though Griffin is wilder," she said, feeling herself flush and wondering if the word "wilder" had triggered another line of thought.

Unbeknownst to them, the very scene, including the picnic party, was being painted by an artist down creek, sheltered from their view.

William Hart loved painting this peaceful landscape and decided, on the spot, to add in the merry young couples. A few deft brush strokes deleted the cow that had formerly held the foreground.

"I'm glad you chose this area," enthused Belle. "We've never been here without our parents. They worry that a raucous element gathers here in the summer."

"Well then, I'll be sure to mind my manners," smiled Peter.

Since the outing had been instigated by Peter, he had packed the lunch hamper. There were wonderful watercress and butter sandwiches, fried chicken, cider, jam tarts and, to their surprise, a bottle of dandelion wine—homemade, of course. He had even carefully wrapped in napkins four small etched cordial glasses.

"I made it myself this spring," he said, pouring the honey-colored brew.

Tess caught Belle's eye, a silent query of, "yes or no." Should they drink it? It wasn't that they were not allowed a small glass of wine or an aperitif at a special dinner. But that was at home, not in public. Finally, Belle took a small sip and smiled at Peter.

"This is delicious," she said, carefully setting her glass on a rock. "Is it a family recipe?"

"Yes, it's my Gram's recipe. You need to pick scads of dandelions, and then you add oranges, raisins, honey and yeast. It bubbles up in a loosely covered jar for a month or so before it's ready to strain and bottle."

"So, we're partaking in a science experiment," said Luke. "So the girls needn't feel uncomfortable being seen imbibing in public," he said jokingly.

Tess was pleased that Luke had diplomatically acknowledged their predicament, and with such grace. He seemed older and more self-assured than this past summer, which was only a couple of months ago. She could sense a subtle recalibration in her thinking.

The atmosphere once again loosened and the conversation flowed. The brief freeze of uncertainty had dissipated. The warm sun cutting through the cool air was welcome. The merry picnickers made for a glowing tableau on the red-checkered blanket. And they radiated from within, thanks to the distilled essence of springtime in the dandelion wine. The boys grew a bit playful and competed in doing handstands and cartwheels. Belle thought Peter seemed more interested in impressing Luke than her, and said as much to Tess.

At last, Luke and Tess rose and walked on the trail that climbed to the top of the falls. It seemed easy out-of-doors to fall into their familiar pattern of observing and commenting on plant life and rock formations. They nimbly climbed to the top of the falls where a field of goldenrod was still in bloom.

"Look! There is a swarm of butterflies—monarchs. What a treat!"

"Yes, if Belle had her pad and pencils, she'd probably do a sketch," said Tess. "I'm always intrigued how they swarm together and know when to fly south. There are so many of them … hundreds."

"Yep, and you can count on seeing them every fall," he said, pulling her close and kissing her.

Tess enjoyed the moment, fully … then broke away and skipped back down the path. Turning back, she said merrily, "You know we can't."

Catching up and smiling, Luke said, "Don't know what came over me. Must have been those butterflies cast a spell."

"Or the dandelion wine," she laughed.

Peter and Belle seemed to brighten at the sight of them. *Maybe Peter is shy or reticent when on his own*, Tess thought. Belle was keen on seeing the monarchs, so the foursome dutifully trudged up the hill together. Many of the elusive creatures had fluttered away, but those remaining kept them enthralled for several minutes.

Belle told Peter of her nature sketches, and he seemed genuinely interested. As they rode back to the stable, Tess thought about Luke and how it would probably be a while before they were together again. When they arrived back at the house, Uncle James was waiting. It was a bittersweet good-bye, with promises to write.

The girls looked forward to their private review of the day, but first they needed to help Maggie with the dinner.

Once at table, Isabelle announced that their cousin, Abigail Bush was coming for a visit and would arrive by train the following Thursday.

"I was thinking," she said, "it might be nice to invite a few of the Emma Willard faculty for dinner Saturday. After all, Abby is a graduate of the school and still likes to keep in touch."

"Fine with me," said Papa, "just keep it to a reasonable-sized group. My week is going to be busy and I don't relish a major event on the weekend. Besides," he said, lowering his voice, "I don't like to see Maggie overdo it."

"I'm suggesting Winifred help her with the service."

"Fine, fine ... "

And so it seemed that there would be some more excitement in the house next weekend. Tess and Belle exchanged glances. Henry, who was still of an age to be left far out of the loop, used the period of brief preoccupation to snag another cutlet. He was annoyed to have been left out of the riding excursion, but somewhat mollified that Belle promised to ride with him on the following weekend.

Once they had finished their nighttime ablutions, Belle closed the door to Tess's room and flopped on the bed coverlet. Finally, they could review the day and share their thoughts.

"So, it was fun today riding with the boys, don't you think?" Tess looked expectantly at Belle.

"I did have a nice time. It isn't often that we get to ride—that is, except on the farm at Grandma's. And, I must say, Luke made a good show. I thought Peter was out of line with the dandelion wine. He put us all on the spot. I told him so, too—while you were walking the falls path. He said he was sorry, but he didn't seem all that contrite."

"Well, I agree, but I think he wasn't up to mischief. Did you see how excited he got when he was talking about making the wine? Maybe it *was* sort of like a science experiment. Maybe he didn't have anyone else to share it with."

"That's an interesting defense," Belle laughed. "Did you think it tasted good?"

"Hmmm ... well, a little syrupy, but, all in all, I liked it. I almost spilled the beans to Maggie, though. You know how she made that apple wine last fall? I almost asked if she'd ever tried dandelion recipes."

"You never know with Maggie. She has a way of slipping information to Mama—especially if she doesn't approve. To tell the truth, I wouldn't mind trying to make dandelion wine next spring—but that's a long ways off."

"You know, Belle, I just had a funny thought. By next spring we'll know more—if Peter is a real friend, if Luke and I should consider a more serious relationship, or even maybe you and Peter."

Belle looked thoughtful. "I'm in no hurry to form a relationship with Peter, or any man. What about you and Luke?"

"I wish I could see the future. I feel something in me is changing – like I have a foot in two worlds. Part of me wishes to travel … see more. Yes, being with Luke is within my grasp, I just don't know."

"As Grandma says, 'You can't tell a book by its cover, but first impressions count.'" Belle laughed and threw a pillow at Tess. "Not to change the subject, but what do you think about Cousin Abigail's visit? I overheard Papa tell Mama that they shouldn't take sides if Abby was having marital problems. I think it has something to do with her being involved with Miss Anthony and Mrs. Stanton."

"Mama really likes Mrs. Stanton and Miss Anthony—thinks they're doing important work. She said we might even visit the Stanton's in New York City—as early as next spring. She's never said a lot about Abigail. I can't wait to ask her about the suffragist protests."

Belle yawned. "I know their work is important, but I find it boring reading," she said, dragging her blanket toward the door. "Night, night".

Before sleep, Tess reread Luke's last letter before putting it back chronologically with the others at the bottom of her 'hope chest'. She wondered if he thought to save her letters.

The next weekend is going to be very interesting, thought Tess, pulling the quilt up to her chin.

three

CURRENTS

ANNA

When Anna awoke she was aware that she had been dreaming about the woods in Griffin. But who was with her? What were they doing? The images totally evaporated as she padded down the stairs to turn on the coffeemaker. *Dreams*, she thought, *they are as enticing and mysterious, sometimes even as foreboding, now as they were fifty years ago.* She swallowed those first delicious sips and opened the *Times*. "The world news still sucks," she said aloud—one of the privileges of living alone. "Thank the gods; Em is unlikely to have to go to war." She made a note to join Cara and Brianna in the Wednesday war protest at the Capitol.

Well, this is interesting, she thought. *It seems a small Thomas Cole sketch has been stolen from the Hyde collection in Glens Falls.* News of this sort always caused a little prickle of apprehension and guilt about the small Thomas Cole hanging in the upstairs spare room. It had been in the house from its earliest days, though Anna was not sure when it had been purchased or by whom. Her sister Jenna probably had more of the details. The truth is, though valuable, the painting didn't inspire her. It was a wooded waterfall scene, but dark and murky. It probably just needed a good cleaning—that's where the guilt came in. Long ago, ten years or more, she and Jenna had discussed getting it restored, but they found the process was pricey. They'd considered selling, or giving it to the Albany Institute, but couldn't quite bear to part with it. It was a last thread to their heritage. And so it hung—a pitiable remnant.

Anna resolved that this summer, when she visited Jenna on the Maine coast, she would force a decision. Maybe Jack and family would join her on Cape Porpoise this year—it could be a welcome getaway.

Anna brushed her silvery blonde hair, threw a red sweater on over her grey turtleneck, and headed out the door. She decided to buy a latte and take it to the shop. As she walked along the park she thought, *Why these niggling reservations about Ned?* He was a type she found off-putting, but surely he was trying to be helpful—wasn't he? And there was nothing in particular for him to gain in helping them. Anna realized that it was his flirtatious manner that bothered her—not with Cara, who encouraged him. But there was something kind of over-the-line in his attentions to Em. *Actually*, she thought, *maybe the real question I should pursue is why I feel that Miles is trustworthy.* After all, she had little information to go on there, either. *Funny how the hidden messages in the subconscious worked.* Though, for the most part, Anna considered herself rational and analytical.

Maybe there was nothing sinister about Ned. But, she had learned over time to be cautious. Sure, as a young woman she'd encountered and endured the muscular groping of inept men, who were just that. But it wasn't until the incident in the park three years ago that she'd become hypervigilant about unwarranted advances. And, of course, the recent photo fiasco had sharpened her antennae. The thing is, in the earlier incident she hadn't seen him coming. It was near twilight. The touch of the stranger's hand was rough and sweaty as he grabbed hers. She pulled hard, but his grip was tight. He pushed her to the ground. She needed to break the connection. Her scream, thank God, was heard by some guys kicking a soccer ball. They shouted "What gives over there!" and the man had run fast. Later, she couldn't describe him, only that he wore dark bulky clothes. His eyes had been blue. Had they locked with hers? Were they angry or vacuous? She couldn't say. After walking her weak knees home and locking the door, she scrubbed her hand, glad that was the only body part in need of scrubbing; though she did it in the shower for good measure.

Later, sitting in the wingback chair in the safety of her library, shades drawn, wrapped in a pink flowered comforter, she had thought it through. She wasn't going to be a scared woman. She would continue walking in her beloved park. But, she upped her running program and began working with weights. And most important, she kept her antenna up . . . and her antenna had resonated in the presence of Ned.

NED

Ned had never been introspective. Truth be told, he valued his skill as a competent liar. He would havta say about himself that he was amoral. Ned was drawn to sexual escapades and quick to sense when a woman was a likely player. However, after some narrow calls with underage girls, he tried to confine his appetites in that direction to porno pictures. He'd been caught a few times by boyfriends or parents; in the worst cases, law enforcement had come after him. So, he'd resolved to stick with mature ladies. Nevertheless, he was susceptible when confronted with young, juicy prey.

He figured his predilection was like being color blind, on some level Ned knew something was wrong, but he really didn't understand how others saw it. Lusting for the young wasn't exactly a disability, or so he thought.

Ned did have a dark side that periodically caused him problems in his interactions with people, especially women. He tried so hard to toe the line. It all seemed unfair to him. He had been at his worst in Vietnam, though he'd been in trouble before that, too. In Nam, the girl had probably died.

She, the girl, was just lying there when he awoke, her eyes open and not moving, cold. He had tried to rouse her. He had even thought, albeit briefly, of finding her mother or whoever the older woman had been. He didn't know the girl. He didn't know the language. He high-tailed it outta there. He'd been too stoned to remember clearly. Nam... that whole scene was a nasty business. If he thought about it, which he really didn't, he might feel remorse. Pondering questions of good or evil never occurred to him. That is, unless he was caught out at something. At the moment he seemed suited to living in a small town off the beaten track, dealing antiques.

ANNA

Anna stepped into the Daily Grind and ordered three *lattes*, for her, Cara and Stan. They were helping unload a shipment of roses for the Sally Stoddard wedding.

As Anna entered Bella Fiore she could see Cara was energetically slashing open the boxes of flowers while Stan plopped them in large plastic buckets of water.

"Hey there—just what I need," said Cara, reaching for the steaming cup.

Anna was pleased to see that the workday was well underway. Cara had assured her that she and Stan could handle early morning customers, so she settled into her office to do the inevitable pile of paperwork. Sometimes, a few hours of sorting bills and answering e-mails was actually soothing.

By noon Anna had finished the priority paperwork, and the outside cases and displays were in good order. Stan said that he could handle the customers while Anna and Cara went for a quick sit-down lunch. They bustled up Madison Avenue to Debbie's, a spot with a few outside tables, which was appealing in the spring sun. They both ordered the tuna with sprouts special and iced tea.

"You'll never guess who sent me an e-mail," said Cara, sipping her tea.

"I hope our lunch break is long enough for me to list the possibilities," countered Anna, daintily chomping through the pumpernickel roll.

"Okay—it was Ned—you know, the guy who has the antique shop in Wells. We'd exchanged cards at the diner."

"And … ?"

"And it was just a friendly note—said how it was fun meeting us, especially me—how smart Emma was—let's see … oh yeah, how he comes to Albany fairly often and would like to have lunch sometime. He said he'd be happy to treat us, if we were around. Waddaya think?"

"Well," said Anna hesitantly, "there's something about him that makes me uncomfortable. To be honest, I was hoping not to run into him again. Hey, it's no biggie." Anna took in Cara's puzzled frown.

"Honestly, Anna, you are just voicing your usual cautious reservations about the male of the species—and throwing cold water on a possible nice relationship, too. There's no harm in reaching out to new people. After all, you yourself said that was one of the stellar aspects of the Net. "

"I don't think I said 'stellar'—besides, that was after a few glasses of wine. All I'm saying is I wasn't drawn to him. No crime—right?"

"I guess … but I am concerned about this tendency of yours to nip things in the bud."

"Yep, that's me—a florist willing to prune any errant buds poking out," she said, laughing and making scissor fingers.

"If not careful, the pruner might turn into a prune," parried Cara, but in a jocular vein.

They'd once again achieved an amiable balance. Anna thought it best not to try to sort out publicly any apprehensions she had about Ned—not now, and not with Cara. And Cara had made some valid points about her attitude. Still, she felt that there was something tangible, some real basis, in her reaction to Ned. And she *had* hoped that their paths wouldn't cross so that there'd be no need to confront him or her own wariness.

✈✦

As luck would have it, work mushroomed over the week. The Stoddard bride decided she needed larger bouquets and more chiffon streamers adorning the church pews, several of the restaurants had upped their standard weekly orders, and one of their early-season suppliers had workers on strike. To make things even more hectic Amy Stoddard, the mother of the bride, was a long-time friend.

Anna nodded to Stan as she walked the long aisles of the greenhouse. The plants had wintered well; there were beautiful tulips in bloom, along with azaleas and forsythia. Eager green shoots of a bountiful summer crop waited expectantly. She gave a long sigh, however; there were not many substitutes she could recommend to the Stoddards if the second batch of tea roses didn't arrive from her supplier. *Weddings*, she thought, *so much drama and emotion packed into one day, such compulsion by the bride for perfection, as if her very life depended on one revolution of the earth. Then again, perhaps it should be such. Ah, I feel a reverie coming on.* Smiling slightly to herself, she sat on the faded, rugged bench near the watering trough and crimson azaleas. The sun through the glass was as warm as summer in San Quirico.

San Quirico seemed long ago, like a dream. She and Nick had been in their twenties. He needed to heal from his war experiences in Vietnam. She hankered for adventure and independence. The Novelli's had relatives in Tuscany—Nick's Uncle Nunzio, who lived in San Quirico. What had begun as an extended vacation grew into an eight-year commitment that might have lasted their lifetime, if Nick hadn't gotten sick. Even now Anna recognized that San Quirico had set the major trajectory for her life. As she idly watched a large bumblebee stumble from one lush fuchsia crater to the next, she mused that, yes, it must be like that for most people—making innocent decisions in their twenties that catapulted them through a lifetime. Then, at her age, when you'd become conscious of the possibility of choice, you were dumfounded, frozen—afraid to change what, after all, had been largely a circumstantial direction.

Almost everything they had learned about growing things had come from Uncle Nunzio. At first they had been content to revel in the Tuscan countryside, often taking long walks to the picturesque surrounding villages. They would start out in the early morning, packing cheese, fruit, bread, water and wine. A favorite walk to Montalcino would take them through undulating hillsides with richly colored, green and gold fields bordered by cypresses. There was an old twelfth-century chapel in a woodsy copse along the way. It was a sanctuary in every sense, a cool respite for their overheated bodies in a setting that housed generations of memories. They always stopped there to rest before climbing the path to the small, walled village. Summer-long the village was profuse with vines of lavender bougainvillea hanging on every wall; potted geraniums poked out from every courtyard.

As time went on they realized that Uncle Nunzio could use a hand in the vineyards, so they began doing some of the more menial tasks like weeding and hauling wheelbarrows full of cuttings. They were young and fast, if not knowledgeable. Nunzio would say *stupefacente*, and they would all laugh. Later, they learned the business, eventually buying acreage nearby, though mostly they continued to help Nunzio and made an informal partnership. She still kept up with Nunzio, now in his early eighties. It had been a full two years since her last visit—maybe a quick trip in the fall was in order.

"Hey boss," called Stan, entering the greenhouse, "you hidin' from us or what?"

"Nah … just trying to figure out the possibilities for the Stoddard wedding."

Stan plopped down on the bench next to her. "Well now, we been in tighter fixes then this. Criminy, we got days before serious worryin.'"

"Good advice, as usual—time for me to go inside and do something useful," said Anna, rising. *Stan's a good egg*, she thought. Truthfully, he and Cara were indispensable or, as Nunzio would say, "good old shoes." She went inside and tended to some late-afternoon stragglers—an older man buying flowers for a woman he'd hoped to impress who wanted "nice but not too flashy, you know—elegant but understated"; and a woman hurriedly picking a bouquet to bring to a dinner party. Anna enjoyed assisting the gentleman and wished him well.

She was happy to close shop and get back home. The thoughts of a luxurious shower, slipping into her "jammies," a glass of wine, a tuna melt sandwich and watching her DVD of *Casablanca* were very appealing.

As she walked by her home office, however, she saw her answering machine blinking two messages. She pressed the button, in spite of herself. One was from Em, sounding happy about her research; the other was from Miles, proposing they go on a photo shoot. Anna sighed and thought, *for the moment I'll stick with plan A and head for the shower.*

She and Em had a nice talk. It seems that Abigail Bush was proving to be the real McCoy. According to Em, old Cousin Abigail did host a follow-up meeting in Rochester to the famous Women's Convention of 1848 in Seneca Falls. Abigail was a resident of Rochester and must have convinced the pastor of the local Methodist church to hold the meeting there. Of course, there would have been the temperance tie-in, too. Now, they just needed to find an approximate date of birth for Cousin Abigail.

Just one thing was gnawing in Anna's thoughts. Em had decided to take a pass on coming to Albany this Friday, saying she had promised her new friend Alan they would bike ride that Saturday. It wasn't the fact of the change in plans that disturbed Anna. Something seemed off in Em's voice. *Oh well,* she mused, *it's probably just teenage self-consciousness about the boy thing.*

Anna decided she'd finish *Casablanca* and then return Miles' call. If he was still at Ned's number, good—if not, she'd catch him tomorrow or leave a message.

The phone rang twice.

"Hullo, Owl's Nest Antiques. How can I help you?"

"Miles! I'm surprised to get you directly."

"Actually, I'm here for the week. Ned's on a buying trip. Ya know, even we hermits have to be useful once in a while. But I do have time this weekend to take you to some great places for photos. I was supposing you didn't get to take many shots last time you were here, what with the weather and the girls."

"I guess you sized up the situation about right. Sure, I'd love to try for some scenic photos—weather looks pretty good, too."

"Great, Anna. I'd hoped you be free. Try to get here around ten. It's a bit of a walk—I'll pack a lunch and all."

They said their good-byes and hung up. Anna poured half a cup of tea and sat into her reading chair, thinking, *Now, that wasn't so difficult, was it?* With a little luck she might well finish the portfolio she needed for the upcoming exhibit.

She pulled out some of her favorite photo books—Nathan Farb, Den Linahen and, of course, Stoddard. Always, Stoddard. Then she decided to take the books and tea to her room. One advantage of sleeping alone in a king-sized bed was space for books and magazines on the side. She eventually drifted off, her tea cooling in the blue Wedgwood pot on the nightstand. A jumble of dreams followed.

In one dream she was back in San Quirico. It was late afternoon— no, closer to early evening. She was in the vineyard surrounded by green and gold—leafy vines and taut young pinot grapes. The sky was burnished and golden, cusping on deep orange. As she climbed the steep hill, the sun grew large and became a heavy blood-red before dropping to the horizon. There was a figure at the bottom of the hill—following her?—moving away? Was it Nick or Nunzio? Miles? Suddenly the figure was close behind her and panting. It was her grandpa—no, her father. But it grew too dark to be sure, and he didn't answer her. And then the dream dissolved and evaporated as she awoke.

Lying in bed, she tried to pull back the wispy fragments of the dream. It was always pleasant to be transported back to the Tuscan countryside, yet unsettling to confront a mysterious personage there. Also—how in the world did the notion of Miles enter *that* scenery?

Fully awake, she wiggled her toes and stretched, thinking about the kinds of photos she would need to round out the exhibit. She felt buoyed by the prospect of the Saturday photo shoot. But it was only Wednesday, and there was a mountain of work at the shop.

As luck would have it, Cara and Stan managed to find a small supplier on the Internet who promised to deliver the scads of tea roses so important to the Stoddard bride. They all breathed a deep sigh.

"Tell you what, guys—dinner is on the boss tonight. Really, you saved my bacon—once again."

Stan beamed. Cara laughed, saying, "Well, this is the stuff of high drama around here. What do you think, Stan—Italian?"

"Pasta and vino—always good by me. That is, unless Anna has another hankering," he said deferentially.

Anna felt pleased. Her mood was buoyant all afternoon. Five-thirty sharp, they doused the lights and turned the key, walking three abreast to Café Buona Notte.

Their tongues well lubricated by the first bottle of brunello, they shared heretofore occluded reminiscences about their early lives.

"I have to say, it wasn't too likely I'd end up working in a florist shop in Albany," said Stan. "Of course, I always liked growing things—was working on a ranch in Missoula in my twenties. That is, before I got in the insurance business. Anyways, after I married Janet and got the business going, I expected we'd move to California—like San Francisco, or like that. Then Janet's old aunt in Saugerties calls her and asks if we'd consider staying with her a while. Long story short, we decided to give it a try. Well, as you know, Janet got sick and passed. But I stayed on with old Aunt Laura—and she did okay by me. I wasn't sure what to do next, when I saw the sign in the shop window last year. To be honest, never expected to stay on," he added sheepishly.

"Oh sure," spouted Cara. "What about Katy, the girl you've been seeing? Wouldn't she be surprised if you up and left?"

"I guess. Look, you gals are somewhat older. I'm just thirty-eight years old, for Chrissakes. I'm not saying I would move—just that I *might*."

Cara snorted, "So you think Anna and I are over the hill?"

"Hardly!" said Stan laughing. "You have more dates than most teenagers—though I guess the boss lady is too busy for such non-sense," he added.

"You bet!" Anna laughed, and quickly quaffed her drink.

Anna checked her camera equipment while savoring a second cup of coffee. It was early Saturday morning; the *Times Union* hadn't even been delivered yet. Through the white frame kitchen window she could see the dawn coaxing some blue into the sky—the sign of a good day. She put some water, cheese and fruit in the cooler, then remembered bug spray and netting—just in case. Supposedly, the black flies had waned. But it was still spring in the Adirondacks.

The Northway was lightly travelled at this hour. It actually felt relaxing listening to the new Springsteen CD while trying not to exceed the speed limit. She figured any troopers stuck on duty early Saturday morning would be unlikely to show mercy.

Her thoughts were mostly about the kinds of scenes she hoped to find for photos. She figured that, with luck, she'd find pond life and wildflowers, which could nicely round out her "Adirondack Sessions." When she thought of Miles and his role as guide, there was a feeling of ease. He didn't seem one who would chat to fill up the silences. At least, that was the hope. She knew that she felt some stirrings of physical attraction at the diner, but she thought that was probably a momentary thing. Who could account for such nonsense? Keeping an eye on the clouds and the light, she was optimistic about the prospect of fine photos. It was good they picked the diner for a meeting place. She already wanted more coffee—and a bathroom.

"Hey! Anna, over here!" Miles hailed her from the corner booth. He smiled as she got closer. "How about a cuppa before we head out," he said, hailing the watchful waitress.

"Mmmm … perfect," said Anna, inhaling the steamy vapor. "Just what I needed."

"Well, I kinda thought you'd like to look at these quad maps and decide where we'd best go. See here?" he said, pointing to some features on the map. "Here we got the Tenant Creek Falls area—pretty nice pine woods and waterfalls. Another nice spot is the Middle Murphy Lakes road. There's plenty of stuff up north of Speculator, too, though a bit more of a drive."

"I'll tell you, Miles, I'm not too terribly fussy—as long as I can get some water shots and maybe some wildflowers."

"In that case, I'm thinking we'll go up Route 30. I know a path along the Jessup River. There's also the Kajamuk River by Speculator. If ya like rocks, we might try Chimney Mountain."

"Sounds great. I'm feeling lucky," Anna laughed.

The day was starting well, thought Anna, as she pulled the Subaru away from the curb, with Miles relaxing in the passenger seat.

By the time they got to the Kajamuk trail, they already had had a workout. The walk along the Jessup had been more overgrown than Miles remembered. Still, Anna had found an amazing cluster of trout lily, fresh with dew and perfectly lit by the morning sun.

The Kajamuk was a proper, well-marked trail. Miles had said they might even find an interesting cave, providing he could remember the side trail to it. Anna was intrigued by the possibility of an interesting photo or two, something a little different from the standard nature portfolio.

At the moment Miles seemed drawn to something by the edge of the pond. He was bent low to the grass. Anna noted his lean muscled torso as his green plaid shirt pulled across his back. She thought living in the woods probably kept him fit. He beckoned to Anna with a wave of his right arm while simultaneously signaling quiet with index finger to his lips. There in the grass was a newborn fawn.

"Maybe you can get a quick shot," he whispered. "Be careful not to touch. The doe must be close by and we don't want to spook her."

Anna focused and clicked, using a long-distance lens in order to bring out the detail of the soft fur and shiny muzzle. The baby animal didn't appear alarmed.

They walked quietly in silence for a few hundred yards, almost reverently.

"That is not something you see every day!" Anna whispered excitedly. "Do you think the mother will return?"

"I expect so. That is, if she's around and okay. We were pretty careful."

"Should we check on our way back?" Anna turned to Miles with a worried look.

"Nope," said Miles, looking ahead down the trail. "Look, Anna" he said with the slightest tinge of annoyance, "We're in the woods. You know, Darwin in action. No need for rescue services here."

Anna felt rebuffed and a little irritated, but decided to hold her tongue. After all, spotting the fawn had been a bit of good luck.

"How about we stop for a bite on the other side of that bridge up ahead? I packed a pretty good lunch," he said, looking warmly into her eyes and trying to erase any black line he may have crossed.

A quick scout found them a picnic spot upstream—a flat rocky surface to sit, surrounded by a pine needle cover. The sun felt warm radiating from a deep blue sky.

Indeed, the lunch looked delicious. Anna thought her two withered oranges and morsel of Jarlsberg cheese looked pretty meager next to this. Miles had spread a lovely faded green-checked linen cloth across the rock between them. On it he placed two delicious-looking baguettes filled with salami, provolone, and roasted peppers. There were also grapes, pepper shooters and two blue bottles of Saratoga spring water.

"Umm …" said Anna, chomping a baguette. "I didn't realize I was this hungry."

"Glad you like it. I always get a good appetite walking in the woods. So, how about that fawn picture—you think you'll use it?"

"Well, I never know 'til I see how it turns out. I mean, sometimes great opportunities don't get you what you hoped for."

"Kinda like life, huh," he smiled. "You seem so absorbed when you look through the camera. I'll bet you're pretty good at it. You been doing it a long while?"

"Yes and no … I began way back—then stopped. I picked it up again about five years ago, found I still had a knack. Besides, well, it's just important to me." She paused. "I mean, it's something I'll do whether I'm the best or not. Does that make sense?"

"Sure … um, could you pass the olives?" He seemed intent on his food. "Is there a story here—about this stopping and startin'?"

He had definitely caught her unawares. She took a breath and plunged ahead. "Okay, you asked … this might be boring."

"As a kid I loved cameras, or maybe I mean making images. My grandpa even helped me make sun images with photo-sensitive paper. Next, he bought me an old Brownie camera. No one and nothing in the neighborhood was safe after that. He let me use what used to be a pantry for developing prints. Anyway, I pretty much kept up my hobby through high school, then college. By the time I met Nick—we were both students at SUNY Albany—I'd already had some shows, won a few prizes—thought I was hot stuff.

"It was Vietnam time. Nick had briefly been in Nam, but was discharged because of a shoulder injury. He'd soured on the war. For a while we were rabidly antiwar—you know, organizing buses to march on Washington, holding speak-outs and so on." She glanced apologetically at Miles and took a breath.

"We decided to move to Italy, partly to avoid the war and partly to help his Uncle Nunzio run his vineyard. For me it was all a big adventure. We married and settled in San Quirico, first with Nunzio, then in a tiny cottage near Nunzio, an ancient house that had stood there for centuries. As you might imagine, it was a wonderful place for a photographer. I still have boxes upon boxes of my work from those days. Well, to cut to the chase, eight years down the road Nick got very sick—lymphoma. Jack, my son, was seven. Nick was in remission and we felt hopeful, but we wanted to be near specialists. We decided to use the knowledge we had learned from the earth to open a florist shop, Bella Fiore, in Albany.

"Somewhere along the way, I took fewer pictures. When Nick died, I stopped altogether. You know, I was busy running the shop and parenting, but also my focus was more inward. I think I may have spent some years not really looking outward." Anna's eyes misted, in spite of herself. When she looked at Miles, she saw he was seriously attentive.

"Anyway, about five years ago, I unpacked my cameras, added a digital set-up and started shooting again. And so, here we are," she said, smiling comfortably. "That's the story."

"Well, I expect that's more like the cliff notes. It sounds like your life has taken a lot of turns to get to this point in the road."

"Yes, twists, turns and detours—like most people our age. And what about you? Surely there's a story as to how you've come to live in a cabin in the woods."

"Yep, there is—and I just might tell about it ... sometime. But, the one thing I know about pictures is that you need the good light. So what say we pack up and walk a bit to that cave area I was telling you about. Not sure you can get a good photo, but it's pretty interesting."

"Good point. But you're not off the hook for your story," she said lightly.

"We'll see. Besides, it's just one of them fucked-up Nam vet stories," he said quickly, picking up his pace so she had all she could do to keep up.

As much as he enjoyed Anna's company, Miles was sorry he'd gotten into personal stuff. Talking was not something he did often or well. But the cat was out of the bag, so to speak, and there was not much he could do about it now. Maybe if they covered some distance on the ground, she'd drop the subject. *Jesus, I'd forgotten how curious women could be.* He suddenly felt exposed, like one of those guys under the bright lights. Actually, he'd once been one of those guys. And he'd done years of counseling to forget that.

The next mile went fast and quietly. Anna was determined to keep pace and not complain, though she knew she was probably missing some good shots. There were some nice clumps of fern on rocks she hoped to catch on the way back. This cave spot had better be worth it, she thought. *What the hell's his problem, anyway?*

"Hey, Miles! I see a good shot!" she shouted breathlessly. "Over here—a lady's slipper flower."

Miles loped back and peered closely at the beautiful pink blossom. "Haven't seen one of these in two years" he said. "They seem to be getting rare."

"Yeah, especially in peak bloom like this."

The light was perfect. Anna couldn't believe her good luck. After taking four shots, all looking pretty good, Miles surprised her by taking an old beaten-up Canon 35 ml from his pack.

"Don't really know if this camera works anymore," he said, "but might as well give it a try. It's a beauty," he said, referring to the flower.

Anna bit her tongue, deciding not to caution him about light settings and shutter speeds.

They put away their gear and slowed to a moderate pace as they continued on the path towards Kajamuk cave.

"Ah ha! There it is—up there to the left."

Indeed, it was a quirky place, unusual in its formation and location. It consisted of a single above-ground scoured room, with a large aperture in the ceiling that lit up the room.

"Wow! This is neat!" said Anna, standing within the tall fifteen-by-twenty-foot room. "It's the kind of cave a kid might imagine. Actually, it's almost like being inside a large camera—you know, like the entrance is the lens and the ceiling hole is the shutter. "

"I thought you'd think it was pretty interesting. I don't know they've ever figured out if its natural or some kind of remnant of an early mine. One of those mysteries, I guess."

They spent some time trying to get shots from within and outside the cave. Though it was an intriguing spot, worthy of recording, Anna just couldn't seem to capture it on film. She got one possible inside the cave with light pouring through the ceiling, but then the light waned as the clouds thickened above. It was frustrating.

"I hate to say it, Anna, but I think a storm is brewing. We probably best head back."

Anna, too, had noticed the clouds gathering. She nodded and put away her camera gear. She knew it was at least a few miles back to the car and didn't relish being caught in a downpour. Besides, she already had taken plenty of pictures—some very promising ones, too.

They walked back briskly, but companionably, stopping once to note some monarch butterfly eggs under milkweed leaves. It was Miles who spotted them.

"Look here, Anna, on the underside of the leaf—these tiny specks are monarch butterfly eggs. I just love finding these little guys, then watching for the butterflies later in the summer."

"Actually, I've never seen the eggs," she said, peering closely. "Late last August I was lucky enough to come across a swarm of monarchs in a patch of milkweed. Seeing the air full of fluttering orange and black wings was thrilling—got a few pretty good shots, too."

The rain droplets began increasing in volume and intensity, and their stride quickened until they were jogging in tandem—Miles a length ahead. Anna was surprised at how soon they reached the trailhead parking lot. She unlocked the car, grabbed a towel from her pack and eased breathlessly behind the wheel. Miles took the towel when she'd finished and gave his hair a cursory rub. Anna turned the wipers on and fiddled with the radio dial. A pleasant Mozart concerto unobtrusively filled the space as they crossed the metal bridge leading to the rutted dirt road near Miles' cabin. She'd decided it was only fair to drop him home, rather than back at the diner.

"How about a cuppa tea?"

"Well I … well, sure."

"Ya might as well just pull off here. The road gets worse nearer the cabin."

"Just a sec … I've got some dry stuff in the trunk."

The sky had brightened enough to put a dull sheen on the wet leaves. The sun's rays flitted in and out of the clouds, casting briefly deciphered shadows.

Once the woodstove and lamps were lit, the cabin was cheery and inviting. While Miles was preparing tea, Anna changed into dry clothes in the bedroom—the one and only bedroom. She noted that, although it was a simple room, it had a queen-sized bed with an attractive blue-patterned quilt, a night stand, an antique wardrobe that served as a closet, a comfy looking beat-up maroon plush armchair and one wall with a built-in bookcase filled with books. There was a window that overlooked a patch of earth, freshly hoed; presumably there would be a garden. It was not the room of an uncultivated woodsman, thought Anna. Not everything was as expected. It was all rather intriguing.

Entering the main room again, Anna hung her damp shirt and socks on the wooden rack near the wood stove, where Miles had his socks hung.

"I presume you don't mind?" she said.

"Nope," he said, putting a teapot and bowl of oranges on a little table in front of the maroon plush sofa, which was no doubt at one time the companion piece of the bedroom chair.

"Ummm ... Constant Comment," she said, enjoying a sip of one of her favorite teas. "Delightful."

Miles nodded. "Yep ... so, you think you got the pictures you were after?"

"Depends ... I mean, I'm pretty sure some of the ones I took near the pond were good, at least the light was right this morning. I'm excited about the fawn shot—now that one could be a real winner, the kind of photo that goes to competition. Of course, I got some good wildflower and mushroom pics ... the lady slipper might be great, too. Yeah, it was a good day. Thanks. It was terrific, in fact."

"Happy I could help. I could see how important it was back there a few weeks ago when you were at the diner with your granddaughter and Cara. So, how is Emma's search coming along?"

"She thinks she may have found some family connections linking Tess, the girl in the letter, to nineteenth-century suffragists—pretty interesting. I expect once summer vacation rolls around, Em will pester me to no end to help with tracking our ancestors. She's excited about the photo of the fellas in Griffin. Anyway, we're having fun." Anna smiled. "She even has Cara interested."

"Yeah, Ned mentioned that."

"Oh?"

"They had dinner in Saratoga last Friday. Thought you probably knew."

"Well, we had a busy week," Anna said lightly, trying not to show her surprise. *Surely, Cara would have mentioned it*, she thought. It was uncomfortably puzzling.

Neatly changing the subject, she asked about the garden out back—a safe topic. As it happened, Miles had more than a casual interest in planting and growing, volunteering the information that he had studied plant biology at Clarkson before going to Vietnam.

Miles told her that when he was a kid he had helped his father and uncle build the cabin as a retreat and hunting lodge. Most deer seasons he'd join them for the annual hunt. After his dad died and his Uncle Brian grew older, the place lay empty and unused. Time passed. Then, after what he termed "a rough patch," he came here and stayed. That was some years ago.

He had pretty good carpentry skills and still did some commissioned work. He occasionally shared a workshop in Wells with another carpenter.

As the afternoon light faded and the sharp edges of the landscape softened, so, too, had they altered their initial impressions and misconceptions of each other. The hard edges of noon had become rounded and luminous with late afternoon. They were drawn to and curious to probe the shadows—perhaps not today, but in the near future.

Anna rose and pulled on her blue sweater. Miles, rising from his chair, offered to walk with her to her car.

The woods at dusk were muted green and close. They walked, each enveloped in private thoughts.

As Anna unlocked the car door, she turned to Miles. Feeling fleetingly awkward, she proffered her hand. Miles smiled and hugged her instead—just enough, neither an advance nor retreat.

"Glad you got enough pictures."

"There are never enough," she laughed.

"Well, I hope you'll show me the ones you got today."

"Absolutely!" she said.

Miles ambled slowly back to the cabin. It was twilight and the trout might be bitin'…worth a try for a good dinner.

As the car slowly eased down the dirt road and over the one-lane bridge, Anna fiddled with the radio dial. Finally, she put in a CD of Patsy Cline songs. Thinking about Miles' innocent hug gave her a sexual thrill—no doubt about it. She liked the guy and knew he'd enjoyed the day, too. She even felt pleased that her initial assumptions were off—she who relied on the ability to astutely size up a new acquaintance. And what about Miles' impression of her? What had he thought before today?

She dearly hoped today's photos were spot on. She couldn't wait to get to the point of editing and mounting.

Later, as she drove down the Northway near Clifton Park, she remembered Miles' comment about Ned and Cara meeting for dinner. It was so unlike Cara not to mention that. They were close friends and in the course of a week knew each other's social calendars, especially when it came to mutual male acquaintances. *Oh well,* thought Anna, *Cara must have her reasons.* They usually stopped for a bite Tuesday after work. *I'm sure she'll 'fess up then,* chuckled Anna to herself.

The work week was busy. That, and the absence of Stan's assistance, kept Anna a bit harried. She'd looked forward to developing and editing her photos, but was too tired to make much progress by the time she reached home. Stan was apparently having a bout of stomach flu, but sounded better on the phone—hopefully he'd be in on Thursday. Wednesday night she and Cara decided to meet at the new wine bar down the street. The prospect of a few hours of relaxation and girl talk seemed inviting.

Cara was already seated when Anna arrived. The place was dimly lit and cozy. *Perfect,* she thought, sliding into the booth across from her friend.

"nero d'avalo—I took the liberty," Cara said, gesturing toward the bottle.

"Very nice," said Anna, taking a practiced sip and carefully letting the bouquet and flavors do their magic. "Good choice."

"Well, the good thing about being long-time friends is that you don't have to guess about wine and stuff."

"Ummm . . ."Anna gave her best bemused wicked smile and held it. "Nope, hard to keep secrets at this stage."

"What's that supposed to mean?—and that's not a subtle look, I should say."

"You know, your dinner date with the antique dealer, Ned."

"Well, it never came to pass. He called and suggested we meet in Saratoga, but then canceled. He seems nice enough—we had quite a long phone chat. I know you have your reservations, but I love a Latin flirt. I'll have to admit he can be a little suggestive."

Cara paused a moment, swirling the wine in her glass. "But, all in all, there's something about him I'm not drawn to—can't quite put my finger on it. So, I was just as happy to miss the dinner. You know me, got to go with my gut."

"Well, I like to think you have *some* good sense, at least," replied Anna.

Grinning, Cara said, "And the photo trip?"

Anna launched into a lengthy description of the hiking trip and the kind of photos she'd captured. She eventually got around to mentioning Miles—the nice lunch and the tidy cabin.

The conversation was relaxed and easy. It circled back to their thoughts about trust and instincts. They agreed that at their stage in life they'd learned a bit about reading people. Then, Anna told about her surprise at having made incorrect assumptions about Miles. She had been thinking stereotypes, really.

"Yeah, but Miles was presenting as a backwoodsy guy—lots of brawn, not too educated, kind of a hermit, right? Maybe he uses the woodsman thing to keep people at bay, or he likes to hide in a cloak of mystery." Cara was really getting into this, thought Anna.

"Hard to say—really. I did enjoy the afternoon—and his willingness to show me some new places. You know, I did talk some about my past—which is not my style." Anna paused, looking into her glass.

"Any really big revelations—stuff I don't know about?" laughed Cara.

"Hardly," chuckled Anna. "Not to change the subject, but are you still planning on going to the peace demonstration Monday?"

"Sure, I expect so. The thing is, that it all seems so hopeless this time around. The Middle East is such a puzzle. When we protested Vietnam, everything seemed clear and possible—you know? Of course, we were younger—which counts for some. Also, now I feel more timid—or at least unpracticed. In the old days I'd hop on a bus to D.C. and feel righteous, but now … "

"Yeah, I know the feeling. I'm doing it because of Emma … I worry about the kids. Also, it was *your* idea we go stand on a corner."

"I know, I know … good thing I've got you to nudge me along. Otherwise, I might just settle in and enjoy myself."

They sighed collectively and sipped their wine.

It was a balmy evening so, after bidding good-night to Cara, Anna decided to take the long way home. She enjoyed walking and sifting through her thoughts, planning the day ahead and thinking about the day past.

It's good to know the story behind Cara and Ned, she thought. It had made her uneasy to think that Cara would be secretive about something like that. She guessed it was because Cara was one of the few friends she had come to rely upon. Perhaps her single state made for greater reliance and trust on female friendships. Anyway, Cara had explained away Miles' mention of the dinner date in Saratoga.

She supposed she'd show Miles some of the photos—once they were mounted. In fact, she resolved to work on the proofs tomorrow. It was a pleasurable thought. She also resolved to call Em and invite her for the weekend.

Emma enjoyed what she termed her "research visits." And for Anna it was nice having Em around. Anna began pulling down some bowls and dishes for breakfast, but there was no hurry, really—Em, like most teens, liked to sleep in on Saturdays. But Anna liked the morning routine of coffee, newspaper and kitchen prep, even though it would be hours yet before Em stirred.

The kitchen was warm and comfortable in the late spring sun. Morning birdsong could be heard through the partially open window. *Amazing,* she thought. *How do they do that? Such a variety of warbles and twitters—are they courting or just announcing themselves?* It was awe-inspiring to think of the seemingly infinite number of living creatures—the whole substrata from microscopic cellular to pulsing, visible things—and humbling to think that the overwhelming majority of them would forever be unaware of her existence.

She took another long, delicious sip of her mocha java and turned her attention to the *Times*. As usual the wars in the Middle East dominated the news—more deaths for American troops, and who knows how many Iraqi and Afghan civilians. *It all seems so perplexing,* she thought, quickly moving on to the crossword puzzle.

She was so absorbed in finding the six-letter Italian word for "sandwich" that she didn't hear Em's bare feet padding up behind her.

"*Panini's* the word, Gram—I think."

"Hmmm … so it is. So, what do you say to pumpkin spice pancakes?"

"Super. Can I do the measuring and flipping?"

"Sure can!"

Anna found these moments in the kitchen with Emma to be one of the little joys in life—Em standing in a pool of morning light, faded jeans and a sunflower-yellow t-shirt, blond curls hastily pulled back with a band, smiling, fully awake and eager to go. Em was already perusing the recipe, then climbing on a chair to reach the favored brown pottery mixing bowl.

"Em, while you're up there could you please reach Great Gramma's blue dishes?"

"Okay, but not the cobalt glasses—remember about it making the milk look icky?"

"If you say so," laughed Anna.

The warm, spicy pancakes, made even more delicious by the prospect of a promising research adventure at the State Library, put Em in a particularly chatty mood. She quickly bussed the dishes to the old white porcelain sink and ran up the stairs to stuff her backpack full of what she referred to as "The Tess Papers." She had made a loose-leaf binder with tabs that contained copies of all the letters from Luke to Tess, as well as notes, articles, genealogical research, and what Em called "clues." *Nicely organized, just like her father,* Anna mused. Emma flipped the pages, explaining what she had found, while gulping hot chocolate as Anna sipped a second cuppa.

"The thing is, Gram, as I've been saying—Abigail Bush, the suffragist, *must* be the Abigail in the way-back family. I mean, how many

Abigails could there have been?"

"Well, I agree that it sure looks promising, but it's amazing how even very unusual names can appear over and over again. Remember all the hits that popped up for 'Rose Bush'?"

"Yeah, that's so totally weird when parents do that to a baby."

Emma looked out the window, lost in thought. Anna discreetly peeked at the editorial page, not wanting to interrupt Em's reverie.

"Gram, I've been thinking—even after we find out some things about Tess and Luke and the rest, we can't know everything—lots of stuff. I mean, are there clues we've missed? When will we know if we've found everything possible? I mean, Tess was a kid like me— probably had hot chocolate here too. I guess this is a different table and all—but you know what I mean?"

"Hmmm ... "mused Anna, "well, let me give this a try ... We've found a bunch of letters about people in our family who are long gone. And, nobody we know has first or secondhand information, so there's that. But the letters have some dates and lots of information, so there's that as well."

"And so?"

"Em, hold on, don't rush me!—I'm thinking out loud. Where was I? ... Okay—we're in the process of peeling away layers of our past, but it's tricky—like peeling oranges or hardboiled eggs. Along the way—on our search, that is—there are lost clues and even dead ends. But if we keep going, there will be some connection, some continuity—clarifying a picture of Tess and the others. How clear? How perfect an image? That's the mystery ... Am I making sense here?"

"Yeah, except for the eggs and oranges," Em grinned. "I guess I just hope we find a lot or enough. It's so much fun—like, I don't want it to end. You know, like this here hot chocolate—it was *sooo* delicious and now it's gone." Em was enjoying teasing Gram.

"Well, my dear, it is important to learn to savor the moment." she parried. "And speaking of moments, we'd better skedaddle to the library. Just put your cup in the sink. Let's go!"

It was a good day. Anna and Emma found plausible sources linking Abigail Bush to Tess and her family. Abigail's date of birth meshed perfectly with the likely age when she visited Tess's family. She was also clearly *the* Abigail Bush who had hosted a women's suffrage meeting in Rochester. Em's speculations and clues had paid off this time. They even joked about the nicely peeled layer of history.

Later, just before dinner, Anna's sister Jenna called. Anna enjoyed hearing from her and wished she had been the one to initiate contact earlier in the week, as planned. But Jenna sounded as chipper as ever and invited them all to visit her home in Cape Porpoise in July. Em was excited by the prospect and later actually did some dance steps when Jack said he thought it was a great idea.

After Jack and Emma got in the car and headed back to Barnfield, Anna poured some tea and sat in the library by the window. She always felt a tinge of sadness when they left. But her mood lifted at the thought of what a fine day it had been. The summer was falling in place, too. She and Jenna would have some good long walks on the beach—show Em some of their favorite spots. Goodness! It had been almost a year since Emma had last visited Jenna and Aaron in Cape Porpoise.

Anna decided she might as well mount the rest of the photos from her Adirondack shoot.

TESS and BELLE

Tess was surprised at how quickly the months had passed since Abigail Bush's visit. She was grateful for all the guidance Cousin Abby was able to provide, especially for suggesting the discipline of writing daily in her journal.

When her famous cousin had visited in September the world had seemed simpler, even if her own direction had been less certain.

Abigail had been a strong supporter of women's rights since the 1848 convention in Seneca Falls and had many tales to tell about Susan Anthony and Elizabeth Stanton. Some of the stories were personal and funny, but clearly all of the women who were active in the movement faced difficult struggles. Humor was evidently a way of lightening their heavy burden.

Tess found herself writing in her journal about the progress of the suffragists along with her notations on her own daily life. The incident that had captured Tess's, and indeed the rest of the Country's, attention was the suffragists' attempt to vote in the last presidential election. Miss Anthony and thirteen other women had bravely cast ballots at the polls, only to be arrested for their efforts. And that was not all. Miss Anthony also refused to pay the fine that would have acknowledged her ballot to have been illegal. Instead, after wrangling with the authorities for months, she delivered a powerful speech. Tess, Belle and Mama read and reread the speech and the newspaper accounts. Mama said she agreed with the idea of women having the right to vote, but thought Miss Anthony was causing women harm by being so radical. Even Papa said it was a wonderfully crafted speech.

When Tess and Belle were alone, they mused on the likelihood that they'd be able to vote in their own lifetime. Belle thought that it would definitely happen in the 1890s. Tess wanted to make sure she didn't forget Miss Anthony's words, so she copied them into her journal. She especially liked the part:

> "… it was we, the people, not we, the white male citizens, nor yet we, the male citizens, but we, the *whole* people, who formed the union.… And it is a downright mockery to talk to women of their enjoyment of the blessings of liberty while they are denied the use of the only means of securing them provided by this democratic-republican government—the ballot."

Within the family, Tess and Belle felt comfortable expressing themselves and exchanging ideas. They also knew many girls in their classes at Emma Willard who loved a good debate. Mr. Durand, Belle's art teacher, was rather outspoken on these matters, too, which Belle confided to Tess was a huge relief, as he had become her primary mentor.

"Honestly," Belle said, "I think I wouldn't be able to continue lessons if he thought otherwise."

"Couldn't his sensibility regarding color and drawing be considered separate from his politics? I can't imagine that his ideas on the world could override artistic talent."

"Hmm … you might think so, but to me we are a sum of our parts. I do not choose to see a beautiful scene painted by someone with ugly thoughts. Anyway, I enjoy being *simpatico* with my favorite teacher. You know what I mean?"

"Yes, yes I do," sighed Tess. "I rather wish Luke demonstrated some support for our ideas of the future. It's not that he disagrees openly with me—he mostly jokes or totally ignores anything I say of a political nature. Of course, I may be to blame for not fully expressing myself in my letters. But I don't feel that these thoughts are welcome to him. You know, I used to enjoy just thinking about summer in Griffin, and sometimes I still do. But, I'm not feeling quite the same about Luke."

Belle looked up and patted Tess's hand. "Maybe you should have a serious talk when you see him next. It's always good to know where friends in your life stand."

Many years later Tess would still reflect on that conversation with Belle. That particular moment stayed with her—the pink-striped wallpaper, Belle looking at her with that focused stare, the flowered quilt pulled up to her chin, the touch of Belle's hand. That image, from time to time, would insinuate itself in the forefront of her thoughts. Not that it was a particularly dramatic moment; rather, it was one of those ordinary mundane scenes that nevertheless become memorable. Perhaps it signaled an unfurling of her thinking. She was beginning to stretch her wings.

As it happened, the following summer of 1874 found Tess in Boston helping her Aunt Clara and Aunt Anna with chores at their small but elegant inn, The Blue Iris. It was there that Tess found her own, individual voice. Her chores, as such, had involved seeing that fresh flowers were in the vases at all times and that all the guests signed up for breakfast and dinner choices.

In mid-July Tess had the rare opportunity to meet, again, Mrs. Stanton and Miss Anthony. It was her charge to address the invitations to a tea being held for the two famous suffragists at The Blue Iris. There were to be presentations by the two women and an opportunity for the forward-thinking women of Boston to sign petitions supporting women's voting rights. It was part of a determined, whirlwind tour of the country, mostly organized by Miss Anthony, which was to culminate in the delivery of piles of petitions to the President and Congress.

It was a splendid event that day at The Blue Iris. There were bouquets of red roses, blue cornflowers and Queen Anne's lace on each linen-covered table. The elegant silver tea service and blue-and-gold-rimmed china were set. And the food … well, Anna and Clara were famous for elegant, sumptuous meals. In fact, after the scones, puff pastries and tea breads were devoured, Aunt Anna declared privately that as many women had probably attended for the food as the talk.

Since Miss Anthony and Mrs. Stanton were guests at the inn, Tess was allowed to join an informal gathering of women in the private parlor as the briefly acknowledged youngest in the room. She sat curled in a dark leather wingback chair. She was not expected to contribute to the conversation, so her thoughts and observations remained her own.

It was a lively evening full of an exciting exchange of ideas about women's rights, the continuing plight of women as second-class citizens and the need for women to be able to cast their ballots. It was on these points that Miss Anthony glowed with animation. She could truly sway a group with the force of her passion and personality.

Miss Anthony and Mrs. Stanton were not young; in fact, they were older than Mama. And some of the women appeared even older than their revered guest speakers. Yet, they all seemed excited about the "inevitable progress" of women. But the question in Tess's mind was, would they who were gathered here tonight live to see it?

Mrs. Stanton said that she suffered from hand cramps when writing, and Miss Anthony was heard to complain about the toll that frequent travel took upon her. Why did they put such effort into a dream? Tess felt ashamed to admit that she assumed that Miss

Anthony and Mrs. Stanton would not live long enough to accomplish these fine goals within their own lifetimes. But the wonder of it was that they were determined to forge ahead regardless. Tess contemplated what the older women might think. After all, she and Belle were in the summer of their lives, where hope came naturally.

Ideas seemed to her harder to hold and appreciate than, say, a completed work of art. The thought of persevering for grand ideals juxtaposed with the process of creating a beautiful artwork was a new insight for Tess. The "idea" of an idea was amazing, but elusive, akin to Belle's butterfly paintings—before the creatures were captured on paper.

These ponderings so intrigued Tess that she resolved to put her thoughts in a letter to Belle that very evening before bed. Belle would enjoy thinking about this, too.

Tess politely bid good-night to the assembled women and retired to her room to write. She thought about the day as she dozed.... *It could be said that some great ideas evolve and migrate over time, likened to the beautiful journey of the monarchs, enduring and incomplete.*

four

TRUSTING

Anna had put in a long workweek at the shop. She definitely felt entitled to spend a few days preparing the photos for the show. Her goal was to submit the photos for review by Monday, then hang the best ones by the middle of the next week.

The early evening walk home was so pleasant that she began to dawdle as she crossed into the park. *Drat!* she thought, *I need a good rainy evening.*

Once she began laying out the photos and matting board, however, her energy level kicked up. She realized that many of the photos she had taken on her outing with Miles were really good, actually kind of "wow." The fawn in the grass was winning in the way all baby pictures are. The lighting on the pink lady slipper was great, even sexy. Probably the best one, however, was the pond landscape reflecting billowing yellow and grey storm clouds. She found a perfect shade of grey matte board to set off that photo. *Very, very nice*, she thought.

It was after ten o'clock before she realized that she had worked straight through the dinner hour. She felt satisfied and energized as she perused the fridge, finally deciding on peanut butter & orange marmalade on whole grain bread with a generous glass of zinfandel to wash it down. Back in her office workroom she set the framed photos out for view as she ate her simple meal.

It was enjoyable to critique the color and composition, the technical successes and happy accidents—akin, really, she assessed, to her work in the old days which, of course, landed her thoughts back in the vineyards of San Quirico. But, it was all pleasant reverie—waves of Tuscan memories happily colliding with scenes in the Adirondacks, artichokes morphing into thistles. When the phone rang, it seemed almost natural to hear Miles' voice.

"Hey, Anna, hope it's not too late to call. Anyways, I'm coming to Albany Friday after next and wondered if you'd be free for tea—well, maybe even dinner?"

"Hmm … no, it's not too late. I just finished mounting photos for the show. Actually, the show opening is on Friday. I mean, I'd be okay if you came … if you want."

"Terrific! What luck—I've been real curious how they turned out."

After they hung up, Anna mused about how easy it was to talk with Miles and wondered if she'd have thought to invite him if he hadn't called.

It had been a few years since she'd exhibited. There were definitely 'butterflies.' And, of course, the presence of Miles was a factor, adding a little to the butterflies. Then again, he'd already met Cara, and Emma seemed pleased that he'd be there because she wanted to talk more about Griffin. So, Anna guessed that Jack, Em and Cara, at least, would want to get together after the opening, and she supposed that Miles would join them. Dee was on one of her extended sales trips, so Em and Jack would stay over. It was comforting to think that she'd have buffers, if need be. Then she thought, *Oh my God! This is silly! … It's just tea, or whatever.*

Gallery 41 was just a block from the floral shop, making last-minute adjustments easy. A lot of the small storefronts on the street were making a game try at panache. Long gone were the old neighborhood green grocers and butchers. For the past thirty years there had been an ebb and flow of various incense/paraphernalia shops and bookstores. In spite of the downturn in the economy, the current spate of art galleries, boutiques and ethnic restaurants looked promising. Gallery 41 had just hosted a juried show of potters, which had been well reviewed. So, all in all, it felt like a local, "big deal" to be showing there. Anna could have reminded herself that she knew the owner—but then, why not just savor the moment? She'd been out of the public eye for years.

Jack and Emma arrived early enough to go to the gallery with her. Guido, the gallery owner, was in rare form—bussing all three of them on both cheeks with a "Ciao Bella!" He'd already set up a table with white linens and laid out clear plastic cups. There were red and white wine—respectable labels—and Pellegrino water. Jack had surprised her with an elegant fruit and cheese platter, and Cara, bless her heart, had made a tray of tiny butter cookies. And the flower arrangements, over-the-top ostentatious, were from her very own shop.

"Geez, Gram, what if somebody wants to buy the flowers instead of the pictures?"

"Oh hush, Em! It's not about selling."

Guido laughed, "So, where's my commission?"

Anna excused herself to give a last check in the ladies' mirror. *Hmmm … skinny black dress, pearls, lucky gold cameo earrings. She smiled, No lipstick on my teeth. Looks like I'm as ready as I'll get. Now all I have to do is hold a drink and be gracious.*

Anna was happy to observe that Em and Jack were smiling and talking animatedly together as they walked the exhibition. She felt a momentary, visceral, start of surprise to see Miles enter the gallery with Cara and Ned. He hadn't mentioned Ned when they had last spoken … *oh well.* And Cara? She had let Ned onto her Facebook page. *Guess I can't be picky about anyone who's interested in the show.* Had she time, she would have acknowledged feeling a shade of disappointment. As it was, she barely registered a quick hello to Miles before an assortment of people began to pour through the doors. Luckily, Em had sought out Miles and was steering him towards Jack. Anna couldn't help smiling to herself. It was all out of her control now. She glanced at Miles and shrugged the universal unspoken "What can I do?" apology.

The evening was going extremely well. Sure, wine and cheese never hurt—but still, people seemed genuinely interested in the photos. An older gentleman regaled her with stories of a mother bear and cubs he'd seen near Kajamuk cave. He thought they probably used it for shelter—although, truth be told, it was unlikely they'd take residence in a place that smelled of human scent. Miles meandered over as the bear tale was winding down. He had thoughtfully filled a small plate with fruit and cheese, which he handed to her.

They managed to break away from the crowd and circle through the display. Miles had a talent for admiring each photo without a lot of chatter—she liked that. Looking at the fawn picture, he paused.

"You know, Anna, these are terrific—even better than I thought possible. I mean, not that I thought they wouldn't be great." The edges of his ears reddened at the possibility he'd seemed to offer a back-handed compliment. Anna grinned. She was amused, not offended. They moved on, each reflecting on their recent photo excursion together as well as the work at hand.

"Anna, I've been thinkin' … being here at the gallery and all is super. Don't get me wrong." He paused. "When I called earlier this week, I was hoping we might get to spend some quiet time … talking and the like." His ears were redder now. Finally, he raised his hands in exasperation and chuckled, "Help me out here—I'm kinda out of practice."

Anna laughed, "Well, if you're asking for a rain check on lunch, the answer is affirmative. And, by the way, I'm a bit out of practice myself."

Em and Guido were heading their way. Em had lots of Griffin questions for Miles, and Guido said Anna needed to talk to a gentleman who was interested in buying a picture. So she left them chatting in front of a photo of monarchs on goldenrod, poised for flight, an older piece that she'd decided to add at the last minute. She followed Guido to try to clinch the potential sale.

She saw the prospective customer was Tony, and she was pleased. She had admired the décor of Ambrosia when she had gone as his guest with Cara. She quickly scanned the room for Cara, wondering if she knew Tony was present—and wondering what she had arranged, if anything, with Ned. Honestly, sometimes Cara expected her to be a co-conspirator. If her flirty ways weren't so good-natured and charming, she'd be damned irritating.

"Hey, Tony," Anna said amiably.

Tony was quite taken with several of the photos. He bought two outright—the scene of clouds gathering over a pond, and the watchful fawn in tall grasses—which he said were for his vacation home on Lake George. He also asked if she'd be willing to do an enlargement of the lady's slipper photo, which she, of course, readily agreed to. He planned to use that one over the fireplace in Ambrosia. Anna was very pleased. Having her photo showcased at one of the major trendy restaurants was a coup she hadn't expected. He also mentioned how pleased he'd been with the flower arrangements Bella Fiore had done for him. Anna was flush with good will and appreciation.

"Why don't you and your entourage stop by the place after the show," he said. "Cara tells me you've assigned her to look after your friends from the North Country; they might enjoy a little Albany nightlife, such as it is. Bring Jack and Emma, too. Treat's on me."

Anna happily agreed to invite the gang. She smiled to herself, So that's how Cara had finessed the situation—somehow making Ned one of *her* friends. Anyway, this did solve the "what to do after the show" scenario.

The jaunt to Ambrosia went well. In the subtle game of musical chairs, Miles and she managed to sit next to each other. Though Cara walked to the restaurant linking arms with Ned, in the final seating she squeezed between Em and Jack, thus enabling her to maintain her favored position with Tony—who was obviously pleased to see her. Unfortunately, because of the seating arrangements, Ned had to lean close to Em when he conversed with Cara. At one point she saw him put his hand on Em's shoulder and whisper something that made her laugh. *Was it her grandmotherly imagination, or did Ned intend to take liberties by touching Emma?* Jack, who usually picked up on any breaches of proper boundaries, was turned towards her and Miles, thereby disarming his usual keen radar concerning Em. He obviously wanted to be sociable—and maybe evaluate his mom's new friend.

As they stood *en masse* in front of the fireplace where her photo would eventually hang, Miles managed to secure a lunch date with her for the following Friday.

The next morning at breakfast, she, Emma and Jack had fun analyzing the previous evening. Jack thought Tony had made an astute selection in picking the lady slipper photo for his fireplace lounge. It was eye-catching and a rare view—even sexy. And he found Cara's "love triangle" highly amusing. Emma said Ned promised her he would check around for more old pictures of Griffin.

It was on the tip of Anna's tongue to ask Em what she thought of Ned, but then she realized she didn't know how to express her own uneasiness about the way he touched Emma. She didn't want to raise suspicions without cause. Maybe she was just an old biddy—an over protective gramma ... Usually this was just the kind of thing she would discuss with Cara, but obviously that wouldn't work this time. Cara had already chastised her for being mistrustful. Then she thought, *Jenna—of course*. Thinking of her sister made her smile—and also reminded her that she meant to call Jenna this weekend.

Turning her attention back to Em and Jack, she said, "So, is the last weekend in June still a good time for Em and me to head east to see Jenna?"

"You bet," smiled Jack, "as long as Em takes her violin to practice."

Emma made a face. "*Actually,* I like to practice. I think it might be very romantic to sit out by the Cape Porpoise lighthouse ... the strains of Mozart competing with the crashing waves."

Emma could always find drama in the moment.

As she kissed them good-bye, Anna promised Em they'd go back to the library soon to continue their research on the Giffords.

ANNA and MILES

When Anna arrived at the Palace Diner, Miles appeared to be comfortably reading the newspaper in a booth by the back wall. He was wearing glasses, something she hadn't seen him do heretofore. He arose and smiled as she approached.

"I finished early at the doc's," he said, gesturing to the paper. "It's really good to see you." He cupped both her hands, then deftly slid her purple cashmere coat off and hung it over his brown suede jacket nearby.

It didn't take long to assemble the pieces she'd left drifting at the edge of her wonderings. He occasionally borrowed Ned's car for out-of-town—in his case, out-of-woods—errands. His turn of phrase made Anna smile.

Today he'd scheduled his yearly physical at the Veteran's Hospital—the one he'd canceled last week when Ned asked to tag along for the photo show. As she had thought, he spent most of his time at his cottage in Griffin and used his bike for trips to Wells, Northville and the like. The past two years, he helped Ned at the shop one or two days a week if Ned was traveling—mostly in the spring and summer. He and Ned hadn't met in Nam, but that was the original link. Most of the time, he helped another guy with his carpentry business. Back a ways he'd been a cabinet maker, had his own business.

He noted her quizzical expression. "Nope, no big health problems—in fact, pretty excellent for a gent my age. Ya see, once you've been in the military, they keep track of you—free checkups and such." After a pause he said, "Um, that might be enough about me. What's in the folder?" He smiled, looking directly, curiously.

Anna really liked the way he had of homing in, concentrating.

"Well, you mentioned on the phone how much you'd liked the monarch butterfly photo that Tony bought at the show last week ... so I thought you might like to see these," she said, opening her portfolio.

Some of the photos went back a ways, like the time she encountered a whole swarm in a field of goldenrod. She had one spectacular close-up of two butterflies landing on a day lily. Miles was rapt, and very complimentary. They both accepted another cup of coffee from the young waitress with snakes tattooed on her left arm—who also admired the pictures.

"Anna, do you ever think you might be recording the last of a species? Who knows when the balance tips that final hair's difference? I guess our generation is the first to get alarmed about how fast the changes are accelerating. Take these beautiful, majestic creatures with their mysterious life cycle—fascinating. Ya know, I studied them a bit—way back, when I was at Clarkson." He hesitated, looking up to gauge her interest. But as it so happened, monarchs were a particular interest for Anna, too. Realizing their mutual passion for the subject, they gave in to the moment, talking, challenging, and interrupting.

"Did you know that the milkweed they eat makes them poisonous to many predators? And that they can fly thousands of miles to reach their destination in Mexico?"

"Not only that," said Anna, "but the monarchs that fly back north the next year are a whole new generation—several generations. Scientists still aren't sure how and why they behave as they do."

"Yep, they're intriguing and appealing alright. Ya know, I once read about a couple who found a monarch with an injured wing. Using tissue and Elmer's glue, or some such, they managed to repair the wing and then nourished the butterfly with sugar water. The problem was that, after all that effort, it was too late for the poor butterfly to continue its migration. So, ya know what they did? They went to a truckers' diner and asked if anyone would carry it south—they had a little container, I suppose. Well, I gather there was a good deal of snickering and snorting, but eventually one of the guys agreed to carry the monarch south and release it. Honest, a true story."

Anna shook her head and laughed, "I can't top that one!"

They talked on … some about Anna and Emma's research on the Gifford's and the clues in the Luke and Tess letters, some about Miles' garden, and some about photography—in general, and Anna's in particular. When Miles invited her up north for another photo expedition that following Saturday, she easily said yes.

She walked him to his car and they briefly embraced good-bye—rather like old friends. As she walked back to the shop, a good long walk, Anna had time to reflect.

Miles was more than he'd seemed at first glance but, of course, that would always be the case. It was a fact that he lived alone in the woods and appeared comfortable in that setting—actually comfortable in his own skin, too. Apparently, he'd once been on a more conventional track—degree from Clarkson, Vietnam, some sort of carpentry business. There were many years not accounted for. But he wasn't particularly evasive. It didn't sound like he encouraged visitors—yet he was seeking her company … wasn't he? She realized she actually knew very little. Nevertheless, she liked him … and bottom line, she trusted him. Sure, the mystery was appealing. She supposed she could arrange to take Em with her Saturday. After all, they could explore the Gifford link at the library and still fit in some time for photos. She sighed. Truth be told, she needed to try having a simple adult relationship with Miles. That shouldn't be such a surprise. On the other hand, it *felt* surprising.

I think it was the talk about monarchs, she thought—their mutual curiosity about something awesome and mysterious that propelled her back to Griffin on the prospect of a photo shoot … at least that seemed true to her. *Imagine! Monarch butterflies each year strive to arc in time from cooler climes in the American northeast to specific areas, even favored trees, in Mexico, beginning every autumn, in the autumn of their lives, to replicate the long struggle of historic swarms that flew in the same path before them … thrilling to consider, really.*

CARA

The celery had lost its crunch. Cara sighed, thinking this probably meant she'd have to go for groceries today—and on her day off, too. But for the moment she padded back to the living room with a cup of tea and sat in her comfy, oversized, flower-splashed chair—orange and pink flowers. It could be thought garish, she supposed. On more than one occasion, she'd posed on it naked—well, at least, been naked on it—and received compliments. On the other hand, both she and the chair had probably looked a lot better twenty years ago when she'd bought it. She smiled, thinking about the time Alonzo, a visiting professor at SUNY, had done a watercolor of her in that very chair—quite lovely, as she recalled, loose and impressionistic in style, she looking young, creamy and voluptuous, the flowered chair seeming to envelope her in a rakish, bawdy gesture. Alonzo had given her the painting, which she promised to always cherish. They had been passionately involved at the time.

One day she came home to see an empty wall in her dining room where the painting had hung. Somehow, Alonzo managed to smooth her ruffled feathers, promising to return it right after the spring "New Artists" exhibition. She had even gone to the gallery opening and endured the sly looks and knowing smiles. She hadn't realized that she was so recognizable from the picture. Well, true to his word, he'd returned the painting and they'd continued their snuggly ways, he hinting of marriage. He to be her '*marito*'.

Then, one day, she was at a gallery in Saratoga. How astounded she was to see a painting reminiscent of hers, but with a blue chair and a voluptuous brunette staring out flirtatiously—by Alonzo, of course. To add insult to injury, she recognized the young gallery owner as the "subject," who then nonchalantly shared that her *amore* had done the painting.

Upon arriving back at her apartment, Cara, without a moment's hesitation, her face pink with anger, her chest heaving, headed straight for her workroom, found a linoleum cutter, carefully removed the glass, and slashed the painting—*There! Done!* The next day, when Alonzo unwittingly arrived carrying a bouquet of irises, she sweetly thanked him with a kiss on the cheek. But then he saw the ruined painting and burst into tears—*"Dice non vero!"* She felt a twinge of regret until she realized it was all about the painting, and not their supposed potential marriage. And so, another lover was excused to take his leave. The kicker was that Alonzo achieved a modicum of fame and her painting would now have some value. But, that was 1990 something—over twenty years ago. She smiled to think, *there's a story Anna hasn't heard.* Inexplicably energized, she hopped from the chair and prepared to tend to her errands, humming as she went.

Cara pulled into the library parking lot, realizing that it would have to be a short browse and thinking that she should have shopped for groceries last. She was hoping to find a quick read about earlier antiwar demonstrations—something to galvanize her and Anna to join the neighborhood peace rally. She'd been confident in her activism back then. Of course, some of the losses experienced in Vietnam had been firsthand. When Jamey Nussbaum, a former classmate at Music and Art, was killed she had grieved for months. In truth, however, the extent of her memories of him was his offering her a stick of spearmint gum before band practice in their senior year. But she could still almost see his pleasant, freckled face. Well, maybe she would try reading something current about Iraq or Afghanistan instead. That could give her some ammunition for countering her sister Cally, too, who was usually in step with the current politically conservative war policies.

Cally, named Calendula by her literary parents was arriving for a visit on her way home from Montreal, home being Hoboken, New Jersey. It wasn't that she wasn't fond of her sister—she was. But sometimes it seemed they were from different planets, or different eras, though Mom swore they were blood. Cally was older by two years, so they had shared some activities and friends growing up. She was now an accountant married to an accountant, apparently happily. Work and finances seemed to occupy most of their time.

Howie, their only son, had spent his early years at boarding school. Nevertheless, he's a cheerful kid, thought Cara, now doing well at McGill. Well, if he'd stayed around the house he might be a sourpuss like his father who, thank god, would not be visiting. The thing is, both Cal and Jerry were of a serious, fastidious bent. When they were together in a room, a cloud of ponderousness could seep in from floor to ceiling, like fog rolling in from the sound. And the picky, neat part—two years ago when they were visiting she'd arrived home from the flower shop to find them scouring her oven!

Well, it was going to be a short visit. She'd prepare some of Cal's favorite foods for dinner—artichokes stuffed with parmesan and anchovies, lemon chicken, a good sauvignon blanc, and dessert. Besides, Anna would be there, too—she was good with Cally.

After spending Christmas day with Anna's sister, Jenna, who was so easygoing and uncritical, she'd been jealous—in fact, so bothered that she'd had a heart-to-heart confessional with Anna. Anna, as usual, heard her out and then pointed to Cally's genuine interest in Cara's music and her admiration for what she called Cara's "style."

Cara continued musing while she sorted her library selections, finally choosing a weighty Thomas Friedman book on the Middle East. *Well, no reason this visit couldn't be fun.* And she'd been wise to keep Tony out of the picture, too. Cally tended to be at her most critical when it came to Cara's choice in men.

Tony and she had theater plans for the evening at the Repertory Company. The current thespians were good at musicals, and she particularly liked *Always Patsy Cline.* Maybe she should announce Cally's Friday visit to Tony at dinner. On the other hand, she wouldn't want him to have too much advance notice. He might be tempted to set up one of his famous platonic outings with Rita, whom he referred to as his "old pal." That might very well be true, but Rita was not so "old," and she was very pretty. For Cara, trust wasn't such a big issue, but she did her best to foster rapt devotion. Displacing the competition was instinctive. She would definitely be at her most engaging tonight—wearing the teal number with revealing décolletage couldn't hurt either.

JENNA

Jenna was happy to hear from Anna and glad to know that she and Em would be visiting in early July. Though she and Anna talked every few weeks, they hadn't seen each other since Christmas at Anna's. And Anna hadn't been to her home in Cape Porpoise since last summer. Aaron would be pleased to hear that Emma was coming again too. She had so enjoyed going out on the lobster boat, tooling around the bay dropping pots in the early morning and then circling back in the evening to retrieve them. Aaron was a friendly, loquacious guy and liked company, even kids. For her part, Jenna was happy to relinquish her role as second mate, especially after a hard day at school. So, having a bright, capable fourteen–year-old on the boat listening to Aaron's stories while she and Anna relaxed on the deck drinking lemonade sounded like heaven.

Actually, she had no complaints since they'd moved from Portland five years ago. Aaron had worked as a private detective then, having taken early retirement from the Boston police force. She taught at a Portland high school at the time. Well, none of it went as they'd hoped. He got caught up in investigating drug dealers, and she found that particular school administration impossible to work for. When she heard of an opening at Kennebunk Middle School she jumped at it. Eventually, Aaron managed to wangle a job as a consultant for county law enforcement. He also found part-time work on old Captain Perkins's lobster boat. None of Perkins's sons wanted the business, so when the captain retired, he allowed Aaron to buy a half share of the business, causing some consternation amongst the local fishermen. But, in two years time, Aaron had made a lot of friends thanks to his hard work and sunny disposition. Jenna found the school to her liking, too—small classes and a few really good students most years. She opted out of teaching summer school this year, just so she could putter in her garden at leisure and spend more time with Aaron.

One of the things she missed most about Anna was the time they used to spend gardening together. As young single women, before

Anna moved to San Quirico with Nick, they cultivated a community garden plot together on a vacant lot in the city set aside for that purpose. Three or four afternoons a week they would spend a few hours first planting, then weeding, and eventually harvesting their produce and flowers. It was all very communal; after the first year, people fashioned makeshift sheds for their garden tools and brought second-best chairs from home to sit in. She and Anna loved relaxing on the discarded wicker settee they'd found at curbside and lugged to their plot, watching the sun set after finishing garden chores.

Later, after grad school, she'd spent the summer in San Quirico with Anna and Nick. Their vineyard and gardens were amazing. Uncle Nunzio was courtly and funny. She still considered it one of the best summers of her life. But then, that was some time back now. And then there were the way-back days when they'd created their first gardens under Aunt Clara's tutelage on State Street near Washington Park in Albany. Aunt Clara had especially loved delphiniums.

Gracious! she thought, *I'd better get back to grading these finals before bedtime.* She smiled, thinking how surprised Anna would be to see how extensive her garden was this year. Some of the perennials would be in bloom by the end of June. She hoped they'd stay for the Fourth of July clambake, and supposed they would.

MILES and ANNA

Well, no denying the weather was holding, thought Anna, as her car eagerly surged up Route 30 towards Wells—no, actually Griffin. Miles and she had elected to bypass their usual meeting at June's Place, the little coffee shop in Wells. This time they'd meet at his cabin to look at maps and then decide where they might walk with their cameras. She'd packed a few treats in a cooler, assuming a picnic lunch would be in order.

Last night she and Cara had gone to an antiwar rally. Cara had been the instigator for attending the demonstration, saying she wanted to get off the sidelines and be counted again. It was the first time either of them had expressed themselves publicly on this particular war—the conflicts in Iraq and Afghanistan. They'd decided that it was a way to at least voice their opinion about current politics and its disastrous policies. Many of those standing with them were their contemporaries, people who had probably been activists in the Vietnam era. In fact, they recognized some acquaintances. The rally had been orderly and serious, not wild and intense like in the '60s and '70s. Still, they'd felt good about bearing witness.

Jenna would be interested to hear about her small burst of activism, and they'd no doubt have some good conversation around it. Anna wondered if she'd broach the subject today with Miles.

As she crossed the rickety iron bridge over the creek and parked off the dirt road, she figured it was still nearly a mile to Miles' cabin. They hadn't decided where exactly they'd hike, although she assumed they'd probably drive somewhere to get to a trailhead. Of course, Miles didn't have a phone at the cabin, so she couldn't call ahead. She stood by the car feeling slightly irritated. Should she take her full pack? *This hermit in the woods life could be damned inconvenient*, she thought.

She laced up her boots, took some heavy stuff and a liter of water out of the pack and headed up the trail to the cabin, swatting a few black flies on the way. About a hundred yards from his cabin, Miles met her on the trail. He was smiling as he said, "I heard you a mile away." He offered to take her pack, which she declined.

"I unloaded the heavy stuff and put it in the trunk," she said.

They walked amiably the rest of the way. Anna slung her pack on the bench in front of the cabin and sat down. She checked her watch and saw that it was just 9:16 a.m.—plenty of time for planning and a good walk.

Everything looked as pleasant as she'd remembered it—actually nicer, as there was more green leafy foliage, even some tiny shoots in the garden.

"Could that be lettuce?" she said.

"Yep, a little early, but I thought I'd give it a try. The rest are indoors waiting. How about a cuppa coffee while we figure out where we'll walk—sit here or inside?"

"Yes to the coffee, and out here in the sun is lovely."

This was a pretty spot. *I wonder if he feels compelled to spruce up for visitors.* The bench and picnic table were neat. There was another, smaller worktable and chair about thirty feet distant under a tree. There were small blocks of wood and wood shavings on the ground. She was surprised to see a tiny carved figure. She walked over to it and saw that it was a bird figurine, unfinished but delicately done. She turned to see Miles setting a tin tray with coffee and muffins on the picnic table.

"Nice," she said, pointing to the carving.

He looked pleased. "Thanks. Doin' it's a lotta fun—especially up here in the boonies."

The sun actually felt warm through her flannel shirt as they sat companionably side by side studying the area topo map and drinking their coffee. The apple muffins were delicious, as it turned out—homemade, too.

"Okay, we've narrowed to two choices. One, we can backtrack near your car and go over this here mountain ending up near Wells. It's pretty—partial views on the mountaintop and a side trail to a pond. The other choice is to get in the car and drive to that piney wildlife management area we were talking about."

They decided on leaving the car and started on foot. They opted to pack fruit, ham sandwiches, cookies and water, reasoning that would keep them until they returned. It would be a substantial walk; no sense in being burdened by a heavy pack, though the cameras and tripods inevitably added weight.

The beginning two miles were easy, mostly on an abandoned logging road. The side trail leading to the mountain was overgrown and hard to find. Since they had maps and a compass, they agreed to bushwhack for a bit and return in fifteen minutes if the going was too tough. As luck would have it, they reached a marked trail within a half hour. Anna felt relieved, and Miles admitted as much, too. Now they could set a good pace.

This part of the trail was a gradual climb through old-growth pine strewn with boulders. The pine-needle floor was soft and quiet. They spotted purple trillium, hepatica and hobble bush. The trail began to steepen and grew rockier. Sometimes Miles had to push or pull her over the granite hulks. They were breathing too hard for conversation during the last half mile to the summit.

"Whew! That was a real workout," said Anna, foraging in her pack for lunch.

"Yep, they musta moved the peak up farther since last time," he said, grinning. "I'm glad we decided on sandwiches *and* cookies."

They settled on a sunny ledge with views to the north. They'd made such good time so far that a short period of relaxation was warranted.

Once Anna felt refreshed by a rest and food, she began to tell Miles about her and Cara's experience at the local antiwar rally.

"You know, it has been quite a while since I've participated in a political rally. This one is ongoing, weekly, in the 'burbs' of Albany—to call attention to the continuing war in the Middle East and call to task the current national leaders. You can bring your own sign or hold a ready-made one. Basically, you stand as an orderly group for an hour or so. It felt a bit like a vigil. The group also brings in speakers to the local community center. In most ways it was a great experience. Not unexpectedly, I suppose, it's flooded my mind with visions of the past.

"But what is unexpected is the resurfacing of events, people, my early life as a Vietnam War activist, my life in Italy—really, things so long-buried as to be almost forgotten. And some of the images recalled weren't anything special at the time, and cognitively or emotionally aren't now ... like this woman, Pat, who made posters with me at the Peace Center. That's all we ever did together; don't think I ever knew her last name. And Nick and I sitting by the statue of Moses in Washington Park drinking Boone's Farm strawberry wine. Surely there are more consequential memories," she laughed. "Oh, and another thing—almost all the rally people were at least our age. Maybe that's why it all seemed too orderly ... kind of bloodless."

Miles was listening carefully. He was pensive, absorbing her words.

"Well, this is a different time. In some ways it's a harder war to understand. 'Course, a lot of our perceptions, collectively, changed after 9/11. Still, lots of us didn't think we belonged in Iraq, still don't—nor in Afghanistan, either. But I guarantee one thing—if they reinstitute the draft, this war will take on the familiar rosy bloody glow—it won't be so remote if families live in fear of their sons' and daughters' numbers coming up. War stinks. And this one has a particularly rotten stench." There was a bitter bite to his words. They sat in silence for a moment.

"About memory, Anna," he said in a more relaxed manner, "that's got to be one of the most fascinating parts about being human, especially memories of the distant past, even childhood recollections. Some scientists claim half of what we remember might not even be true—never happened. Like crime scenes and such—you compare two or three witnesses and they'll all swear to something different."

He sighed, "Anyways, I always welcome a pretty memory, especially if it's in a beautiful setting—with a lotta colors. And other creatures, like the monarchs we talked about at lunch last week. What is it that enables them to head to Mexico each year—another kind of sensory memory?"

He has such a warm smile, she thought, as he rose and slung on his backpack. They decided to take a side jaunt to the pond nearby. The early June day had grown unseasonably warm. Maybe they'd even cool their feet in the water.

There was a clear trail to the pond. They sighted an inviting rocky clearing in about fifteen minutes. After shedding their sweaty hiking socks, they dangled their feet in the cool water. Anna peeled an orange for sharing. The water reflected clouds and the distant pine-rimmed shore. The only sound was that of Miles skipping stones. Anna couldn't help but follow suit. The ripples distorted the beautiful reflected image, making fluid abstract pictures.

Miles calculated that the village of Wells was probably less than two miles distant. They were still full of energy and, truth be told, Anna found the thought of an ice cream cone very appealing.

"There's something about ice cream," Anna said. "It brings back all sorts of childhood memories. I suppose vanilla is first. I mean, most moms start offering that first. You know, milky white, pure, bland. My favorite ice cream memory has to be my great Aunt Clara making strawberry ice cream. She would cook a custard concoction, cool it and add heavy cream and crushed strawberries. There was a metal container with a lid and handle that fit into a larger wooden bucket loaded with ice and rock salt. My sister Jenna and I would spell each other cranking the handle until Aunt Clara deemed the ice cream ready to ripen, meaning the whole kit and caboodle got covered with a canvas tarp and more ice. Meanwhile Jenna and I got to lick the wooden paddles that had beaten the creamy mixture … mmm, a delicious memory."

"Let's see now," Miles countered. "I don't recollect makin' the stuff, but I do remember my dad and Uncle Jim walking me down a dirt road in Minerva to a little general store—seemed like it was miles from the camp where we stayed. Every time I'd complain about the walk, Dad would mention that if I was "good" I'd get ice cream."

"So, what'd you get?"

"Vanilla—of course."

Miles looked quiet, pensive. "My daughter Evie liked vanilla ice cream. I enjoyed taking her to the park in Ithaca and buying from a little stand. She'd sit in her stroller throwing bread crusts to the pigeons and squirrels while I fed her." He seemed hesitant. Anna knew to respect the silence and wait. But finally she said, "And … so? Does she live near here?"

"Well, Anna, I'm not so good at telling stories—and for awhile I kept the past hidden even from myself. But a few months ago old thoughts, images, whatever, would, ya know, just pop up unbidden. So, I mentioned it to my counselor at the VA—probably another story. Anyways, he says something like, "Well, is this a good or bad thing?" And after some more thinking and talking I decided memories were just that—simply images of sometime back when. So I don't panic any more, especially when a good one bubbles up—like about me and Evie in the park. Actually, it's something of a gift to recall it. She was only two years old then. Her mother, my ex, Una, left with her that same year."

As they continued walking, Miles told her about meeting Una when he was stationed in Germany. They married and came back to Ithaca, where his mother was living. They'd all been happy that first year when Evie was born. He finished his degree in biology at Clarkson College and worked as a lab assistant at Cornell. Una soon grew restless with the married life, however. And he started having sleep problems, nightmares and such—later diagnosed as post-traumatic stress disorder. He thought Una was taking classes, but by the second semester she was skipping class and hanging out smoking weed in the beautiful gorges near Cornell. His mom was watching Evie while he worked. One day, his younger sister, Georgina, saw Una in a compromising situation with Hopkins, a visiting professor of sculpture as famous for handling his students as for molding clay. Georgie gave her what for, and Una swore it was an innocent flirtation and promised to toe the line. Georgina was sworn to secrecy. One day, he arrived home to an empty house. Una was smart enough to leave early on the day he worked late at the lab. She absconded with Evie to the West Coast. She claimed to be staying with a girlfriend from Germany—that she was just homesick, but would come back. Time went on. During spring break he'd flown to Los Angeles to find the address she'd given. There was no such place.

Miles turned to look at Anna, "So, that's the shorthand version."

Anna knew full well there was more to the story and they would have more to say as time went on. She reached and patted his arm. "To be honest," she said, "you've left me speechless."

"Well then, it's a good thing we're most of the ways to town. Would it be okay if we make a quick stop at Ned's shop after the ice cream— while we're here?"

The ice cream shop was by the lake. It had a sunny outdoor deck with picnic tables. Anna ordered a double strawberry in a sugar cone. Miles ordered a plain vanilla. They watched a pair of geese with some goslings swimming in the lake below. It was a welcome distraction—a quiet moment watching the lake.

When they entered the store, at first they thought Ned must have stepped out.

"Hullo ... hullo," called Miles.

As they walked to the back office, they saw Ned hunched over his laptop, absorbed and typing. When he saw them, he looked startled and closed the PC.

"Sorry—didn't hear you," he said, quickly rising and walking towards them, closing the door behind him. Miles picked up the small package someone had left there for him and they chatted a bit.

Ned mentioned that he had an old box of pictures from the Griffin area, purportedly, and said he'd be in touch with Anna and Emma after he sorted them. Anna noted that Ned seemed uneasy with her. She wondered if it had to do with Cara—whether or not he and Cara were dating. While Miles and Ned chatted, Anna browsed in the books section of the store. He had a pretty good collection of Adirondack history. Also, she had to admit that there were some nice pieces of jewelry, and she spied a few Eastlake Victorian side chairs that she'd think about—the upholstery was a hideous pea-green, but the chairs themselves were well made. She could re-cover them.

Miles called to her; he had found a book about Griffin, *Ghosts of Griffin*, written in the early twentieth century. They negotiated a pretty good price for it, though Ned seemed a little pained to let it go for a bargain. Being gracious did not come easily to him. Anna put on her most appreciative smile and dropped the wrapped book in her pack. The doorbell clanged behind them.

NED

Ned watched them leave, instinctively staying in the shadows lest he be seen. He hadn't expected this turn of events. Were Anna and Miles in a relationship? That didn't seem likely. Miles, who was fairly open and affable with him, hadn't dropped a clue. *Nope*, he thought, *didn't see this comin'*. Though, upon reflection, he wondered if Mr. "monastic woodsman" might not be trying to get a little piece after all.

But the thing that bothered him most was almost getting caught surfing his usual porn sites. He made sure to keep that private. Another prick of unease came when he thought about how he'd left a note on Em's Facebook page this morning—just an innocent "hi, how's it going" kind of thing—but, still. And another thing, he should have gotten a better price for the Griffin book—and the bitch knew it, too. "Jesus," he said aloud, "I'm getting sloppy."

He felt the day turning sour. For every little break he got, something always went south. He was thinking of calling Joan, the realtor in Saratoga. She was always good for laughs. Maybe he'd call Cara, too—sleuth things out about Anna.

Ned continued to stand at the shop window, biting his nails, as he watched Miles and Anna become small in the distance. Only then did he reach for the phone. Much to his disappointment, neither Joan nor Cara answered their phones. Well, so much for the hopes of either sex or gossip. Joan seemed less available lately. And with Cara, a little gossip was the best he'd likely get. Maybe they were both home and screening their calls. *Whoa! No need to let those thoughts creep in.* Once he succumbed to morose thoughts, he'd stew for days.

The door chime tinkled. Luckily, a couple came through the door looking for old picture frames, which he had aplenty. Turns out they had a bunch of family pictures they planned to mount and frame. He could tell they were impressed by his collection. They shot the breeze for a while. Really, he was in his element now. He might have overcharged them on some items, but not as much as he could have.

After they left, he decided to check his PC and surf a bit. After all, no harm in doing a little pretend chatting. He found it exciting when they flirted or made suggestive comments. After a bit of that, he decided to go to June's Place for the early bird special. Perusing porno always made him hungry.

MILES and ANNA

Miles and Anna walked amiably together, packs on backs, to the north end of town. Miles chose a different route back. It was somewhat easier in that it went part of the way on a dirt road. They were able to keep a good pace, only stopping once for a water break. At sight of Route 10 up ahead they broke into a jog, racing each other and laughing. As they crossed the old iron bridge to Miles' trail to the cottage, they were winded.

"Whew! Anna, I think you might even beat me in a sprint."

"So, not on cross country, I guess," she said with amusement.

"Ya never know—I could twist an ankle or something," he countered. "Anyways, I've prepared a meal for us—hope that's okay."

"Sure, I've got some cheese and crackers and homemade guacamole in a cooler in the car. I was thinking we'd be hungry after the hike. I brought a bottle of red, too, though I've the impression you might not drink?" she said as a question.

"Truth is, I don't drink much—but I allow for the occasional glass. And you're right to think there might be a story about it, which there is. But the thing with addictions is a long while back. So, I'm startin' to ease up on myself—ya know? Of course, one good reason not to drink is that it's just one more item to carry home in my backpack."

Anna thought how genuine Miles seemed. He was proving to be a person of rich character. She was glad they were becoming friends—if that's what it was.

When they got to the cottage, he poured them both a tall glass of cold water direct from the spring. It was early evening and still warm. Anna sat outside while Miles busied himself inside with the meal preparation.

Anna felt very relaxed sitting outside Miles' cabin. While he busied himself making dinner, she pulled a notepad from her pack and made notes about the photos she'd taken. It was a good habit, she thought—kept the scenes fresh in her mind. Also, if it turned out to be a while before she got around to developing and mounting, she'd still be able to accurately label and file the prints. The *Ghosts of Griffin* book was a good find too … looked to be a bunch of personal recollections on the area.

The delicious aroma of roast meat and onions broke through her reverie about sky and water reflections—something spicy, too.

"Hey, Anna, how about some wine, cheese and crackers?"

"Sure thing." *Once again that nice open grin*, she thought.

They pulled two Adirondack chairs into a circle of sun near the fenced-in garden, a rickety camp table between them. The late-afternoon sun cast a warm glow on the greenery and cottage. The only sounds were from the cascades in the nearby river and birdsong—rustling leaves too. It had been a while since Anna had been surrounded by nothing but natural sounds. She leaned back and closed her eyes to just feel the pleasure of it.

"Tired?" Miles asked.

"On the contrary!" she said. "Just fully listening is wonderful, you know? I remember from my school days thinking about what it must have been like for the Indians to be in the forest. My sister Jenna and I would play Indian princess at Aunt Clara's camp on Lake George. This would involve hiding in the woods listening to nature sounds—and, of course, the padding moccasins of handsome braves. Unfortunately, the motor boat sounds usually prevailed—though we did our darndest to pretend they were some early, and now extinct, water creature. I still sometimes wonder what it must have been like living here before the Europeans arrived."

Miles looked thoughtful. "Well, guess it wasn't so noisy for the early settlers, either. Imagine what it musta been like makin' your way up the Hudson or as far as Lake Champlain after havin' lived in London or Amsterdam. Definitely a whole new world—and I never gave much thought to it all when I was a kid. Do ya think youngsters like Emma are different? Speakin of—how's she doin' on solving the family mystery? She seems like an unusually persevering sort."

Anna enjoyed talking about Em and their trips to the library. She realized in the telling that she was really happy that she would be taking Em with her to visit Jenna this summer—actually in a few weeks.

When Miles mentioned Ned and said maybe he could help, it felt like a piece of ice had dropped on her chest. She hesitated, and then sat forward.

"Miles, I can't tell you for sure why, but Ned makes me feel ... uncomfortable. And I can't put my finger on it. Maybe he's a great guy, but ..." she trailed off, hoping Miles would say something to ease her misgivings.

Miles looked thoughtful—and puzzled. "Ya know, Anna, I'd like to tell you I have a handle on Ned, but I don't. He seems like a good sort—willing to give a hand now and again. He's originally from Brooklyn—as you can tell. He once mentioned his stepfather had taught him antiques—don't think he has living family. He seems to like the ladies—no surprise that. But, as you know, I don't pal around much with anybody—wouldn't have settled here otherwise. I kinda hate to admit it, but it's one of those guy friendships. We've both been in Nam. Talk a bit about that. Go fishin' once in awhile—he don't hunt. He likes to have me watch the store once a week—though it's been more days lately. In exchange he gives me a ride to Albany or the nursing home in Minerva—my uncle's there. I'll give this some thought."

Instinct and intuition are, at very least, mysterious and unreliable predictors of events in the future. Still, most of us persist in noting when we're prescient. Anna found Ned threatening, but couldn't say why.

Miles frowned, and then smiled. "What say we head in for some venison stew."

Anna felt the apprehension evaporate as she pulled her chair to the table. She was pleased and impressed by the look of it all—an old-fashioned blue-flowered linen cloth, a white milk pitcher with purple iris and white yarrow. The dinner plates were pale yellow, as were the napkins. In the center, on an ancient cutting board, was a blackened pot containing the aromatic stew. Two large rolls and a plain glass bowl of salad greens completed the picture.

"My, my," exclaimed Anna, "I must be company."

"Yep, don't generally use a cloth and such—nevertheless, it's my regular stew. Also, my table's no stranger to flowers, and I regularly use the votives to cut down on running the generator for light. The irises grow wild by the river. Did I mention I planted milkweed—well, transplanted—in hopes of attracting monarchs? Well, we'll see." Miles took a sip of the wine Anna had brought. "Nice," he said.

Indeed, Anna was charmed by the whole scenario. She hadn't had any particular expectations for the day beyond the hike. So, everything else came as a revelation.

Miles noted that Anna looked very attractive when she relaxed and smiled—or maybe it was the wine and candle light. The day he first met her—was it only a month ago?—he had found her pretty in that harried pinched way—like independent, working, city types. She was quick and feisty alright, but under the hard surface there was gentleness. He suspected she'd developed a useful veneer of armor, as had he—as had most by their age. And how old would he guess she was? He liked the way she tried to be precise and choose her words in telling her past—like it was important she tell the truth. Yes, siree—Anna didn't try to bullshit.

In response to his question, she told him about how she and Jenna had spent their teenage years being brought up by their widowed grandmother, Anna, her namesake, and their great aunt Clara. Their parents had died in a plane crash in the Berkshires—her dad had piloted a small Cessna. It was six months before the wreckage was found. She and Jenna had held the fantasy for over a month that their parents were hunkered down on the side of a mountain or maybe living in a cave. They were safely ensconced in the Bleeker household by the time the remains of the plane and their parents were located.

She said, "Believe it or not, Jenna and I still think of our childhood as pretty happy. Of course, maybe there's been some sifting and shaping over the years. Do you find that to be the case? I mean, about the way-back times?"

"Now, I'm not avoidin' this," he smiled, "but let me throw another log in the stove first."

It had been so long since Miles had recollected, or at least voiced his recollections, that it took some ummms and pauses as he proceeded to talk about his days in Saranac Lake and Ithaca. His father had been a logger—last of a dying breed, literally He was trying to roll a bunch of logs down an incline when he slipped and a furious mass of logs rolled right over him. His mom was mad at both him and the company. After all, he was fifty years old and had been promised a safe desk job in the main office. Mom? Well, typical of her, she had moved them within the month to Ithaca. Miles had felt uprooted and bereft but was, after all, just a kid. His mom was always a great one for, as she would say, "soldiering on." All in all it was okay, he supposed.

They continued in this vein, talking, exploring, revealing, until Anna realized night had fallen. It was time to go. Miles grabbed two flashlights off a shelf and they proceeded down the path back to the car. The cocoon of darkness provided over the trail felt almost protective to Anna. They walked two abreast, arms occasionally touching, two separate beams highlighting the forest. The car was now just in sight. Anna used the automatic key and beeped the door open, then threw her pack on the back seat. She shined the light briskly around the car— just so she'd spot any rocks or stumps that needed to be avoided.

"Oh, drat and hells bells!" she exclaimed.

Miles bent close to the right front tire. For a moment they stared in unison. Finally, Miles pressed on the black sidewall.

"Yup, flat as a pancake," he said. "Ya know, it's probably best you stay at the cabin for the night. Jerry's garage closes by six. In the daylight I can put on the spare."

Anna felt resigned to the turn of events—no, on second thought, not at all unpleased. She had a change of clothes and a sleeping bag in the trunk. Also, she'd noted an outside shower next to the cabin. There seemed an element of adventure to the whole thing.

"Miles, honestly, I hate to put you out—but I guess you're stuck with me for the night."

"Well, I got plenty of coffee—even eggs and bacon, it so happens. Don't worry about it."

They walked back under the dark canopy of trees, this time guided by the faint light from the cabin.

After a cup of tea and some more conversation, Miles offered her his room. She declined and opened the futon, neatly placing her sleeping bag on top. Miles placed a cup of water and a flashlight on the stand next to the futon and went to his room. They said good-night.

Anna had planned to browse through the week-old *New Yorker* in her pack, but the gas lamp was dim—anyway, she was sleepy. She lay down awkwardly in her clothes, then decided to be comfortable and stripped to underpants and a T-shirt. She blew out the light.

At first it seemed she'd doze right off. The room was cool, bordering on cold with the window open. The futon was actually quite comfortable. There were no ambient street sounds or flickering city lights. She could barely hear the river; maybe it was wind sweeping the trees. *Jees-zuz, it's so dark and quiet*, she thought. In spite of her best efforts, sleep wouldn't come. She felt restless and nerved-up. Peaceful images of the trail they'd hiked relaxed her, but then snippets of the day's conversations would begin to alert her. She tried her surefire method of body relaxation, starting with her toes. For a while she lay in a half-dream state. Then she thought she heard a creature outside. A twig snapped—but no, or it seemed quite distant. Finally, she crept out of her bag, stretched and took a sip of water.

"Anna?" said Miles sleepily, turning on his side. "Is something wrong? Are you cold?"

Without a word, she slipped under his covers. "Shhhh," she whispered, close to his ear. He hesitated, then touched her face and smoothed her hair. He reached under her shirt, and she deftly pulled it over her head. They lay close and kissed, gently at first. It was strangely new and intense, yet, of course, familiar...

"It's not that I didn't mean it," she said, sipping her coffee. "It's just that it wasn't planned—can't really explain it. Did it surprise you?"

"Hell yeah!—but a good surprise." He stirred a heaping teaspoon of sugar into his green enameled mug, looking thoughtful as he spoke.

"Would you have made a move if I hadn't?" Anna was trying to find a level of comfort. It was hard to proffer a disclaimer without sounding coy or disingenuous. She hoped not to descend into sounding "I don't usually … etc."

"Well, Anna, probably not—not right yet at least." He was struggling for words. "I don't see many people, ya know? The counselor at the VA says I'm kinda walled off." His ears reddened. "I mentioned you … he thought it was a breakthrough when I said you were becoming a sorta friend. I couldn't have imagined us in that way before last night—not that I hadn't noticed you were pretty—especially that night at your show. Ya know, I don't live with expectations. Last night was real nice. So tell me … "

"Hmm … You'd think one of us—well, I, in this case, could articulate what happened. Okay, as I've said, I would have driven off until another day—if not for the tire problem. I actually almost fell asleep—it was comfortable on the futon. Some noise or dream fragment woke me a bit. I got out of bed and noticed your door was ever so slightly ajar … I could hear you sleeping."

"Snoring?"

"Well, anyway, I peeked in." She raised her shoulders in a Gaelic shrug. "Whatever possessed me … maybe I knew if I didn't, it would never happen … and though I'm even confusing myself—I'm not sorry."

Miles got up and brought the steaming pot of coffee to the table, setting it directly on the worn wood. He sat across from her and gave her hand a brief pat. "It was a nice surprise. I guess we'll just see what we will see." He smiled, catching her directly in her eyes.

She exhaled. The tension left her. There was no need to say more.

Miles got the spare on the car, and once Anna got to Jerry's Garage, they fixed the tire. She left Miles by the river fishing—where she'd first encountered him on her trip to find the elusive town of Griffin.

NED

After closing shop, Ned headed for June's Place. The turkey special was good. It was a quiet night, not much conversation. Of course, it was early, which probably accounted for the sparse clientele. He felt at loose ends—agitated.

He waved good-bye to June and sauntered up the road and over the river, deciding a long walk might be the ticket. But, when he got back to his apartment, he still felt restless and uneasy. No calls on his machine, either. *Damn*, he thought, *might as well take a run over to Miles' cabin.* Sure, Miles might be surprised—but he did drop by now and again. He'd bring some old lures with him as a pretext. Surely, Anna would have left by now. Maybe he could weasel some info about Anna from Miles—and about Emma, too. *Excellent plan*, he thought.

As he drove over the old iron bridge near Miles' he spotted Anna's car. He hesitated, then backtracked and eased his car down a narrow road into a pull-off safe from view. *Well, well—this might be interesting.* He figured he'd hide out until he saw Anna leave. He walked along a fisherman's path on the shore opposite Miles' cabin. He could see the dim light from the cabin. About an hour passed—still no sound of Anna's car. By now he was doubly curious. What was going on? Shielded by the cover of darkness he decided to cross the bridge and walk the alternate river path to Miles'. The moon was near full. He could go most of the way without shining a light. The open river provided reflection, too.

It was slow going—especially the last quarter mile. He was aware of how clumsy he'd become in the woods. Twigs cracked. Branches swished. In fact, the colonel in Nam had reamed him out on a regular basis for being a klutz. He circled the woods behind the garden. *What say!* The cabin lights were out. He briefly thought of abandoning his mission. But a mangy, dog-like curiosity took hold. He could hear his breathing as he slowly crawled the fenced garden's edge. He stood out of sight close to the main-room window. It was quiet in there alright. Feeling some success, he walked near the open window. Damn! He stumbled on a log and fell. He heard someone now—footsteps on the floorboards. He ran, quietly as he could, down the main path for about half a mile and then cut to the river path. *Jesus! What was I thinking? Miles is a crack shot—probably still has the infrareds too.* He sat in his car until he was sure Miles wasn't out there, and then eased his car up to the main road—hightailing it home.

The following afternoon, as Ned was getting a coffee-to-go at June's, Jerry from the garage was mentioning how he'd had to change a flat tire for some lady hiker-tourist type who had run over a broken bottle in the woods near Griffin.

Ned, back at his store, stirred the coffee—three sugars. *Well*, he thought, *could be all innocent.* If Miles only had a phone or a computer, he might call him and nose around. It was always best to interrogate while the incident was fresh. *Damn Miles and his lack of technology!* And he wouldn't even get to see him until after his Connecticut buying trip.

five

WINGS

The drive back to Albany from Griffin was only two hours, but Anna's thoughts and recollections covered a lifetime, with *Scheherazade* providing an amiable background. It was true that she'd acted impulsively—out of character, really. But, if that was really true—why didn't she feel more anxious or even remorseful? She knew "it" might or might not happen again … Oh hell, the bullshit-o-meter came on—of course it was likely to happen again! Still, it also seemed altogether possible that they might just be casual about the whole thing.

In theory, she liked the idea of living in the moment. She and Cara had just been talking about that. Cara was sure to have an opinion about the event—that is, if she confided in her. As things stood, the confiding of personal tidbits usually only traveled one way—from Cara to Anna. Sure, Anna mentioned her feelings about Dee and Jack—and maybe her concerns about Em. But, truth be told, Anna didn't normally have an intimate personal life to share.

Cara, and sometimes Jenna, teased her occasionally about her celibate lifestyle—the kind of teasing that assumed she long ago had cast her lot and was resigned to it. And resigned she was, or so she'd thought.

She was not one to make too much of a diversion from usual patterns, yet she had a suspicion that it wouldn't be healthy to just ignore this sudden turn of events.

And what about Miles; could this be unsettling or destabilizing for him in some way? No, probably not. Damn it all to hell—she had no one to blame but herself! She took a deep breath and changed the music to an Elvis Costello CD. Actually, she liked it that Miles had said they'd "see what they'd see."

It was a good thing that she and Em would be leaving for Cape Porpoise to visit Jen in a few weeks—give her a chance to sort her thoughts.

Miles enjoyed fishing in the river. Last week he'd caught a nice brookie. He was hoping for good luck today—it would save him a trip to the market. Tomorrow he'd be filling in for Ned at the store. It'd be more convenient to do a food shop then. Ned always left early on his buying trips—left a key out back. Truthfully, he was not prepared for any nosy chitchat either. Ned definitely had his radar up in regard to Anna. Miles had noted him spying through the curtain after Anna had purchased the book about Griffin and they'd left the store. His years in the war and his current life scouting through the woods had taught him to note small movements. It was one of those automatic instincts by now. He chuckled, *Old Ned must have spent less time in the field in Nam.*

He didn't know quite what to think about Anna. She was warm and soft and smelled good. She was nice and a good sport, too. He believed what she said about not planning to bed him—he liked that. He hoped she understood that he wasn't one for expectations. She seemed to be comfortable about his ways.

The last woman he was with, several years back, had tended bar one summer and then moved on. She was alright, and had found him convenient—hadn't even mentioned she'd be leaving when she moved. They'd never really become friends. When she'd gone, he didn't give it a second thought.

It was a fact that he and Anna had started to be friends. Now, there was this unexpected sex thing that he didn't know what to make of. He chuckled again, *Guess my counselor won't be so bored next session—if I get to mentioning it.*

ANNA

When Anna got to her shop late that afternoon, there was a pile of messages waiting. There were two new summer weddings—very good—sundry flower vendors advertising their stock, credit card bills and reminder sticky notes on her computer, one saying that Emma had called because she couldn't reach her at home, another reminder from Cara that she was entertaining her sister Calendula and having a dinner party. *I already RSVP'd*, thought Anna—*didn't I?*

As she sorted the rest of the mail, Cara breezed through the door, returning from a dentist appointment.

"I *so* can't be seen with this ugly Novocain-swollen lip—I think I'll deadhead some of the hothouse plants, if you don't mind. By the way, I tried to reach you last night. Were you away?"

"It's a long story." Anna grinned in spite of herself.

"Soooo … worth a talk over wine?" Cara peered over her specs, her swollen lip making a comic smile. The door jangled. "Uh oh, gotta hide," said Cara, scooting out the door to the greenhouse.

Anna knew they'd go for a drink after work. It was their custom. However, she wondered just how much of her escapade she should, or would, divulge.

The client who stepped up to the counter was one of Anna's favorites. Brianna, originally from Jamaica, owned a bakery on Lind Street. Every week she bought two bouquets, one for her mother and one for herself. They'd become pretty good friends and went to the movies and dinner together, especially in the winter months. Summers, Brianna seemed to host vast hoards of family who loved to explore the Berkshires and Adirondacks.

"Anna," she exclaimed, "blue is one of your best colors." Anna glanced at the bucket of bluebells next to her. "No, no, I mean on you—your shirt," she laughed. "Yes, very good."

"Thanks. Actually, it's my favorite color. So, what's up with you?"

Brianna sighed, "Everything is great—lots of family staying with us. Business is very good. My niece, Angela, is helping with the baking.

You'll have to come by and try her chicken roti—superb. I see there's a new Quentin Tarantino movie coming in September."

"It's a date!"

Brianna ended up buying two bunches of bluebells mixed with daisies. After she left, Anna glanced at her image in the mirror across the room. Maybe, Collette, the French author was right—maybe *it* was good for the complexion.

After work she decided to go home first—check the mail and call Em before meeting Cara for drinks.

She reached Em on the first try. Unfortunately, Dee was evidently hovering in the background. Anna felt Em had something to say, but was holding back. Nevertheless, they had a good chat about their upcoming trip to Cape Porpoise. Anna took a quick shower, fluffed her hair and headed to Ambrosia to meet Cara.

EMMA

Emma marched up the stairs to her room with her MP player. Mother was such a pain sometimes. All Em had asked to do was go to a movie with her friend Amy, but no … instead, she had to practice her violin for an hour. By the time she finished, it'd be way late. It wasn't that she didn't like to practice. The thing was, she thought it was about time she got to make decisions for herself. After all, she was a good student and the top violinist in the school chamber ensemble. Mother seemed to like Amy, so that couldn't be it—*though if she knew some of the stuff Amy did, she'd freak.* She supposed some of the problem was that her mom traveled so much for her job that she tended to over-parent when she was around. Today, however, she just didn't care what Mom's reasons were; it was plain unfair.

She'd wanted to tell Gram about Mr. Silver—Ned—sending her a note, too. It was a little odd to hear from him, but she had allowed him to be a Facebook friend. It was fun to be talked to like an adult, which she practically was. Ned might be able to help her and Gram, too. But with mother listening there'd be gazillion questions—for no good reason, either. Honestly, these days Mom was always suspicious, which was ironic because kids at school thought she was a nerdy goody. It was weird to have to protest her "good reputation." Even Amy sometimes taunted her about never trying pot—not that it really bothered her.

Besides, she was worrying about Amy these days. She knew Amy was cutting herself and that you had to have some kind of serious problem to do that. Amy showed her all the little scars on her underarms she had made with a razor blade. It was icky. But she'd promised not to tell, and Amy said she'd stop. Still, she wondered if it was really serious. What if Amy bled to death some day and Em hadn't ever told anyone? That would be pretty terrible.

CARA and ANNA

Cara was comfortably seated in the back banquette of Ambrosia, head bent intimately next to Tony, by the time Anna arrived. They both seemed glad to see her. Tony excused himself after some talk about neighborhood business and walked them to the lounge, where her enlarged lady slipper photo hung over the fireplace.

"Gets a lot of compliments, Anna. People really love it."

Cara gave Tony a proprietary buss on the cheek, and she and Anna went back to their booth. Sal, the waiter, came over with a cheese platter and uncorked a mellow Nero D'Avalo. "Salute," they clinked together.

Cara was still preoccupied with Cally's visit, and Anna was trying to be attentive to Cara's obsessive menu-planning for the prospective dinner party. Then there was the subtext. It is curious how the stew of family memories continues to simmer—a *soupçon* of hurt, a dollop of kindness, a dash of forgiveness added periodically over time. She and

Cal were, as she was saying, "Definitely not two peas"—though peas were among the few vegetables Cal ate.

Anna knew this dinner thing was making Cara anxious, but she couldn't get a clear read on it. She knew that Cally was two years older than Cara—an accountant married to an accountant and working in Manhattan. Apparently, they'd often been at odds as children—Cal the serious student and Cara the impulsive, creative one. In their college years Cara at one point dropped out of Julliard to live on a commune in Vermont, while Cal persevered in her advanced degree in mathematics at NYU. They were both musical and could be comfortable together in that context. It seemed that Cara's main bone of contention was that Cally still felt free to offer unsolicited advice—usually framing it in a critical way. It all seemed like generic piddling family stuff to Anna.

Cara was saying, "Why, in the family lottery, couldn't I have gotten a sister like Jenna? You two always seem like great pals. She's so easy-going—even laughs at your silly puns. Cal's so … well, edgy."

"Don't know if you're looking for a real response, but I'd just chalk it up to plain old sibling rivalry. Besides, I think you're exaggerating—Cal loves it when you play the piano."

"Maybe," said Cara, swirling the wine in her glass. "So, how come no sibling stuff between you and Jenna?"

"Think about it—no parents might be part of the answer—though I've never really given it a thought before. Do you ever think maybe you're stuck on some hurt feelings in the past that might no longer have relevance? Like, Cal borrowed and ruined your favorite sweater, or your mom liked her drawing better than yours? You know, stuff that doesn't factor anymore."

"Jeeze, Anna, you got me on the couch here." Cara looked pensive. "One true thing I can say is that none of my family liked or understood my early commune/Vietnam protesting days—and that forever framed their thinking. Remember my Aunt Roslyn—the one who provided my inheritance? Well, one day she took me aside to tell me I was in her will to no small amount. But, in doing so, she shook a finger at me and said, "I just pray to God you won't do anything foolish with it." No matter that at the time I was a hard-working music teacher in a respectable public school. Roslyn had me cast in a mold."

"Did you want Cally to be more supportive back in your Vermont days?"

"Yeah … probably."

Cara smiled at Anna and joked that she could have a second career in counseling—she was feeling more optimistic, even content, about preparing a meal and assembling a few congenial guests for a pleasant evening together.

Anna said, "On a more practical, solvable matter—I think you should make a simple meal—like that delicious roast lemon chicken, mashed potatoes, peas, chocolate cream pie—maybe those spicy carrots you do—a sauvignon blanc?"

Cara sighed. "Not very showy, but doable—and Cally'd like it, except for the carrots and the fattening pie."

They both laughed.

"Oh my God!" Cara exclaimed. "You almost made me forget to ask—about your hike with Miles. So, is there more to the story? I know you must have gotten home real late. You usually pick up before 11:00."

Anna was sure she didn't want to elaborate. On the other hand, she didn't wish to be exactly secretive, either. She took a sip of wine and cleared her throat.

"It's kind of a roundabout story. One of those days that didn't go quite as planned. It started in an ordinary way. We hiked—a good, long hike over a mountain and into Wells. Where, by the way, we stopped at your friend Ned's store. Well, when we got back to Miles' cabin, he had prepared a tasty meal—venison stew. We were having a good talk, time went on and he walked me to my car. The dirt road where I park is about a mile from his cabin—there's just a path to the cabin. Anyway, I had a flat tire and decided it would be better to accept his offer to stay the night. So, that's why I wasn't home."

"Is that it? Did he make any moves? Is this woods guy turning into a relationship?" Cara coaxed in her merry, mischievous way.

"Actually, he didn't make any moves." Anna could state this truthfully. "I think we might become friends. I like him. He wears well." Anna sat back, hoping she'd concluded the story.

Cara leaned in with a wicked smile. "So, did you wear him well?"

Anna couldn't help laughing. "You got the cliff notes—that's it for tonight."

Cara gave Anna's hand an affectionate squeeze. "You know, it wouldn't be the end of the world if you let yourself unthaw and have some fun—as you may remember, there's nothing quite like it!"

Anna smiled without comment, thinking, *Yep, she's got that right.* But what she said was, "Hope you don't mind changing the subject— but when I saw Ned in Wells at his shop, I realized I'm still uneasy about him. Also, I don't think he likes *me* either. It's hard for me to put my finger on it—can't point to any particular reason. I thought you might help me figure it out."

"Hmmm … Actually, I think he rather likes you—at least, he's been curious about you, especially the research you and Em have been doing on your Griffin ancestors. I've only been out with him twice, including the time at your gallery show. He's the kind of guy who comes across as worldly and sexy—at first. He has that dark, dangerous look I find titillating. In my opinion, with him a lot of what you see is veneer—scratch the surface and you get an authentic plywood background. Except for his knowledge of antiques—that rings true. I know he embellishes on his past—or I suspect he does. Now, that doesn't mean I've totally given up on him." Cara's voice dropped to a whisper, "Knowing another guy is expressing interest keeps Tony on good behavior. I noticed Ned left a message on my machine last night. When I return the call I'll keep my antennae up."

Anna took the long way around the park on her way home. She wondered if Cara had intuited the deepening of her relationship with Miles. At first it had seemed so. The funny thing is, her friends, even Cara, were so used to her celibacy that they'd be blind to seeing her in a different light.

Anna was pretty sure that she'd eased Cara's anxiety about her upcoming dinner party for Cally. And maybe she had helped Cara stir the past—you never know what new thoughts might come to the surface. Thinking to include Brianna on the guest list was a good move. She was a smart, relaxed conversationalist—might bring one of her fabulous cakes, too.

In sifting through some of their conversation, Anna wondered if what she'd posited about the reason for the lack of sibling rivalry between her and Jenna was true. In the end, she concluded, there was no accounting for the peculiarities of family dynamics.

She was beginning to feel silly about voicing her reservations about Ned to Cara and Miles. It was beginning to seem that he was merely someone beyond her range of comfort, slightly foreign to her. Perhaps it was simply that. After all, neither Miles nor Cara found him particularly disturbing. She was about to let it go—then the image of Ned's hand on the small of Em's back at the photo show, touching and rubbing, came to mind. *That's it*, she thought. *He has boundary issues, and I'm the protective Gram.* And then she thought, *I haven't traveled this far in life by discounting my intuition.*

ANNA and JENNA

After work the next day, Anna decided she might as well firm up her plans for visiting Cape Porpoise. Jenna was very amenable to them arriving the last week in June and staying through the Fourth of July. They'd be there two full weeks.

"I'm pretty sure Jack and Dee will be okay with it. You sure you want to put up with us that long?"

"Are you kiddin'? One week never seems long enough. There's a lot to do here, and Aaron is looking forward to Em's help on the boat."

"Jen—"Anna paused, "Cara and I just went for drinks and were talking about sibling rivalry. I couldn't recall us being particularly contentious—is that true?"

"Jeepers, Anna, you city folk are awfully introspective. Sounds like you must have been low on old-fashioned gossip," Jenna laughed. "But, no, far as I know we didn't act that way growing up. Of course, Aunt Clara would never have allowed it anyway."

They both laughed, thinking of Aunt Clara the disciplinarian.

Anna felt buoyed by the prospect of a two-week vacation by the sea and some time with Jen.

MILES

Miles decided to ride his bike to Wells. He needed to pick up his mail and stop at the local "All Days" convenience store before heading to Ned's shop. His left knee was bothering him—the bike always got the kinks out.

Ned had made an unexpected visit yesterday—said he'd like to do a little shore fishing in the river, so they spent about an hour or so casting and reeling in. The thing was, Ned's tackle box was pathetic. He was short on lures and his pole setup hadn't seen much use. Miles gave him some worms and then helped him land a medium-sized trout.

Ned seemed eager to walk back to the cabin and shoot the breeze. Actually, that's when the real fishing began. He definitely tried to get some juicy gossip about Anna—said the guys at the garage had mentioned fixing her tire last Saturday. He even tried the old buddy stuff—asking if she'd stayed over and they got it on. To Ned's disappointment, however, Miles saw it coming and had no problem deflecting his questions. Nevertheless, Miles was greatly relieved that Ned would be long on his way to Hartford by the time he arrived at the shop today.

As he pulled into the post office parking lot and secured his bike he thought, *I'm not as concerned as Anna about Ned—but I'm glad she put me on alert. Sure, Ned was just acting like any guy might—still,*

I've never been much on kiss and tell. Of course, I usually don't have anything to tell. He saw his reflection and realized he was smiling.

He threw his mail in his pack—plenty of time to read while minding the shop. He stopped at June's and got the special and a Coke to go—her hot meatball sandwich was his favorite.

It was Tuesday, not likely a busy shopping day in Wells. Ned had given him a duplicate key that turned the deadbolt to the outer side entrance. Ned said he liked having him on the premises keeping an eye on the shop. Miles supposed he *did* provide some protection. He always did a complete walk-through and a quick survey of the merchandise before sitting at the desk behind the counter. He noted that one of the Eastlake chairs Anna had admired last Saturday was still there—and caught himself thinking it'd be nice to buy it for her. Quick on the heels of that thought, he reminded himself that being cautious was his stock–in-trade. *Damn, before I know it I'll be getting cautious about being cautious. After all, I don't have to buy it just because I thought about it.*

The door to Ned's back office was ajar, so Miles walked in to check that all was in order. Ned had left his private PC on. Miles didn't intend to snoop, but the screen saver gave him pause. On first glance it was just a photo of two nude women cavorting under a waterfall—the kind of picture a lot of guys would find appealing. What Miles found disturbing, however, was that on closer inspection they looked more like girls than women. It was only a mildly erotic scene, nothing explicit or tasteless. Still, it bothered Miles to see it. Maybe Ned thought of it as "arty." Actually, all the women he'd seen Ned with were buxom babes with quite a few miles on—not slim adolescent types. *Oh well,* he thought, closing the door behind him, *it's his business—not mine.*

Ned had left him a small list—a customer who might call about a bronze deer figurine, a woman in Minerva who was having an estate sale, and someone who might stop by for an end table. Other than that he was simply available for "whoever/whatever." Most likely, business would be slow until Thursday, when Ned was due back. Miles had agreed to open up from 1:00 – 6:00 p.m. It gave him a chance to use the phone and the computer—the pay was almost beside the point.

He sometimes called his uncle in Minerva. Occasionally he sent an e-mail to his sister Georgina, who lived in Boston. Though, of course, he never had much to report.

Oh, and there was elderly Mary Lou, too. Still getting around pretty good, but depending on him to fix the inevitable failures of an aging house—circa 1875, she'd said. They'd grown close over the years. He wouldn't take money, even for what was at times significant carpentry. But he did accept barter for the use of her car—at her insistence. He also didn't mind a bit taking her on grocery jaunts. She'd been willing to hear him out on the sense of using a walker while her sprained ankle healed, too. They both had an affinity for the woods; she was a "46'er" and had some great tales. Her old, hazel eyes took on a sparkle at the mention of the High Peaks. *Yep, she was a fine friend.* At the thought, he gave her a call, telling her he'd be by Friday to fix the kitchen window jambs. She said there'd be chocolate chips waitin'.

Now he could add Anna to the growing, though still miniscule, list of friends.

Maybe I'm turning into a social butterfly—not likely. But it set him to musing about monarchs and whether or not his "butterfly garden" would attract them. It was Mary Lou who had told him there were flowers other than milkweed that would attract the critters, and it was she who termed it a "butterfly garden."

His reverie was interrupted by the door jingle. A youngish couple began browsing the shop, which left Miles alert, though in the background—unless they had questions. Ned would have liked him to interact more with customers, but they both agreed it wasn't his style. The guy was looking in a locked case at antique timepieces, the woman at glassware. They both thumbed through old Hardy Boys and Nancy Drew books. They were an attractive couple in that sporty, mid-thirties way. The guy wore pressed khakis with a navy plaid shirt, and the woman was in a short denim skirt with a yellow-flowered camp shirt. *Must be on a holiday.* Miles went back to the newspaper. He looked up to see them heading his way and made what he hoped was a friendly face. "Can I help you?"

"We were wondering about that old chair. Eastlake, isn't it?"

"Well, it's in that style—mightn't be authentic though. Confidentially, it's a bit overpriced to my way of thinking." Miles couldn't believe he was saying this.

"What about this other chair—the Mission-style one?"

Miles walked around the counter to the chair in question and looked at the tag. "The wood's beautiful—oak with the original finish. A pretty piece." He paused. "I could knock 10 percent off this one."

"Hon, I actually like this one better than the Eastlake—what do you think?"

"Okay by me."

After Miles helped "Hon" and Marty get the chair in the car and waved good-bye, he returned to the counter, wrote "sold" on a tag and tied it to the arm of the Eastlake. He sighed and sat back behind the counter. He started to write an e-mail to Anna, then thought, *No, it'd be nicer to hear her voice.* For the moment, he went back to the paper. He'd wait until about 5:30 to call.

ANNA and MILES

Anna heard the phone ringing as she unlocked the door thinking, *Hope it's nothing about that flower shipment—probably shouldn't have left the shop early.*

"Hullo, Anna, it's me—Miles. Just thought I'd say a quick hello since I'm near a phone—sittin' Ned's store while he's in Connecticut. Is this an okay time? You sound out of breath."

"Hi—sure—glad to hear your voice. The phone was ringing when I opened the door—thought it might be business. If there's a problem with orders or a persnickety customer, Cara or Stan sometimes call me at home. So, how's everything out in the woods?" she said lightly.

"Good enough, Anna. Speakin' of flowers, my friend Mary Lou says you can plant specific flowers to attract butterflies—maybe you've got some ideas on that. Anyways, that's not why I called. I was wondering if you'd like to go on a date—dinner or a movie or something. I've use of a car this coming weekend." He waited.

"Oh gosh, I'd love to get together—problem is, I promised Emma we'd do more library research Saturday—she'll be staying over Friday night—maybe or maybe not on Saturday. I mean, you could visit the research library with us—you'd mentioned wanting to see it. Well, probably not." Anna took a deep breath; she felt herself rattling on. *Damn!*

"Hmmm … can't say as that would be a date. So, I'll need a rain check on that." There was a pause on his part. "Ya know, I would like to see the library—if it's not an imposition. How about me taking you and Emma to lunch? We can figure a date for later."

They made arrangements to meet at her house on Saturday and walk to the library. Anna was glad she'd be seeing him—even a chaste library visit supervised by Em was preferable to waiting and wondering. She also realized that, as a habitually single person, she left very little space on her calendar for new friends. Up until last Saturday the thought of romance, or even a dalliance, never crossed her mind. And now, the warm timbre of his voice was still reverberating through her body. She thought, *Damn it all to hell! I'm supposed to be past all this.* But, no, she was the culpable one—she had started it. Miles had as much as said so last week. And who was Mary Lou?—not that she gave a rat's ass, of course.

Anna turned on *the news hour*, heated a bowl of pea soup and poured a judicious, but full, glass of pinot noir.

MILES

Miles was glad he was going to see Anna Saturday. It was not exactly the date he'd planned, but still ... Actually, he hadn't had much of a plan beyond dinner somewhere. True, he'd had erotic thoughts before sleep, but that didn't translate into the reality of forming a plan to land her in bed after a dinner date. It did seem to him ungentlemanly to make a date that appeared to have the express purpose of coupling. On the other hand, she'd taken the initiative the first time, so it should fall to him to make the next move. *I do believe it's easier landing trout*, he thought, as he locked the shop and unlocked his bike from the lamp post.

He was glad he'd called Mary Lou, too. She was happy to hear that he'd moved his visit up a day, and she could lend him the car for a few hours. He was anxious to get the Eastlake chair out of the shop.

MARY LOU

Miles had expected Wednesday to be quiet, and it was. The day was overcast, dark grey. *Just as well*, he thought, *a good excuse to close early*. He wrapped the chair in a drab army blanket, placed it on the rear car seat and drove back to Mary Lou's house.

Her house was just a short ways north on Route 8—roughly three miles, as the crow flies, to his cabin.

She greeted him all smiles at the door, minus her walker. "And don't you say a thing. It's parked in the kitchen where our tea is waiting."

He followed her down the shadowy oak hall to the bright kitchen. He was pleased to admire his paint job. The dark blue walls nicely set off the white cupboards and woodwork, though he'd had qualms about covering the dark oak chair rail features with paint. She'd sensibly decided on linoleum tiles over his suggestion to sand down the floor boards—said it'd be less slippery.

"Now I could have made cookies, but I got to thinking about cinnamon toast, an old-fashionedy thing—hope you like it. I use lots of butter, sugar and cinnamon, and run it under the broiler 'til it bubbles."

"Ya know, I haven't had this in … I don't know when—really delicious." This was no lie, and he was happy to see a full platter. The scent of cinnamon – universally appealing.

"So, will you be showing me the chair? I think there's a little story you might tell me here." She impishly peered over her tea cup. When she saw him hesitate, she said, "Oh, go on—an old lady has to have some entertainment."

Actually, he had wanted her opinion on the chair, so he went to the car and carried it right into the kitchen. "Waddaya think?"

"Honestly?—Very nice, except for that dreadful upholstery. Also, it might be a little delicate for a big fella like you. Unless you're thinking of someone smaller sitting on it. Am I on to something?" She was clearly enjoying this tease.

"Well, Mar, remind me never to do anything like rob a bank under your eagle eye."

Once he'd mentioned Anna's name and how they'd met, Mary Lou was all attention. He told her about Emma and the family letters, how he and Anna had twice been hiking, that Anna had a flower shop and was an accomplished photographer. He hesitated, and then told her that Anna was becoming a friend, he thought.

"You know, I thought there was a story, and this is a humdinger. I have to say, I think this is a good thing. Of course, I figured a man must have his reasons for living in a god-forsaken cabin in the middle of nowhere—and I'm not one to pry. But, I've gotten a sense of you over the last five years and kind of wished you'd find a nice woman. Also, you're not as soggy solemn as you were five years ago. You laugh more. A person your age can enjoy a little companionship. You're a good lookin' fella, too." She laughed with him.

"Soggy solemn! That sounds pretty grim. Maybe I've changed a little. But it's hard to say about these man-and-woman friendships—how they'll take and such. She seems really nice and honest. I like her. Actually, the chair might be for her—that's why I bought it. So we'll see what we see."

He leaned back in his chair and took another cinnamon toast. Mary Lou had made some good points. He had never realized that she observed him so closely. *Then again*, he thought, *we all observe each other and form opinions, which we don't always let on about.*

"In my day I loved a good hike," Mary Lou sighed. "I hope you'll bring Anna by to meet me—and its fine if you leave the chair in the living room until you decide when to present it, too."

They left that subject to consider other matters while he worked on the kitchen window jambs. Then, Mary Lou gave him a hug with surprising strength before he stepped out through the door.

NED

Ned came back from Hartford in good spirits. He'd found some old oak dining room pieces that usually sold well in the shop or at the summer antique fairs. He had also acquired some vintage erotica that he knew some clients would pay a pretty penny for. However, his mood plummeted when he discovered he'd left his computer on in the back room.

Jesus H.! How stupid can I get! He thought a moment about Miles—whether he'd likely snoop in his files or not. He concluded probably not … *but still.* Next he walked through the shop and checked the inventory, looked at the list of "solds." *Good—two chairs, a quilt and a tea set—actually very good for midweek.* But why hadn't Miles written down the name of the customer for the Eastlake? He'd told him that even cash sales should have a name, and preferably an address. *Is it me or him? How hard is that to do?* He sighed, deciding to go upstairs to his apartment and leaf through the new erotica. Those were purchases he needed to be real careful about.

Ned liked the way he'd decorated his apartment. His friend Donna from Saratoga had given him good suggestions—brown leather, tweeds, some old gold-framed landscapes and a faux English hunting scene with spaniels and men on horseback. It was all manly and respectable—except for his bedroom, which Donna had called "scary bordello" in style. Maybe it *was* a little over the top with the mirrored ceiling, scarlet drapes and matching satin spread. He noted that it turned up the heat on Donna's lovemaking, however. *Christ, it's my house, anyway,* he thought, as he poured himself a healthy splash of Jack Daniels.

The thing is, he knew he had to stay under the radar of any authorities—just blend in and not call attention to himself. He'd managed pretty well for the past ten years, too, except for one close call in Cleveland two years ago. But he hadn't hurt the girl; in fact, she'd been more than cooperative. Actually, nothing bad had happened to any of the girls since Nam—and that was long ago. If he thought about it, there was a lot to be remorseful for back then, but he mostly avoided thinking about it. The problem for him now was, he fully understood that some of what he liked sexually was considered wrong in the eyes of the law—but to him it didn't *feel* wrong as long as he treated the girls well. He felt a dark mood coming on and decided to watch the game and save the pictures until later.

When a person recognizes his own dark side, even once, it forever casts an unwelcome light on those heretofore thoughtless romps with the devil. There are reasons for keeping things in the shadows.

EMMA AND AMY

Emma sat on the school steps waiting for Amy. She supposed that Amy was, once again, delayed by something she'd done or not done in one of her classes.

The day was warm, made her think of summer vacation. It was only three weeks 'til she'd be going to Cape Porpoise with Gram. Last year she got to go out on Aaron's boat. He promised to teach her more about lobstering this summer.

The geeky kid next door was kind of fun, too. His name was Watson, and he laughed when he told her it was a name he was meant to grow into. She might take her violin with her—for one reason, Mom would be pleased to think that she might practice. Another reason was that Aunt Jenna said she'd like to hear some pieces, and Watson played the guitar and piano, evidently pretty well—she wouldn't mind showing him that she, too, was a good musician.

"Hey, Em, you been waiting long? Mr. Connelly kept me late to lecture me on being more careful with math homework. He's such a pain."

Amy slouched next to Emma on the cement stairs of the school. She was dark-haired, skinny and a few inches taller than Emma. She liked accenting her pale good looks with light foundation and dark clothes. She often wore dark lip gloss, which she assiduously wiped clean before going into her house.

They both lived within the city limits and had permission to walk or ride their bikes to school if they chose. Now that it was near the end of the school year and the weather was warm, they'd agreed to walk or ride bikes together for the remainder of the term. Em's parents and Amy's mom felt it was safe for them to make the mile journey home as long as they were together, and their homes were only a block apart.

Emma wrinkled her brow. "So, why aren't you doing your math? That's one of your best subjects."

Amy sighed, "I guess. Why do I do or not do anything? According to the shrink Mom has me seeing, I'm looking for attention, or approval or something."

"Well, Amy—it sure can't be approval."

"Oh, right—you got me there. Wanna do homework together today? I got some way cool tunes we can listen to afterward."

"Sure—but can we do it at my house? Mom is home today and she made cookies. You know how she travels so much? When she's home she makes playing "Mom" a big deal," Emma said, rolling her eyes.

"Hey, I'll go for cookies and milk—well, one cookie and skimmed." Amy darted a quick furtive look at Em. She knew that Em thought she verged on anorexia.

Sure enough, Dee had chocolate chip cookies carefully placed on a blue-and–mustard-colored Deruda plate that she had recently brought back from Florence. She had set out two cups and matching plates on the countertop. When she saw Amy, she smiled and set out another plate and cup.

Amy wondered if she was intruding, but Mrs. Novelli seemed welcoming enough. Her own mom might have been annoyed with unexpected company. Their house, especially the kitchen, was usually untidy. Also, there probably wouldn't be cookies set out. Since her mom was between boyfriends, she tended to restrict her diet, hoping the reward for a size four would be a new and improved boyfriend. Besides, her mom was still at work and wouldn't be home anyway. She made a quick call on her cell to her mom's office, letting her know she was with Em.

When Emma saw her aproned mom dash from the fridge with a half gallon of 2 percent milk, smiling and chatting, she felt a little sheepish for her earlier disparaging comments. All in all, she realized she'd lucked out in the parent department. Her mom was always nice to Amy, too.

"So, Amy, any special plans for summer?" Dee asked.

"Well, I'm hoping not to have to go to summer school for math—that'd be a real downer. I'm supposed to work in Mom's office two days a week filing papers. At least that'll give me spending money. In August I'll stay with my dad in Hartford for a few weeks. We're gonna go to Mystic Seaport and maybe over to Tanglewood. We usually have fun."

"Sounds fun," Dee nodded. "When Em gets back from Maine, we'll have you and your mom over for a barbeque."

Amy left out the part about her dad being grumpy at the moment because he didn't get a promotion and her mom being pissed because he couldn't give her more money. *Of course, he wouldn't have to give Mom more if it wasn't for me*, she supposed. Secretly, she hoped they'd get back together. They were only separated, not divorced. Dad didn't even have a girlfriend. Well, at least he said he didn't.

After snack time the girls settled into the sunroom to do homework. When they finished they thought they'd ride bikes to Secret Falls, which wasn't really a secret; it was located on a footpath off a dirt road. All in all, it was safe riding in the daylight. But first they'd check e-mail.

"Whoa, Em—who's the new guy on Facebook? I don't recognize that name, 'goodboy'?"

"Nice of you to read over my shoulder … Actually, he's more a friend of Gram's than mine. Remember me telling about the old letters Gram and I found in the attic in Albany? Well, this guy, an antique dealer up north, has old photos of Griffin going back to the 1800s—can you imagine? Anyway, he likes to chat about stuff like that."

"He seems to like to ask lots of questions. Probably one of those adults who's not used to talking to kids. Does your mom check your mail?"

"Nope, the parents never check—they respect privacy. I'm hoping he'll help us find more pictures. I don't think Gram likes him, so I'm not mentioning his notes—not to Mom, either—she's insanely weird about talking to 'older men.' I mean, what's the big deal. We're almost adults—right? Okay—send!" Em clicked on the icon and then sat back. "Let's ride!"

Dee smiled to hear them clatter down the front steps, helmets in hand. She was glad to have Amy borrow her old bike, too.

Maybe she'd get Jack to go for a bike ride on the weekend. Em was away at Anna's. She might even pack a picnic. Jack was a good guy who didn't complain much about her frequent business trips. Nevertheless, she was aware that there was a growing feeling of distance between them. In truth, she knew most of it was her fault. "Guilt sure is a great motivator," she said aloud, slicing mozzarella for the lasagna.

Their counselor was no doubt right about reclaiming old good patterns or making new ones, and determination was one of Dee's best traits.

ANNA, MILES and EMMA

Anna and Emma arose early Saturday morning, knowing Miles would arrive by 9:00 a.m. Em had asked to borrow a pale pink long-sleeved shirt, which fit her surprisingly well. Anna went for a deep rose shirt that Emma said was "perfect."

"Perfect for what?"

"Oh, Gram—you know you like to look nice." A true enough statement.

Anna never failed to enjoy her lemony yellow kitchen with its blue-and-white-checked curtains, especially on a sunny day, which this promised to be. She poured them each a glass of orange juice, knowing they'd have coffee or hot chocolate later.

Em was organizing what she called her "genealogy folder" to show Miles and take to the library. Anna was making orange cranberry scones, saying they'd have them when Miles got there. In the meantime Em was making do with a small bowl of granola and a hunk of cheese. Anna felt a heightened sense of anticipation—not exactly a familiar feeling. In truth, she looked forward to Miles' arrival. She was perusing the *Times* when the door chimed. Sure enough, Miles stood framed in the jamb, smiling. They lightly hugged as Anna closed the door and led him to the kitchen.

"I thought we'd all need a bite before heading out. Also, Em wanted to show you one of her favorite letters from Luke to Tess—the letter that propelled us to Griffin."

Emma beamed, rising to shake Miles' hand. "You'll like the library, Mr. Duffney. It's way cool." She thumbed through the packet of letters.

"Let's see … okay, here's the one that made us want to visit Griffin. I'll just read a little now, so's we can get going—but I'll show you more when we get back. This letter—all the letters are from Luke to Tess. So we have to guess what Tess said back."

She read, "It is spring again, and the waters leap over the rocks under the falls to rejoice. I wish you could see it."

"It goes on about school in Wells and how he's gonna work in the tannery over the summer. And, of course, there's the other letters— all dated from 1872 to 1876. Luckily, he mentions a few names like Abigail Bush that we've checked out. Tess had a sister Belle. I'm going to see if I can find anything about her today in the records of the Bleekers." She looked expectantly at Miles.

"Well, that's all true enough about the falls. I'm glad you and Anna got to see the spring rush." Miles' deep brown eyes seemed focused inward. "I sure wish I had more old pictures of the place. When I last visited my uncle Brian in Minerva, he said he could swear he'd seen more old photos someplace. The problem is that his memory kind of goes in and out and sometimes his imagination takes over. By the way, Anna, these are delicious."

Spurred on by Emma, they all finished their scones and downed the last cup of coffee. Anna promised Miles a tour of the house when they returned.

Em was walking at such a pace down Madison Avenue that Miles said she must have her Gram's running genes. It was still cool enough that the brisk walk felt good.

The seventh floor archives were exceedingly quiet, even by library standards. They found two tables by a window and set to work. Miles decided to look for his family in the Hamilton County section. Anna and Em continued looking for information about Belle Bleeker. They didn't find anything about Belle, but they found an interesting note in an Albany bulletin about a Dr. Bleeker traveling to the Hancock Shaker Village to treat an outbreak of influenza. Miles found that Isaac Duffney had married one of the offspring of Nellie McCarthy, who had married one of the Girards of Griffin. He also found that Stephen Griffin II, presumably the namesake of the town, had later been a New York State Assemblyman.

After a few hours and some excited whispers, especially by Emma, they left with their notes and copies and were treated by Miles to lunch at the Olympia Diner. Two tuna melts and a BLT later they were strolling through Washington Park towards Anna's house. They sat for a moment in the afternoon sun by the statue of Moses—Miles and Anna on a bench and Emma cross-legged on the grass before them. In spite of the vibrant greens of the trees highlighting the yellow forsythia and purple tulips, they stayed in their mist-shrouded Griffin world, at least for the moment.

Em broke the silence. "So, if Doctor Bleeker went to Hancock village to treat patients, the Shaker people must have been living there then, right? Who were the Shakers anyway—a cult or something?"

Miles and Anna glanced at each other, then at Em. Miles spoke first.

"Since your Gram's not jumping to it, I'll simply say I don't know a lot about them. What I do know is that for some reason or other 'intentional communities' were popular in the nineteenth century. It might have been because our country was fairly new—less than a hundred years old. It seems people might have been experimenting with different ways to live in this 'new world order.' It always seemed to me that just striking out from Europe to come here by boat in the 1800s musta been quite the adventure in itself. You knew once you set sail from the mother country you weren't likely to go back. Yes sir, we were a real frontier. Anyways, one of the distinguishing things about the Shakers was they agreed to be celibate. They were also famous for being hardworking and inventive—big on farming and growing things. I once read they grew medicinal herbs and made elixirs and such in Hancock."

"You mean celibate like nuns and priests? Is that why they didn't last—not wanting kids and all?" Em shaded her eyes from the sun, looking curiously and directly into Miles' eyes.

"Yep, being celibate was a big factor in their demise. They counted on recruits to grow and sustain their mission. They did take in kids, like orphans who needed homes, or after the Civil War, widows with children. Does that sound right, Anna?"

"Yeah, I think you covered it. You know, they haven't quite vanished. Supposedly there are still a few living in Maine. I have to say, you've got me interested in them again."

"Gram, you mean we'll visit them when we go to Aunt Jenna's!"

"No, I mean I'll Google them."

A blue ball bounced unexpectedly in front of Emma and she reflexively punched it back to a younger boy about fifty feet distant, then waved and smiled. Miles and Anna watched the various tableaus at the park, Miles' hand casually brushing Anna's. Anna thought, *Isn't it strangely wonderful that my eyes are seeing the park before me while my mind and body are processing the tactile accident of Miles' hand. Wait, he patted—it was not accidental.* They all stood and walked the rest of the way to Anna's house.

Anna proceeded with a quick tour of the house, as promised, while Emma decided to make "homemade" hot chocolate to go with the oatmeal cookies. Miles was impressed with the house, saying the sitting room library was a gem. When they reached the top of the stairs and she waved dismissively by her bedroom, he held her close and kissed her. She responded. They reluctantly separated, laughing. "Ah, the tables have turned. Who'd of thought we'd be sneaking upstairs for a smooch while your granddaughter's in the kitchen," he said.

"And don't forget," said Anna, "Em thinks I'm celibate."

Then and there, they hastily made arrangements for a date the following Friday evening. Anna hoped nothing was on her calendar for that day, but even if there were, she'd cancel it.

At the sound of Emma's voice announcing the hot chocolate was ready, they obediently went down the curved oak staircase and walked into the sunny kitchen.

"Isn't Gram's house neat? It's so cozy and old-fashioned—I love staying here. Besides, it's close to our research library. My house in Barnfield is nice in a modern way, but as my Dad says, Gram's house has character. What do you think of the hot chocolate? I found cream to whip in the fridge—makes it special."

"Don't think I've ever had better hot chocolate. Your Gram's house is a beautiful example of a Victorian town house, even the inside—except for her modern office. It reminds me a bit of my friend Mary

Lou's house—that is, the inside fixtures. Come to think of it, I'll have to ask her if she knows anything about Griffin in the old days. Her house dates back to the 1870s and is within walking distance of Griffin. I believe the house was in her husband's family back to at least 1875. He's, of course, long gone, which is why she has me help with chores. The car I drove today belongs to her—part of our barter system. Someday when you're out my way we'll visit Mary Lou. She loves to hear stories about hiking in the woods." He sat back in his chair smiling at Emma.

"So I guess Mary Lou is pretty old." Anna hoped she got the tone right.

"Yep, she's gotta be eighty-something—but she's kinda cagey about her age. Some women are, ya know. She twisted her ankle recently, otherwise she's pretty spry."

Em, still focused on the research, reminded them that they had found more mysteries today—like the Mr. Duffney link back to Nellie McCarthy and the Girards, and Dr. Bleeker and the Shakers. She flashed them her notebook where it was all carefully written, including pages she'd copied from records. She was a serious, if young, researcher.

Anna invited Miles to stay for dinner when she realized that evening was approaching. He declined, saying Mary Lou would be expecting him to return the car. He had very much enjoyed the day and warmly thanked Emma and Anna for including him. He noted the attractive picture they made, standing next to each other and framed in the curved oak doorway.

As Miles drove north, he felt … lucky—that was it. Life threw a lot of curves along the way—this one, meeting Anna and Emma in the woods, had been lucky. Probability told him that a guy deliberately choosing to live in a circumscribed pattern in the forest could stand a fair chance of predicting life's events. There would be walks, fishing, gardening, whittling, odd jobs, illnesses, accidents, occasional visits and, of course, eventual death. On that count he'd figured a hunter would find him some spring, stuck to his floorboards. Now, as luck would have it, his prospects looked different. Yep, it was a good surprise—whatever it was.

He saw Mary Lou's parlor curtain move as he pulled into the driveway, and hoped he hadn't made her anxious by his slightly-later-than-said arrival.

Once inside, he saw that Mary Lou had clearly expected him to stay for dinner, and he was glad then that he hadn't taken Anna up on her offer. It would have saddened him to think of Mary Lou sitting here and expectantly waiting dinner for him. The table was set with rose-rimmed plates and clear glass water tumblers. Mary Lou had a large platter of fried chicken and a bowl of buttery mashers in the oven; green beans with shallots were on a top burner. It looked delicious and he said so, pushing Mary's chair closer to the table before he sat.

"So, how'd it go in Albany today?" Mary had this way of cocking her head when asking questions. "Did you have a nice time?"

Miles guffawed. "I see you're not beatin' around the bush—cutting right to the chase. Let's see, where should I start … her house, the big library, lunch, the park, what we might have said? … hmmm." He knew he was teasing her a bit. "Well, let's see … Anna lives right on Washington Park in an old Victorian brownstone. Inside it would remind you of your house here.

"She has a smart little granddaughter named Emma, around fourteen I'd guess, who visits from Barnfield. As you know, I met them early spring by the river while they were lookin' for Griffin." He laughed. "Anyways, Em has taken fiercely to researching people from the old days. She and Anna found a bunch of musty letters in the attic that appeared to be written by a young man from Griffin to a girl in Albany. They've already figured out that the girl, Tess, was a relative of theirs who in the late nineteenth century lived in Anna's house. The boy, Luke, was definitely from Griffin and the girl, Tess, seems to have stayed with her grandmother some summers in Griffin. There are no letters from Tess to Luke, so the fun is in piecing together her side of the conversation. Together, Emma and Anna have already found out quite a bit about the Bleekers in Albany. Anna's maiden name was Bleeker. So they took me to the State Library archives to show me how they find clues and such." He paused, realizing Mary might not care about all the details, though she had been a librarian at one time.

"And this was fun? You musta been desperate to spend time with this Anna, if you ask me."

"Now that wasn't somethin' I was thinking to ask you … Believe it or not, I actually found out some interesting stuff about my own family—possibly connected to Griffin, too. I think one of the Duffney's once married a schoolteacher from Griffin. Her name was McCarthy."

"Any other names crop up?" Mary Lou was getting more curious.

"Not a lot more. Emma was particularly intrigued by a newspaper account of a Dr. Bleeker, probably Tess's father, going to Hancock Shaker Village to treat patients. Emma is thrilled with every little kernel of information—quite a kid." In the telling he realized how much he liked Em, too.

"Now you've got me thinking. My memory is not as good as it used to be. Also, I didn't much pay attention to old-timers' stories before I became an old-timer myself. But I do recollect Uncle Dawson telling a story about someone from Griffin running off to join the Shakers. The only reason I remember it is there was some kind of love story to it—like someone died or a lover spurned—something interesting to it. All this talk of back then, when are you going to tell more about you and Anna?"

"Let's see … I still like her—think she still likes me. And … we have a date for next Friday, without the kid." He smiled broadly.

"I just knew it, you old dog! Life is looking up for you. Now, let's have a piece of this lemon meringue pie and celebrate."

Miles told her he did feel lucky right now. Mary Lou said there was a lot of luck to life. She offered that he keep the car until tomorrow, because evening had fallen. He declined, knowing his muscles needed the feel of a bike ride, and he had a good headlamp. Also, he didn't want to hit something sharp with Mary's car going over the bridge, like Anna had. (And he didn't want to explain about Anna's flat tire, either.)

He felt the thunk, thunk of the tires on the wooden slats of the bridge and then turned right onto the pine-needle-covered path. The house was dark as he approached. It looked small in the moonlight.

NED

Ned felt a certain surge of elation when he saw Emma's Facebook response to his note. She mentioned being on the Barnfield High soccer team and having their last game soon. She said she was looking forward to summer vacation and was going to the Lee Mall to buy camping supplies Saturday. Also, that she was still doing research with her Gram about Griffin and wondered if he had found more pictures.

He felt like rushing off a note to her, but knew he needed to be cautious. She was so pretty. He would love to have a picture of her. No, he'd put himself in danger if he wrote anything like that. He could check the Barnfield High girls' soccer team schedule and, depending, he could just casually happen on the game. He scrolled the Barnfield district school homepage.

Bingo! The game's in Pittsfield tomorrow—just where I might be looking for antiques. It could be risky if parents were around, but he could probably finesse it. He knew how to dress to fit in. Besides, just a glimpse of her would feel good. He'd bring his camera—the one with the telephoto lens. It was worth a try.

And then there was the mall on Saturday. Even if her parents were there, he could give the impression of a kind uncle type wanting to help a kid with her genealogy project. Yes, it was getting clear now. Also he was feeling excited. Damn! That kid's a beauty. He could just imagine her in shorts … or less. He poured a finger of Jack Daniels over ice, sat in his Cordovan armchair and perused his latest cache of vintage erotica. *Damn—the young ones sure are flexible. Most of this stuff was late-nineteenth-century porn, too. Prurient interests probably increased with all the manifest taboos of that era …*

The game drew a pretty good crowd, which was good cover. No one seemed to notice him. He sidled up to a mom and made some chitchat—once he felt sure that she was rooting for the home team.

All the girls looked sweaty and gorgeous. Finally, he spotted Emma and a pretty dark-haired girl on the sidelines. They were laughing, and when Em turned in his direction he got a few quick shots with the telephoto lens. Then he got a shot of the dark-haired girl for good measure. *Oh man—they look so nimble in their shorts and tees.* The coach waved the two girls onto the field and he watched until the end of the period. Not wanting to press his luck, he bid good-bye to the mom next to him and left. *Mission accomplished.*

He downloaded the photos when he got home, and enlarged some of them. He especially liked the one of the dark-haired girl standing next to Emma. He would never hurt Emma; she was so beautiful and precious.

Saturday, as arranged, Emma and Amy met for their summer buying excursion. They liked shopping at the Lee Mall. Amy's mom had dropped them off for a few hours with the usual admonitions, promising to pick them up for lunch. They had each bought a few t-shirts and shorts on sale at Gap. Emma wanted to look at daypacks, but they decided to first stop at the food court and have a Coke.

Emma was surprised to see Ned standing by their table. He was carrying a coffee and asked to sit with them. It seemed he'd been to an estate sale in Lenox and was on his way home. He offered to buy them a second Coke, which Emma declined but Amy accepted. He mentioned he'd found a few more pictures that might very well be of Griffin. Emma said maybe she and Gram could stop at his shop when they returned from their trip to Maine.

Amy was particularly chatty and kept interrupting the conversation about Griffin. In fact, she was so annoying that Emma excused herself and went to the ladies room. When she returned and walked towards them, Amy was leaning in close to Ned and laughing. *Honestly! It looks like they're flirting!* Amy could be such a jerk, but most of the guys she flirted with were at least still in high school. Probably Ned was an idiot, too, though she did hope he would share more Griffin pictures. Anyway, they needed to stay on their shopping schedule. Amy's mom would be mad if they were late for their meeting place. She walked to the table, smiled and didn't sit down.

"Thanks for the Cokes. Amy and I'd better get a move on if we're ever gonna finish shopping."

Amy looked pouty, but stood—extending her delicate hand. "Nice meeting you," she said, tossing her dark hair over her shoulder and smiling.

Ned stood with a courtly, gentlemanly bow. "It was certainly my pleasure happening on you two young ladies."

He watched them walk away. Amy had a provocative saunter. And he didn't think it was his imagination, either. After all, she had given him her e-mail address. Yes, indeed—he might have a new friend on Facebook.

Every season is forever new, year after year. Em and Amy were expectantly awaiting their summer adventures, as was Ned.

Emma thought, each new season heightens our anticipation for change. We sense summer coming. In spring we are alert to unfurling leaves and blossoms opening, and wonder when we can hope to be comfortably, fully immersed in lakes and streams. We begin to wear brighter colors and look for berries at stands.

ANNA and CARA

In preparation for Cara's dinner party, Anna decided she'd make lemon mousse. It was actually beginning to feel like summer. It was only two weeks before she and Em would go to Cape Porpoise. The thought of dinner tonight with Cara and her sister Cally made her downright nostalgic about Jenna. Jenna was going to be surprised at the blossoming of Emma, even though they'd been together over the Christmas holidays. *Thank goodness older folks don't usually change that fast—at least, I hope not.* The thought made her chuckle.

It was such a nice evening for walking, even with the lemon mousse in tow. Cara lived on Finch Street, west of the park. She had bought the building for a song, she liked to say—the humor being that the former owner had sung with her in a choir and had actually been a former lover, too. Cara rented the basement apartment to a male graduate student who did some chores in exchange for reasonable rent.

Anna arrived almost a half hour early, knowing that Cara would appreciate a helping hand.

"Oh honey, thank God you're here! I somehow lost track of time and forgot to make the salad—could you please—while I finish arranging the porch? The oranges and avocado are on the counter. Wow! That looks great," she said, dipping her manicured finger in the mousse. "Yummy."

Anna quickly finished the salad, stuck it in the fridge, and carted a tray of glasses to the back porch. "Cara, you've done a terrific job out here. Your porch is always pretty, but the fresh white paint on the lattice and the profusion of flowers look spectacular."

"Yeah, well I work for this flower shop—they have great stuff," she laughed. "Ron, downstairs, did the painting. Oh no!—the doorbell—must be Cal, never a second late," she rolled her eyes.

As it happened, Cally *and* Brianna stood framed in the open door, Cally carrying a small, chic overnight case and Brianna a canvas sack of goodies.

"Ah, I could set my watch by you," said Cara, air-kissing Cally. This may have engendered a prick of alertness in Cally's posture, but it was quickly dispelled by Brianna.

"Yes, being on time is a very good thing," she said with a Jamaican lilt. "In my family, which as you know is very large, the late one gets the bad seat and the end of the stew—maybe only gravy—maybe only the bone." Her good humor set the mood as they all filed to the porch.

Cally and Brianna were genuinely impressed by the profusion of flowers and greenery in bloom. There were various anemone, spiraea, asters, pansies and ferns, as well as red, pink and orange geraniums and hanging pots of cascading petunias in all shades of blue and yellow. The whole quilt of color was casual and elegant, reflecting Cara's persona to a tee.

"My! We sit in the middle of a garden. Look, there is even a monarch circling the purple flowers," Brianna said.

"Yes, my sister is the artistic one. This is, well, magical," Cally smiled at Cara, taking the liberty to pour them each a glass of the white Bordeaux she had brought. Turning to Brianna, "In Jamaica the flowers were extraordinary. I enjoyed a winter holiday there last year. Do you still have family there?"

"Yes, still plenty family, though many are here, too. My bakery keeps me very busy—very hard to get away. But, I do miss the tropical flowers. Also, since 9/11, travel seems much too hard. Every time I'm at airport I wish for the old days—you know? "

"Yes, I do agree. I travel a fair amount for work—can't get used to all the security rigmarole."

"Do you think younger kids already think its normal?" Anna chimed in. "If you were, say, under ten on 9/11—you've probably adapted. I wonder if kids feel less anxious, or if increased fear is part of their natural state. I mean, the smoldering towers and the planes were unthinkable for us when it happened. For us, 9/11 will always be like when Kennedy was shot—the experience forever etched in memories"

"So, where were you on 9/11?" asked Brianna.

"I was at the shop tending the new arrivals in the greenhouse. Cara and Stan had gone to the Coffee Bean on a breakfast run. They came storming in, saying the Twin Towers in New York City had been hit by a plane. We assumed it had been an accident—turned on the small TV in the back of the shop. Mrs. Simballi from next door and her young niece, Laurie, who had come from the City to Albany for a job interview, were in a tizzy because they couldn't reach any of their Brooklyn relatives—including Laurie's mom.

"After the full magnitude of the disaster was revealed, we closed shop and hunkered down in front of the TV with the Simballis, who were still trying to contact friends and family. Cara and I put together a makeshift pot of goulash, Stan bought some beer, and we all watched events unfold. For the next few weeks after, we were busy sending flowers—either for relief or condolence. You know, even now there remains a sense of unreality to it."

"Yes, that was true for us, too. Of course, much of my family have come recently from Jamaica and live in the City. They came here because they thought they would be safer, as well as prosperous. My two cousins had only been here for a few months. They were so frightened and discouraged—they came north to stay with me. Angela is still with me. It is good. She is a fine baker and I make sure she has time for her teaching program at university."

They all agreed to having similar experiences and feelings—first horrified and terrified, and then eventually slipping into a cocoon of unreality. Was it because they had watched it at a distance, on TV? Cally and Brianna had even gone early-on to the crater where the towers had stood, and they all had at least driven near the site within that first year. The pilgrimage seemed necessary.

Cara sipped her wine, thinking. "Anna and I have recently joined in at a few rallies. Iraq and Afghanistan are terrible wars, and our politicians seem so hapless and inept. The participants at the peace rallies are usually more our age than student age. At first I thought it peculiar—I mean the lack of college kids. I thought, don't they care? But, lately, I've come to realize that our street demonstrations were different—what we did for Vietnam. It was 'our thing.' Kids today have their own thing—they most often use the Internet as their voice. So, protesting is done by them in different ways." She glanced Cally's way to see if she was perturbed by these comments.

"And you've concluded?" Cally asked, with genuine interest.

"Concluded? Dunno—maybe just that each generation has its own variation on old themes." Cara shrugged, rose and went to the kitchen.

Anna was in the midst of telling Cally and Brianna about Miles' experience with 9/11, when Cara returned to the table with the casserole.

"Can you imagine?" she said. "He was in his cabin in the woods without either phone or TV. He knew nothing of the disaster until

September 13, when he went to Wells for provisions. He said it felt so strange—like he'd returned from a time warp."

"Hmmm …" said Cara, setting the casserole down and pouring more wine all around, "I always like hearing stories about Miles." Her expression cued Brianna.

"Anna, could this new friend be in the category of romance? Ah, we all so love a story of romance … look—in the petunias—those two monarchs are having a romance."

The conversation was lightening, which was a good thing. After all, they were not likely to solve the complex problems of America and the rest of the world that evening.

"Cara, where in ever did you find Grandma's recipe! It must be at least twenty, maybe thirty years since I've had her chicken rice casserole. Remember when she helped us make it for Ellen Vanderpool's shower? We thought it quite the sophisticated dish, what with the pimentos and almonds. This is yummy! Brianna's sweet potato rolls are perfect with it."

Cally was clearly touched by her sister's thoughtfulness. And that pleased Cara.

They continued to talk—Anna and Cara telling stories, some humorous, about their involvement in the Women's Movement back in the 1970s. Brianna said that she'd read much about it in newspapers as a young person in Jamaica. In her opinion, it had given her courage to get a small business loan to open her bakery—the idea of the American Dream had pushed her along, too. Cally said that she now appreciated that activists, such as her sister, had paved the way for her, but at the time, back then, she had found the idea of marching and confronting legislators confusing and embarrassing.

"No, that is not it exactly," she said. "From this vantage, I think all the tumult of the '70s frightened me. I was a good student and didn't want to consider that gender might hamper my success. Let's face it; I was Miss Prim back then."

Cally stopped short of saying that she and their parents were horrified when Cara was photographed braless and wild-haired, waving a poster demanding the Equal Rights Amendment at a D.C.

demonstration. Also she had felt alienated when Cara dropped out of school to join a commune in Vermont.

"If you were Miss Prim, then I guess I held the title of Miss Outrageous." Cally smiled at Cara's comment, and Anna and Brianna laughed.

It was a lovely, successful dinner party—perhaps memorable. Cara was pleased, if puzzled. *Then again, current waves of thinking always wash away the detritus of those memories crashing before. And it seems the sediment left to memory can prove fool's gold.*

MILES and ANNA

Miles arrived wearing a blue chambray shirt and chinos. Anna wondered if he'd bought new clothes for the occasion. The thought pleased her. Besides, they went well with her choice of a blue denim skirt, white blouse and lapis jewelry.

Anna noted that Miles was an excellent driver. He had selected Olana as an outing for them before dinner. He'd been curious about it. Also, he liked driving on the secondary roads that followed the Hudson River. He was not used to cultural venues, driving with Anna beside him or going casual dress-up, but all in all he felt relaxed and comfortable—even as he traveled in what was for him a kind of alternate universe.

Anna, however, was in her element, even if her driver was part-alien. At the moment, map open on her lap, she was navigator. As they crossed the bridge over the Hudson River at the village of Catskill, Anna noted the magnificent structure high on a hill. It was an amazing sight, and they were even more intrigued as they drove the winding entrance road to Olana.

The idiosyncratic, Persian-style mansion of Frederic Church, famous Hudson River School painter, sat high on an overlook above the Hudson River. The vast home, built of sand-colored blocks of stone, had many archways and large, curved, cathedral windows. The most striking aspects, however, were the decorative tiles and Arabic script features that ornamented the house in bold colors of blue, green, mustard and gold. Many of the windows were filigreed black on gold-colored glass. The house in its singular magnificence was framed in an equally imposing landscape. It was not surprising to find that Church had spent nearly forty years perfecting his home and grounds. Miles and Anna were duly impressed.

After capturing many angles of the mansion with their cameras, they explored the grounds and views. There were miles of trails along which to pleasantly while away an afternoon. The trails looped down to the bottom of the hill and around the pond before climbing back up to the flower garden that was southeast of the house.

"Can you believe it—see the monarchs hovering in the garden? We're having one treat after another."

Miles was pleased that the day was going well. "I think the garden may have plants meant to attract butterflies. Notice those purple plumy flowers—Mary Lou calls those 'butterfly plants.' She had me help her put some in her garden last year—they're perennials."

"Yes, they're a favorite of mine, too. They're called purple cone-flower. Let's walk back up top to see the views of the Hudson River. I'd like to try a few more photos before we leave." Anna saw that the light had shifted just enough to highlight the mountains west of the Hudson.

"Ya know, one of the things about Church was how much he traveled—Europe, Middle East, South America, Mexico and here, too. Imagine how difficult travel musta been back then. I find it daunting even today."

"So where would you like to go if you could?"

"Dunno - haven't thought much about it. Did a bit of moving about after Nam, as you know, but my current circumstances don't encourage it. Guess one of these days I should go to Boston to visit my sister Georgina. World travel ... I'd havta think about it."

Miles and Anna took some more pictures, Anna of the scenery, and Miles of Anna in the foreground of the mountains. The vista *was* beautiful, he thought. It was easy to see why Church had so often painted this landscape. Miles remarked on how mysterious and magnificent Henry Hudson must have found the river in 1609.

Anna said, "But it's still magnificent and quite wonderful, in spite of the wear and tear of the past nearly 400 years."

"I've hiked into 'Lake Tear in the Clouds', just to see where the Hudson begins. Did it twice, once about ten years ago."

"And?"

Miles laughed, "And it was great."

They picked a small café with an outdoor patio for dinner. The evening was warm enough, and they selected a corner table. Though it was hardly dark, the waitress lit the center candle. "Special occasion?" she smiled.

They both demurred good-naturedly, resuming their conversation. They felt comfortable and at ease together. Anna already knew she'd invite him for coffee when they returned to her house—and that he'd accept. She also decided to tell him about the trip to Cape Porpoise that she and Em were taking the following weekend.

Miles was curious about Cape Porpoise. He and his sister Georgina had been to Ogunquit a few times with their mom when they were teenagers, and he remembered the lovely beaches and ice-cold waters.

"As I recollect, we spent hours walking that long stretch of beach. Sometimes we got out at sunrise to find the best shells. Mom always joined us about 7:00 a.m. with a thermos of creamy coffee and donuts ... got to drive as far as Kennebunkport once."

"Really? You know, that's close to Cape Porpoise. My sister Jenna and her husband moved there from Boston. He's a retired cop. He still does some consultant police stuff, though he likes to think of himself as a lobsterman. He has a permit for a number of lobster traps—actually, lobstering is one of the things Em most looks forward to—well, as an assistant of sorts. Jenna teaches in the local school, so she more or less has the summer off. She and I spent time in Ogunquit as children with our aunties. Do you get to visit your sister often?"

"Well, sorry to say, not so much. I'm a little hard to reach, and Georgina resents that. However, I do make sure we get to talk once in a while. She finds my lifestyle peculiar and doesn't mind telling me so. Maybe I'll try to visit her this summer—though I don't like to always hear the same old, ya know?"

When they spoke of the past, it would seem their paths might have crossed earlier. Unspoken, they both thought about how much of life is determined by circumstance.

They talked more about Maine, beaches, childhoods and lost loves. Their comfort level was growing. They were willing to display for each other these pictures, maybe just snapshots, of their early histories, each anxious to share the patchwork of moments in time.

At the doorway to Anna's house, she invited him in and he accepted. They skipped the formality of coffee and walked hand in hand up the stairs. This time he led the way. After gently undoing the hooks and buttons, they slid between the cream-colored sheets and kissed slowly—almost unbearably slowly, thought Anna. Miles thought how enjoyable it was to feel wanted again. He was entranced by the beat of her heart. She loved the sandpapery feel of his chin in the hollow of her throat.

He left before dawn. They promised to speak during the week. Anna gave Miles her cell and Jenna's phone number. Miles gave her Mary Lou's number, just in case, though he realized the awkwardness of it. Nevertheless, they felt joy as they hugged before opening the door. He gratefully accepted a mug of coffee to go.

MILES

As Miles drove up the Northway, he wondered if he could ever have predicted this turn of events. Thoughts came in rushes.

When he had met Anna and Em by the river, it wasn't anything special. Em was so curious—it seemed natural to show her the pictures. Anna, on the other hand, was so reticent that he didn't particularly take to her—thought she was kinda snobby. *So I'd havta say, the very first impression wasn't great.*

Well, by this stage in my life I know a lot, and one thing I know about is trajectories—jeez, musta shot my first rifle when I was ten—got my first deer at twelve. Then there was Nam. 'Course, I already knew how to aim and shoot. At Clarkson he remembered thinking about direction in other ways. He remembered how he got an "A" on some fool paper he wrote for saying something about needing to aim correctly to get where you wanted to go—probably carried on a bit with the analogy. Ever since, it's been one of those ideas he'd pull out once in a while to measure how he was doing. *Allows me to chide myself for taking a wrong turn, like—what did I expect? But this time?—Just didn't see it comin'.*

Then he thought about how when he tells old 'Bumble'—his counselor, Jake Bumby, about it on his next trip to the VA, Bumble's gonna have a field day. Last month, when he told Bumble about taking this lady on a photo shoot, it was the first time he'd seen Bumble's eyes opened wide in twenty years. *Poor Bumble, ten or more years of talk about huntin' and fishin', and now this.* Bumble had seemed to struggle with this new facet of Miles' life much more than Miles himself did. "Miles, you are comfortable with this? Yes? There are no bad feelings, yes?" *Well, he's a good sort—got me over some rough patches.*

"Damn that car was close!" he said aloud, applying his brake and horn. *Hope I wasn't that much of a jackass at that age!*

He decided to drop the car at Mary Lou's and offer to take her grocery shopping. She was able to do that on her own, but Miles suspected she limited her purchases, not wanting to carry too many bags to the kitchen. She always referred to their shopping trips as "stocking up."

It was such a warm day; her screen door was open to a gentle breeze. "Hope I'm not too early," he said.

"Nope, already had my coffee and pulled a few weeds from the garden. Those raised beds you put in last year are dandy—makes weeding easy as pie. Though, as I always say, making pie is none too easy … "

As they got in the car, Mar said, "I was going to ask if your date went well—but just looking at your face, I know it did." She buckled the seat belt, looking smug as she settled in.

"Gosh, guess I don't have to tell a thing then."

"Oh, go on. You know I want the details—where you went for dinner, who ordered what, and so on."

He told her about Olana and was somewhat surprised to hear she'd been there "back in the day." When she said she remembered how beautiful it was, he described the house and spectacular views in greater detail.

"Yep, just like I remember it," she said. "We stayed late just to see the sun set over the Hudson River."

After he carried the groceries in, they walked to her backyard garden. She cut some lilacs for him, a mixture of deep purple and white.

"I know you don't have these back at your cabin. They're particularly fragrant towards evening and should last a few days in water—case you have company," she added. She loved teasing him.

"Not likely, but you never know. I'll send smoke signals if anything happens. Oh, I almost forgot—I gave Anna your phone number, just in case. Hope you don't mind."

"Ah ha! Guess I'll get to meet her sooner or later."

Miles turned and waved as he peddled down the driveway. He felt a little silly carrying a bouquet in one hand with a pack full of groceries on his back.

Miles was relieved to have his life back to normal the next morning as he sat in his old Adirondack chair—coffee mug on one chair arm, and whittling knife and wood scraps ready on his workbench. Sunlight heightened the multitudes of green surrounding him and cast purple-black shadows under the leaves. The young lettuces in his garden looked about ready to pick. *This is the life I love*, he thought. He'd promised Ned he'd work at the shop Wednesday; otherwise his time was his own. No one was apt to wander to his cabin this early in the summer, no phone to ring, not even a mailman to stop by.

The thing is, he never felt exactly lonely—rather, he felt somewhat blessed, surrounded by an amazing variety of greenery and colorful rocks, all strewn by nature's hand in the dark loamy Adirondack soil. On a warm day like this, it was hard to imagine a better place. He knew that there were people in town who referred to him as a hermit. Maybe that was true, but he doubted any of them had experienced the woods as fully as he did.

Even as he thought this, however, he heard as though in the distance the rumbling bass notes of another melody. If he wanted to, he could still hear and see that black earlier time when he had wandered here to the place his dad and uncle had used as a hunting cabin. His life then had been a mess. For over a year he wondered if he would survive.

The hunting cabin was more of a hideout back then. The trees hovered above, the brambles and rocks blocked his way. When the woodstove went out, he lay de-energized in his smelly sleeping bag, not giving a damn. He lived on fish, game and Campbell's beans. That whole year had been discordant, grey, disheartening, like the presence of death. The woods were hard, sharp, unforgiving. Luckily, Nam and his childhood had given him great survival skills. He had often backpacked as a kid; later, in Nam, he'd faced greater challenges surviving the jungle. Nevertheless, it seemed he was defeated. He often thought he'd just end it. But in the end he didn't give in and didn't give out.

One day he awoke in his cabin after a mindless two-day drinking binge. It was cold, and he could hear rain slashing on his tin roof.

Then he got to thinking about the trajectory thing—*time to point and aim.* And so he did.

But, who was he kidding? The woods could be tough. Sure, it was home and he loved the peace and beauty of it, loved the changing seasons—loved willing his mind to create and his body to push back against the hardship of the wilds. Yep, it was violins and flutes these days, with a few blues guitar riffs to make it interesting. No rumbling kettle drums and mournful pipes and oboes. Why? *Because I say so.* So, was he a hermit? He could see the point of it.

Then there was Anna. He wasn't willing to call it a problem—yet. Nonetheless, visiting Anna had felt like visiting a foreign land. Granted, he had once lived in urban areas, and lived successfully. Still, he enjoyed best having Anna visit him on his own turf. And now there was the possibility of a communication issue. In fact, that was most probable. On top of the usual man-vs.-woman communication puzzles, he'd be confronted with the technology expectations. He was glad he was familiar with computers and phones, but that was it—never planned on owning any of it. Did he care if the world was passing him by? Was seeing Anna a mistake? *Fuck it. Don't need to think about it today.* He decided to do some carving while he had another cup of coffee.

EMMA and AMY

Amy rocked back and forth in the oak rocker in Em's room. Em was folding her freshly washed t-shirts and shorts in preparation for her trip with Gram to Maine. Gram said to pack only one duffel, which she agreed made sense—once she decided on colors for mix and match. Looking at the piles of pink, yellow and green on her bed, she spoke peevishly to Amy, who rocked behind her.

"Honestly, Amy, I wish you'd stop telling me to keep secrets. All this stuff about Ned is kinda icky."

"Like what? He just thinks I'm especially photogenic—and pretty. You're just jealous 'cause he didn't ask you. Though you are pretty ... he did mention that". She looked in Em's dresser mirror and fluffed her hair. "Do you like my hair long or short?"

Em decided on seven of each—shorts, shirts and unders—and stuffed them in her bag. The rest she placed neatly in her dresser. That task done, she flopped on her bed.

"I'd say short hair for summer. And I'm not feeling jealous, just concerned." *Yikes! I sound like Mom.*

"Well, that's kinda stupid. If I *do* decide to meet him, and I might not, it'll be someplace like that park in Barringham—like, by the fountain. Anyway, what if I want to be a model someday? I'd havta get experience—right? Besides, he's very gentlemanly—and old. So, stop acting like you're an adult. You do promise you'll keep it a secret, though—swear to God?"

"Jeez, Amy ... I guess. I thought you wanted to be a veterinarian. You never said anything about modeling. What does Roy say about all this?"

"Roy's a boy—you can't tell boys secrets." Amy wished Em had shown some enthusiasm for her modeling adventure. *She probably is jealous ... but, she's good at keeping secrets.*

ANNA

Anna sat in the comfy beige armchair in her office, her feet propped on the matching ottoman. She was going over her to-do checklist, a task she actually enjoyed. As far as the shop, Cara and Stan knew the drill. Brianna had thoughtfully offered to have her niece help out on two of the late days, which was a relief to Cara. She'd be gone for only two weeks—maybe less. When Cara went on vacation at the end of the month, Em might stay and help out. Jack and Dee were delighted to have Em get some work experience, and Em, for her part, thought it would be fun—and that she might get to continue her research.

Damn! I almost forgot about taking another quick look in the attic. Em is quite the little taskmaster. Well, might as well get to it while the air is cool.

The floorboards creaked as she ascended the stairway. The two bare overhead lights cast corner shadows on the dark wood. Though it was still light outside, the small attic windows were heavily veiled in dust. *Guess it wouldn't hurt to bring some Windex up here soon. I'll go through the three boxes stored under the eaves, and that'll havta be that. When Em is here end of the month, I'll have Jack bring some of the other stuff downstairs for sorting.*

As she had expected, there wasn't anything more that was particularly germane to Griffin, nor were there any more letters from Luke to Tess. The only thing of some interest was a small eight-by-ten oil painting depicting a field of goldenrod and bluebells with a pair of monarchs in the foreground. It was terribly dusty, but appealing, and the gold frame was very nice. It was not dated, but there appeared to be initials in the right-hand corner.

Well, this is a worthy find. I'll bring it downstairs and clean it and bag the trash later. Anyway, I'm ready for a cup of chai about now. Once ensconced back in her armchair with tea and a soft cloth, she got to work on gently cleaning the painting. *This is very well done,* she thought. *Perhaps I should take it to the Institute for cleaning advice—come to think of it that would be a good time to take in the little Cole landscape, too.*

The phone rang. She'd hoped that Miles might call, and indeed it was him.

"Hullo, Anna? Hoped I'd catch you before you take off for Maine. Seems Ned is leaving me in charge most Wednesdays—and I must say, I look forward to the prospect of calling you."

"Me, too," Anna laughed breezily. "Guess what? Tonight I found the most extraordinary item in the attic—a painting of two monarchs! Can you believe it? As you know, my very focused granddaughter is always nudging me to continue looking through old stuff in her quest to 'find Griffin'—especially stuff about the Gifford's and the Girard's—and I do try to oblige her. As usual, I came up short, I think, from her standpoint—but the painting looks pretty good."

"So, is it signed?"

"There are two initials." Cradling the phone in her neck, she wiped at the right-hand corner of the canvas. "Hmmm ... I think the initials are 'BB.'"

"The 'B' could stand for 'Bleeker,' right?"

"Yeah ..." Anna said slowly. "On the other hand there are a lot of 'B's."

"Ya know what I'd do—I'd set Em on the trail. A perfect summer junior-sleuth project and she just might connect some dots."

"Brilliant!" Anna liked Miles' thinking. "I can't wait to show you the painting, too—it seems monarchs are popping up all over."

"It's the season, of course. This is the time of year they leave their cocoons here in the Northeast. Me, being where I am, I've seen bunches of them lately. Then there's Mary Lou, trying to join something called *Monarch Watch*. She's even set up an old computer so's she can e-mail these folks. And she's got me helping her with her butterfly garden."

"But you've been trying to attract them to your garden, too, right?"

"Yeah, there's something intriguing about them. It must be something to see them roosting in Mexico at the end of their journeys."

Anna was surprised. "It's not impossible ..." she said.

"No, no it isn't. I've already begun to fancy getting as far as Albany."

"And there's a plane right there with wings to fly you." Anna wished she'd bitten her tongue. She knew voicing dreams was just that—wishful thinking. Miles needed his known world curled around him.

Miles laughed lightly with her and the tension—if there was tension—eased. They talked about how they'd enjoyed walking on the escarpment overlooking the Hudson and about her upcoming trip to Cape Porpoise. He told her he had a surprise for her that would be waiting for her return.

When they finally rang off, Anna flopped back in her chair. *He always leaves me with a lot to think about.*

MILES

When Miles hung up the phone, he thought, *there is so much Anna doesn't know. I could tell she thought she was oversteppin', but she really wasn't. It isn't like I havta live in the woods. I just do. Anna must realize I didn't always live in a cabin by a river. And it's not some holy grail, either. Christ! Her soft, hushed voice … maybe she thinks I can't afford a trip to Mexico. If there's one thing I've always been, it's a realist. Maybe a little fucked-up, but I've never lost sight, at least not for long, that the cabin is a choice. And I'm grateful for that. Even when I was gnashing my teeth and huddling in the cold, my bank account lay serenely chocking up interest. Well, maybe not so much today.*

When people call me a hermit, I usta think I was a fraud. Now I say, Fuck 'em. There is some truth to it, though—I've been wary of people and of venturing out, I'll admit. And I'm usta conversations with myself—sooner or later one of my selves makes sense.

Miles was tidying Ned's shop when the phone rang. Disappointment—it wasn't Anna.

"Hey, Ned, Rico here. Listen, I've got a line on some choice erotica. You wanted first refusal? You got it, but I need a quick answer. I'm telling ya, this stuff is hot—unbelievable!"

"Whoa—slow down there, Rico. Ned's on a buying tour. I'm minding the shop for him. If you want, I can take your number and have him call back tomorrow."

"You got his cell? I'd like to talk to him tonight—I've other clients ya know." There was irritation in Rico's voice.

"Sorry, bud—no, that's the best I can do."

What was that all about? Must be Ned has an interest in erotica, though he's never listed it in his inventory. Could be it's his personal collection—wouldn't surprise me. He likes to talk about the babes he's known. Oh, well. I'll leave him a note. Of course, there's never a pen handy when you need it.

Miles rummaged through the top desk drawer … paperclips, business cards, rubber bands, rubbers, mints … ah, yes, a pen. He grabbed a notepad and wrote, "Call Rico. Urgent." On the back of the pad was the notation "PW boyoboy." Miles was curious. It was like a puzzle. Then it came to him—*Aha, must mean password.*

Though it was strangely out of character, his curiosity got the better of him. He went to the back office, turned on Ned's personal laptop and punched in the characters "boyoboy." Sure enough, the Windows screen kicked in. There was still the same screensaver of nude women under a waterfall. At a closer look, they were definitely very young. In the shadows by the rocks was another figure, which he'd missed the first time. It was a guy with a mustache, positioned like he was hiding.

Miles realized that now that he had the password he could snoop in Ned's files, but he didn't. He suspected that Ned might have raunchy stuff on his laptop—still, it was personal. That probably explained why Ned was so touchy about the laptop. He never cared if Miles used the main computer up front. For the moment, Miles was just satisfied to have made the correct assumption about the meaning of "PW."

He was beginning to feel a little less like the "techno-boob." That was a good thing, since Mary wanted help with *Monarch Watch* on her computer. Her arthritic fingers slowed her down, she said. This reminded him—he should stop by there and fix the kitchen screen after visiting his Uncle Brian at the nursing home.

ANNA and EMMA

It was a perfect morning for a drive to Cape Porpoise. Anna and Emma both felt like kids jumping out of bed early for the trip. Of course, Em *was* a kid. They had packed the car the night before and watered all of the plants. Coffee was ready to switch on, and cups and wrapped Danish sat on the table. Cara had the house keys.

Anna gave her travel list a once-over, and then they went out the back door to the car. As they drove east on the interstate, the red sun slowly crept to the horizon before popping into view. Em made a joke about it popping up like a beach ball, saying she was already thinking about the beach. Anna told her there wasn't any reason they couldn't do just that this very afternoon.

"Super! Gram, I think I'll start with my turquoise bathing suit. I brought three bathing suits."

"Well, it's definitely beach weather—the temperature is already seventy, and the sun is barely up. Of course, it could be cooler and breezy along the coast. Aunt Jen knows we're anxious to feel the sand and waves, says she'll have a picnic basket packed and ready when we get there. Aaron's out on his boat, but he'll join us for dinner."

"They are *sooo* nice. Did Uncle Aaron say I could go out with him tomorrow?"

"We didn't cover everything," Anna laughed. "I'm sure he's looking forward to your help."

There's nothing like an early start, thought Anna. Funny how it jumpstarts your sense of time—like the sun kicks you forward 'cause you're already in play. I'm glad I thought to let Em pick the CDs this time—I suspect the Four Seasons was a nod to one of my favorites. And I don't mind Green Day, either.

They decided on a pee break and snack in Kittery. It was only 9:30 a.m. They'd be in Cape Porpoise well before noon.

As they pulled into the driveway, they could see Jenna in the backyard bending to weed the garden. She straightened and waved when the car doors slammed.

"Wow! Aunt Jen, this is a big garden!"

"Jen, this is amazing—you've really expanded. How in the world do you manage it?"

"I'll admit, it got a little out of control. If it wasn't for Watson, it'd be hopeless. The deal is, I tutor him for his SATs, plus give him some cash. In return, he applies his young, sturdy back to weeding, lifting and hauling. See over there in the far right corner? That's kind of a community veggie garden. The eighth-grade garden club mostly tends it. They have a small booth at the Saturday farmers market. So far it's working well. The herb garden and flower beds are my babies—well, and the heirloom tomatoes by the back porch."

Anna and Em quickly settled in the upstairs guest room with its two matching twin beds covered with matching pale-cream-and-yellow quilts. If they looked carefully from the west window, they could see a patch of ocean beyond the trees. Hurriedly, they put on bathing suits, shorts and t-shirts before scampering to the kitchen. Jenna was packing a cooler with sandwiches—egg salad and cream cheese with green olives. There also were chips, pickles, iced tea and lemonade, and brownies too. Em sneaked half an egg salad sandwich before they headed down the back shortcut to the beach.

This was a handy path and was used by a few neighbors to either side. It skirted the street and veered through a wooded patch, then turned to a sandy passage between two large boulders before the broad expanse of the beach. Jenna had already staked out their spot with a blanket and two umbrellas. All three sat on the blankets and applied sunscreen. Anna and Emma savored the beach scene—lapping waves, blue sky and hot sand.

"Ahh—worth the trip from anywhere," Anna smiled at Jenna. "The weather's perfect, too. How's about a quick walk so I'll feel entitled to your delicious lunch?"

They kicked off their flip-flops and walked on the hard, wet sand, letting the cold surf lick their toes.

Em hung back on her beach mat. She had spied Watson in the distance, and correctly assumed that he'd stop by to chat. He gracefully folded himself onto Aunt Jenna's blanket. Em felt pale next to his nicely browned body.

"Figured the 'whitey' on Mrs. Curtis' blanket had to be you."

Em laughed self-consciously. But she knew she looked good in her new turquoise swimsuit.

Meanwhile, Anna and Jenna continued their walk, the sounds of the waves and gulls creating a private cocoon for their talk.

"Honestly, Jen, I didn't mean to spill the beans first thing about Miles—though, of course, I meant to tell you sometime over the week."

"Gotta say, this is one big surprise, Annie—and about time, too. For a while now I figured you'd decided to emulate Great-Aunt Anna, your namesake."

"Don't get too excited—this could just be one of those passing things. You never know—you know? Also, I'm not ready to let on to Em or Jack. As you might guess, Cara has begun the 'knowing' looks, however."

Jenna chuckled at the thought of Cara, a favorite of hers. Cara usually had her radar up when it came to the nuances of relationships. And, after all, she was Anna's friend.

"I'm so glad you and Em came to visit. I have to say, walking and chatting with you is something I look forward to. Aaron has been so tied up with work—well, this visit gets him away from all that."

"You mean lobstering?"

"Oh, no—that's his good work. It's the ever-encroaching police work that bothers me. You know Aaron. He feels somehow obligated to help the chief—not that he doesn't get paid handsomely. But a lot of it is tracking drug traffic and searching backgrounds on the computer. Some of it's the same dark stuff that we left Boston to get away from. Honestly, I just wish he'd stuck to his original plan to phase out the police work and go full-time with the lobstering. After all, he already has his pension. We don't need the money. Basically, he's working two jobs just because he can't say no to an old friend. Anyway, he's only lobstering while you're here." Jenna sighed. "Hey, look at that—they've already found each other. Em and Watson."

Anna and Jenna ambled toward the blanket. Emma and Watson were building a sandcastle, of all things. They looked up and laughed when they spotted the adults.

"I'll bet you thought we were too old for this stuff," said Watson.

"We're trying to capture our lost childhoods," chimed Em.

"In that case you should enter the big Fourth of July sandcastle contest".

"Nope, too organized for us—might drain our creativity." Watson was placing shells around a lopsided turret. Em was scraping a moat around the base with a broken red plastic shovel she had found. They explained that their model would demonstrate the effects of global warming in about two hours—high tide.

"So what was the rationale for tidal castle destruction when *we* were young?" mused Anna.

"I guess we were just super-intuitive about environmental trends—or into 'birth and death' symbolism. It's too bad everyone has sandy hands now; otherwise, I'd put out some lunch. I made enough for you, too, Watson."

Emma and Watson ran to the cold waves and rinsed their hands. Jen spread out an old red-checked cloth, napkins and sturdy plastic tumblers, and then unpacked her cooler. They sat semicircle on low blue-striped beach chairs, facing each other and the ocean. Anna and Jenna had both donned t-shirt cover-ups and straw-brimmed hats. The kids were comfortable in swimsuits and baseball caps. They relished the delicious lunch.

"So, Em, Annie tells me you've been leading a family genealogy search. Turn up anything interesting?"

"Way, way exciting, Aunt Jen! It's kinda unbelievable, really. And to think, it all started with a pack of old letters in Gram's attic. I mean, Gram might have easily tossed them—we were housecleaning at the time. Luckily, I saw them and untied the ribbon and started to read. We brought them downstairs to read more, and right away we saw they were full of clues. So Gram agreed to take a road trip to a place called Griffin where this guy, Luke, who wrote to Tess, lived long ago. When we got there, the town had disappeared! I was really sad and bummed—thought we had taken a wrong turn or something. Then I saw this fisherman by the river. Turned out to be this really awesome guy named Miles who knew all about the old days and why the town got deserted. He's still helping us—along with an antique-store guy named Ned who might find more old pictures. Gram got some of the pictures restored, so they're clearer, but we still can't figure out who the people are" Em paused, recalling Amy's revelations about Ned's e-mail and the possible photo shoot.

"So, is this Tess a Bleeker? Did you find out anything about her?"

"She lived in Gram's house—where you and Gram grew up. Yeah, she must have been a Bleeker. When she was a teenager she used to stay some summers with her grandmother in Griffin, and there was a boy there named Luke, who liked her. They wrote back and forth, but we only have Luke's letters, which were all tied together with a ribbon. It sounds like Luke came to Albany, too. We think the Bleekers were probably liberal—there's some mention of the family going to hear Susan B. Anthony and Elizabeth Cady Stanton. Oh, and when we looked at some stuff in the library, it seems that one of the Bleeker relatives, named Bush, was big in the women's suffrage movement in the 1870s. We're pretty positive Tess's father was a doctor and that he went to treat patients in the Shaker village in Hancock. .. Gram, am I leaving out anything, so far?"

"I think you covered the highlights … Miles mentioned that a friend of his thought there was a story connecting someone in Griffin to the Shakers back then—all pretty sketchy though."

"Wow, that's really cool, getting to research your own family like that." Watson was clearly impressed. "Do you think you'll find out more? Like, what happened to them."

"Oh, yeah, I 'spect so. Right now we're collecting info on any names that seem related to Luke or Tess. Later we'll see how dates and events connect. It's fun—like a puzzle."

Jenna gave Anna the "this kid's good" look.

After some splashing and body surfing with Watson, Emma returned to the blanket.

"Gram, is it okay if I go to the village with Watson?"

"Fine, better dry off first—your teeth are chattering. And put some fresh sunscreen on, too."

The kids toweled briskly. Emma pulled a pair of turquoise shorts over her matching suit. Watson volunteered to put sunscreen on her back. They sauntered away from the beach and up the sandy path.

"So … what did you think about the sunscreen action?"

"Don't even go there, Jen. Unfortunately, at our age we know it's not innocent—even when it's innocent."

"Yep, well I know. Do you remember that darling Sorriso boy? They called him 'Sonny.' I think we both had crushes on him. When we'd catch a ride to Thatcher pool, he'd be life-guarding. He'd wink and smile at us, but end up walking Judy Jarvis to the ice cream truck. You once said you thought he'd ask you, but that he didn't want me to feel bad! Anyway, he once rubbed sun lotion on my shoulders."

"Oh sure, you probably begged him to do it."

"Nope, he said I was getting pink, and he smeared it on."

" 'Course, that might be one of those false memories," snorted Anna. "How old were we anyway—twelve, thirteen? Already our day dreams were hardly chaste."

"It's no doubt my imagination, but kids today seem older and more sensible. At least, kids like Em and Watson. But it's true of many of the kids I teach, too. Of course, they are exposed to more information—inevitable with the Internet. So, times do change and the young are the first to adapt … Em has certainly grown since last Christmas holiday even.

"It was thoughtful of Watson and Em to offer to pick some of the vegetables for farmers market, too. I know Watson is proud of the class garden project. Still, it pleased me to no end to realize he thought it worthy of showing off. Em will like those kids at the veggie booth."

Jen's garden was magnificent this year, and Anna thought to compliment her on it. Anna's small plot in back of her Brownstone was puny by comparison. In fact, it periodically verged on letting weeds get the upper hand. Most of her careful tending was in the greenhouse in back of the shop, hothouse plants reserved for others.

EMMA and WATSON

"I almost forgot how quickly the temperature changed once you got away from the sea breeze," Emma said. She could feel sweat running down her back under her bright yellow t-shirt.

"Yeah, well, you get used to it. And it's different when you're actually out on the water. You'll need a sweater *and* a windbreaker when you go out in Mr. Curtis' boat." After a short pause, Watson said, "It's not too long a walk to the farmers market. I figure we'll pick some of the herbs and lettuces and take them in a cooler to our booth. You'll get to meet my friends Sam and Beth. The stand closes at 4:00—but, you don't have to stay that long."

Em found everything about the small coastal town fascinating. Once they passed through the large boulders, they were back on the village streets. The older clapboard homes sat back from the road. Many of the houses looked scraped and weathered by the harsh winters, but they still managed to maintain a sturdy presence bordering on rustic elegance. This was a street that defied the affluent newcomers who tried to snag waterfront property on the pricey cliffs.

They cut to the left, walking on a lane bordering a tidal inlet that ended at the local park, adjacent to the harbor marina. Strong riverine smells rose from the muddy banks—seaweed, salt and rotting fish odors—earthy and not unpleasant.

Em remembered walking through the park and down to the harbor last year. The covered pavilion was new; on the land side it abutted a little cemetery. The marina parking area was close by, which, as Watson observed, was handy for anyone coming to market.

There were a number of stalls huddled under the open-air roof selling flowers, breads, honey, beeswax candles, ornamental plants, vegetables, carved wooden bowls and jewelry. The eighth-grade gardeners called their booth "Porpoises with Purpose," as they were planning to use some of the farm-stand profits for a class trip to Boston.

Sam had smooth, dark skin and kinky, closely cropped hair. Beth was slender and petite with several ear piercings and a small diamond nose stud. They both smiled and waved to Watson. They said business had been pretty lively and they were glad to have additional veggies to sell.

Emma was impressed with how easygoing and friendly they were to her. Beth asked questions about Albany and Barnfield. Sam said he'd passed through Albany several times. They both spoke enthusiastically about Mrs. Curtis, her Aunt Jenna, and said they'd likely see Emma in the garden tomorrow.

It was blasted hot, so Emma and Watson said they'd mind the booth for the rest of the afternoon and give Beth and Sam a break. Presumably, Sam and Beth were going to the beach. Watson took two bottles of lemonade from the cooler, passing one to Emma.

Once seated in the shade, Emma felt reasonably cool. She found that she enjoyed watching the market hubbub and the boats drifting in the harbor. She wondered where Uncle Aaron's boat was. She imagined that he was cruising in some cove a few miles up or down the coast. She thought about wearing a sweatshirt and heavy gloves, helping him winch the traps on a line. He would be surprised at how much stronger she was this year. She smiled at the thought.

"A penny for, Em."

"I was just thinking of being on Uncle Aaron's boat—and about your nice friends." They had been agreeable, though she hadn't actually been giving them a thought at that moment. "I mean, are they close buds, just classmates, good students or what?"

"Let me see … Sam's a real friend. We study together and go for long bike rides. Before and after season we ride to Berwick and Goose Rocks beach—even as far as Camden. In high season the parents get real nervous about the traffic, which is bullshit. We're fast and careful. Beth? … not exactly a close friend. I like her, but she has problems that I'd rather stay away from. You know what I mean?"

"Kinda—I mean, not exactly, but I have a friend, Amy, who I'd havta say is close, who seems to have problems and situations that I'm not sure what to do about … but I'm pretty sure I should do something."

"So, like drugs and stuff?"

"No ... maybe occasional pot, but no serious drug problems. A few weeks ago I was concerned about this cutting thing she's been doing. You know, on her arms." Watson nodded; he'd heard about that kind of behavior. "Anyway, I almost told my mom about it; then Amy said she'd stop—and I think she more or less did. So, we were back to studying together and doing fun stuff. One day we were at the Berkshire Mall and this guy, Ned, who knows Gram and me, sat and had a Coke with us. Remember I mentioned the antique dealer who had pictures of old Griffin? Well, it was him. Anyway, I got up to go to the ladies, and when I came back Amy was all flirty with this guy, which was annoying—but okay. A week or so later she tells me Ned is her Facebook 'friend'—*and* he's thinking of taking her somewhere to take pictures!"

"Is he, like, a fashion photographer?"

"I seriously doubt it. *And* he's way old—like, fifty even. What would you do in my shoes?"

"Hmmm ... well, the cutting thing could be bad. Guess I'd tell my dad about that. But, I don't think I'd tell on the Facebook thing. Parents get so hyper about that kind of stuff. Before you know it, she'd have to give up her phone and computer. Then, if it turned out to be no big whoop, you'd feel like a jerk. Nobody'd want to be your friend. 'Course, the guy could be a real 'perv,' too.... Yeah, I think I'd just keep talking to her, checking to see what was going on."

"You're probably right. Maybe I'll shoot her a quick hello note later." Emma still felt disquieted, but Watson had made some good points. They were interrupted by an older couple—"flatlanders" according to Watson. Nevertheless, he certainly enjoyed telling them all about the class garden project. As a result, they bought a bunch of veggies and threw them an extra ten dollars.

"Gosh, I can't wait 'til people stop referring to me as *young lady*" Emma said.

By 4:00 they were sold out. Watson said he might as well stop by the Curtis's and do a bit of weeding before going home.

Em was so excited about the prospect of lobstering with Uncle Aaron that she hardly slept. She took Gram's advice and laid all her clothes for the adventure on a chair by the door, so when 3:00 a.m. arrived she was downstairs in a flash. Uncle Aaron had coffee ready and was scrambling a mess of eggs. "Cheese in 'em or no?" he said. He whistled while he cooked. Em liked that.

It was still dark as they made their way down the path to the marina, so they carried flashlights. Their first stop was the bait shop by the marina. They carried two pails of ripe-smelling stuff down the dock to where the boat was tethered.

Claude Cutter was waiting for them on the dock. He was a rugged, unshaven guy who looked to be in his mid-thirties. He was already wearing a beat-up green poly-pro hoodie, although the day was warm even in the meek dawn.

"Hey there—you must be Emma. Hope ya had yer Wheaties this morning." He smiled amiably, reaching for the bait buckets.

"Better than that—Uncle Aaron made scrambled eggs and English muffins," said Em, returning the smile.

She thought, *Maybe I'm just a girl kid, but I'm strong and sensible. I remember everything from last year. Besides, I did weight training all last semester.* Nevertheless, she sat patiently while Uncle Aaron went through the safety drill. They already had put on slickers and boots. Claude was steering the neat red–and–white boat through the cove out toward open water, heralded by squawking gulls and dinging buoys.

"Listen up," said Uncle Aaron, "the best way to stay safe is to be alert. Most of the reason we wear these big boots and gloves is for safety—they've saved many a man from getting caught in the ropes while tossing or pulling traps—'course, the boots also help with footing if it gets real slippery on deck here. Once we get out a few miles to our grounds, Claude will set out some new traps and winch in the ones we laid out last week. He goes pretty much on automatic—so stay out of his way. I'm gonna have you help me bait traps over there." Aaron gestured to the pile of traps. "It's smelly, dirty work, but that's how most lobstermen, or lobsterwomen, start. Now, I know you said you wanted 'real' work this year, but if it don't suit ya—that's okay, too."

Em furrowed her brows and looked Aaron directly in the eyes.

"I meant what I said. I think I can do the work. And I'll be careful, too," she smiled. "Show me how to load the icky glop."

If Aaron was surprised at her determination, he didn't show it.

"So be it," he said. "Right this way."

Last year he had noted her rapt interest while she was on the boat, but nothing like this. Of course, then they'd just pulled up a few traps—more like a holiday venture. He'd actually been hesitant about bringing her out today. Because of his work with the chief and Claude's schedule, he needed to get some real lobstering done. Play was not an option. He was seeing Em in a new light. You had to expect kids to change year to year—still, she'd sure taken him unawares.

Once Aaron showed Em how much "glop"—mostly herring—to load in the traps, she worked quickly. By this point she had discarded her slicker for an oilcloth apron. He noted the toned look of her arms above the gloves and how her decisive movements were well coordinated and efficient.

Em looked to the now-featureless strip of shore. The breeze was cold on her back and arms. She rose to get a sweater and slicker. Claude slowed the boat and stood in the cabin doorway. He shot her two thumbs-up. It pleased her because she knew he meant it.

When they got to hauling in the traps, Claude showed her how to measure lobsters and decide whether or not they were keepers or were to be heaved back overboard. It seemed that many of the lobsters had to be thrown back. Em was fascinated by all the other sea creatures besides lobsters that were caught in traps. There were hermit crabs, whelks, sea ravens and the like. In one trap there was a huge ugly fish that Claude called a wolf fish. It had rows of nasty teeth that uncle Aaron said could grind up clams and lobsters, shells and all. Claude said they were good eating. Uncle Aaron said he could keep it—and he'd keep the next, should another be caught.

Although they threw a lot of small lobsters back, Uncle Aaron said it was a good haul. After they cleared the old traps and set out the new ones, they thoroughly cleaned the boat, swabbing and hosing it, to the noisy distress of the gulls following them. Em did the hosing and was glad to be finished. She was more than happy to sit in the sun with a cup of coffee and a ham-and-cheese sandwich. In response to Claude's question, she said, "Sure, it's hard work, but I liked it. Yes, I'd do it again—might even be a lobsterwoman someday." She squinted in the sun and pulled her cap down to shade her eyes. When she saw the look on Aaron's face, she pursed her lips and scowled, trying to appear nonchalant—her version of older—then giggled in spite of herself.

"You had Capt'n Aaron goin' there Emma," Claude laughed.

Yes indeed, thought Aaron, *having Em along worked out just fine. If she were staying longer, she might even become part of the crew.*

AARON

He thought back to his heated talk with Jenna last night—how he'd said he was too busy to babysit a kid who fancied boats when he was behind schedule as it was. And then she'd accused him of losing sight as to why they'd left Boston to begin with. Once again they'd gone in circles over his doing consulting work for the police force. He sighed. She was unlikely ever to understand the bonds he had with the chief—or any other fellow officers, for that matter. Yeah, a good part of him preferred lobstering. But he'd been a damn good officer—plus he had mastered the ability to track people on the computer, not so common in an experienced officer his age.

Anyways, he owed Jen an apology. Em was a good kid—even better, she was a dandy sailor. He could tell without asking that Claude was impressed by her, too. *Yep, Em was admirably focused—kinda like Jen and Anna.*

After they docked and unloaded the catch, Claude and Aaron settled accounts. It had been a better than average day's take. They agreed to set out again this coming Thursday. Claude shook hands with Em, saying she was good crew.

"Whaddaya say to ice cream?" Aaron asked.

"Yum—I think working on the boat made me extra hungry."

Sal's Stand was a drive-up ice creamery in town on the main street. Some of the garden crew from the farmers market was there. Beth, the girl who Watson had implied had problems, gave her an extravagant wave.

"Hey, Em—hi, Mr. Curtis!"

Em waved back, saying "See ya later" as Beth and her two male friends ambled back toward town. Em liked it that Beth was friendly— thought she looked interesting, too. Uncle Aaron looked thoughtful and frowned a little.

"So, ya met Beth at the garden, huh? … Comes from a harum-scarum kinda family. Her dad spends a lot of time away at sea, and her mom had a minor drug bust past spring—claims she wasn't dealing, just recreational using. I'm hopin' a kid like that can stay to the straight and narrow—ya know? It's a lot of pressure. I know the Portland police are doing some undercover work—guess if you were staying longer I'd havta give you some warnings. Your Aunt Jen thinks you give these kids outdoor work, garden projects and the like, they'll stay out of trouble. But, it's not that simple." Aaron sighed.

"Yep, I know. But, the kids think the garden and the farmers market are really neat. Another thing, I've been thinking ..." Em hesitated. "Next year I'd like to try working on the boat, you know, learning the ropes. You don't have to answer now. Honest, I could do it. Please, please let me try!" She gave a winning smile. "You're my favorite uncle."

"And your only uncle, at that. Tell you what, I promise to consider it over the year. You might change your mind, too. And then, there's the parents. Maybe they won't take to the idea. I mean, there are easier and safer jobs out there. I'll tell you this; we were impressed with you on the water today. So, I won't say yes or no. Another thing, I'll expect you to write an essay on just why you want to do such a thing. Deal?"

"Deal. And thanks for the ice cream. Hope it doesn't ruin our appetite for dinner."

They both laughed, knowing that was highly unlikely.

Em was glad she had gotten her courage up to ask about next summer. She'd hoped Uncle Aaron would listen. She now knew he'd consider it, and that was a good start. Em liked the idea of a new challenge. She was beginning to stretch her wings.

As a consequence of their heated conversations of late, Jen had been giving Aaron the cold shoulder, especially after they retired to the privacy of their bedroom.

When they'd remodeled the old house to create a master suite, it'd been lovely—large enough in the main area for a king-sized bed, and to the right a nice sitting room alcove with a gas fireplace, plus a master bath with a whirlpool tub that had a view of the ocean. Sometimes it was their special hideaway.

Unfortunately, of late, the cushy sofa in the alcove was being used by Jenna as a retreat both from him and from the cozy king-sized bed—and forget about the whirlpool tub for two.

It was late. Tip toeing down the stairs, he observed light spilling from under the door of Emma and Anna's room. Hard to tell which of them might be up reading—maybe both? He'd married into a family of obsessive readers.

Back in the bedroom, he placed a small silver tray with two cordial glasses filled with Sambuca and two pieces of chocolate on the coffee table. Jen looked up from her book and smiled.

"Thought maybe we should have a little talk time before bed—that is, if I'm not interrupting," he said. "I've been thinking, you've been right about a number of things. It's true that I've been grouchy and short with you of late—and trying to do two jobs isn't what I'd planned. I was way out of line complaining about takin' Emma on the boat. You know what? She actually was a real help. Anyway, I feel really bad about having you think I didn't welcome having your family here. I guess the stress of helping the chief so much has made me snappy—uncharacteristically, I hope. In fact, I've cleared my calendar for tomorrow. I was thinkin' you gals might want to do a little exploring—and maybe you'd like me to drive."

Jen looked pleased. She bent towards him and gave him a full smack on the lips. "Don't think I'm totally won over—actions always speak louder than words. But, yes, a family drive would be terrific—and I've just the place. Remember Em and Anna talking about the Shakers, the possibility of a family connection? Well, I happen to know they want to visit the Shaker community at Sabbath Day Lake. What do you think?"

"Fine by me. They might like to see one of the lighthouses up that way, too."

Dozing off with the lights out, their shoulders touched. Aaron was thinking how harmony embellished the songs of life, when sleep overtook his thoughts.

A mild breeze kept clouds sailing overhead across the cobalt sky as they neared their destination. Anna could tell that Jen's personal dark clouds had lifted since yesterday and suspected there'd been some making-up in the interval. As for Em, she was simply thrilled at the prospect of seeing a Shaker community. The only nagging thought for Anna was that she'd planned to speak with Miles on Tuesday as prearranged—and today was Tuesday. Well, she could always make a quick cell call this afternoon to Mary Lou—once she found some privacy and cell service.

She had just started toward the museum ticket shop when her cell jingled. Since she was more or less in tandem with the group, she may have come off sounding more formal than she felt.

"Hey, Anna, hope this is a good time—I'm over at Mary Lou's. She's got a bunch of garden chores for me, so thought I'd call while my hands were still clean. By the way, she says she saw three monarchs this morning on the purple coneflowers."

She told him about their trip and how they were all set to tour the Sabbath Day Lake Shaker site. She could hear Mary Lou in the background saying something about old Griffin and the Shakers. The upshot was that Mary Lou was inviting her for tea a week from Saturday to show her the garden. Anna said yes. They'd hash out the details later. *Jeez*, thought Anna—*this is like being a chaperoned teenager, on both ends of the phones.* Nevertheless, she was pleased that she and Miles had some defined plans for her return.

The day was so pleasant that they were all enjoying walking the premises of the Shaker village. Though it seemed a museum of times gone by, they were surprised to find modern-day Shakers in residence. Six of the eighteen buildings were open to the public.

Since 1931 an effort had been made to continue the Sabbath Day community as a residence and museum. The simple white clapboard or brick structures were nicely arranged on spacious grounds. There were ample gardens and a barn housing livestock. The half dozen Shakers in residence tended gardens and grew and packaged herbs, albeit with the help of a volunteer staff. For the most part, they still adhered to the principles set out by Mother Ann Lee in 1778 when she settled in Albany/Watervliet after fleeing England. Though always pacifists, the current members of the sect were especially adamant in their pacifism in light of the conflicts in the Middle East.

Emma was curious whether or not they kept records of all the people who had lived in the community. Brother Eric told her that there were lists of members in the archives going back at least two hundred years. Anna raised her eyebrows when Emma boldly stated that she thought someone of their family may have been a member in the late 1800s. Eric pointed south to the red brick building housing the library, and they quickly walked in that direction.

"Em, there's no reason to think such a thing," whispered Anna.

"I know, but we won't know unless we look." Emma colored in embarrassment. Nevertheless, she was earnest and determined in her intentions.

The record room was cool and musty. As they stood around the long oak table, a kindly grey-haired volunteer brought out to them volumes that listed the Shakers who had lived there from 1875–1885, the dates they agreed as most likely. Aaron decided to walk outside while Emma, Anna, and Jenna persevered.

They found three women named Tess, but no Bleekers. They realized that, even if one of the Bleekers or Giffords had been a Shaker, it was more likely they would have lived in the Hancock or Watervliet communities. Then they came across the name 'Theresa Blecker.' A notation said that she'd traveled to Sabbath Day Lake from Hancock in 1883. Could it be Tess? Was the spelling of the last name a typo or a mere coincidence? The pleasant woman volunteer made them a photocopy of the page and wished them good luck.

They all felt buoyed by the prospect of possibly finding family history, even though it was a very slim and tenuous lead. Anna promised to take Emma to Hancock and the Shaker research center in Chatham. She didn't mention the hazy story about a Shaker from Griffin that Mary Lou had recalled to Miles; there'd be time for that later. Anna had to admit that her curiosity was growing. *Then again, life was full of coincidences and near misses.*

Once back in the sunlight, they wanted an outdoor activity. Aaron drove to the coast and down to Camden Lighthouse. It was one of his favorites, and he regaled them with tales of mariner history. They all especially liked the story about Mrs. Tolliver, whose husband was a smuggler. According to Aaron, Jake Tolliver had a good business smuggling rum from the islands. All was fine until Mina Tolliver joined the Temperance Society. She begged him to quit, and when he wouldn't, she and her matron cohorts poured vinegar in all the rum barrels. Ever after, he stuck with running molasses.

When they got back to the house, Watson was watering the gardens. Aunt Jen suggested that Em take a pitcher of lemonade and a plate of 'chocolate chips' to the porch and invite Watson to join her.

Watson looked intent as Emma told him about their experience with the Shakers at Sabbath Day Lake. He seemed genuinely fascinated by the possibility that one of Emma's relatives might have been a member.

"Yep, it would be sorta interesting anyway. But Watson, if you could see the letters, I'll bet you'd really want to know more about Luke and Tess. It's so cool the way Luke describes the town. And you get a pretty good idea of what Tess must have said in her letters just by his comments—like they both read *Adventures of Tom Sawyer*. Imagine, it had just been published!"

"You want to help me dump the weeds and clippings in the compost pile?"

"Sure—I'll just put this net thingy over the cookies in case we want more later."

Emma could hear a phone ring inside as they went down the wooden porch steps and walked to the back gardens. It was nearly 8:00 p.m. but there was still plenty of light left for several trips to the compost pile. Watson was telling her that he and Sam were going to write up their garden project and submit it to a sustainable-garden newsletter based in Brunswick.

"You know, if more people start thinking about composting and making organic gardens, it could revolutionize whole towns—maybe even more. We heard a guy talk at the college, saying if the movement grew, it would change the way we think. People would want local stuff and be willing to import less foreign products. At least some of it makes sense. Dunno if I'd miss having access to the variety we have in the big markets, probably—but you adapt. We're getting more interest in gardening here—that's for sure."

It was their last wheelbarrow load. They thought they deserved another cookie or two.

Sitting on the porch, they could hear the adult voices through the window. Anna was saying she'd have to tell Em. Uncle Aaron was saying that there was probably no need to get too wrought up. In most of these cases the kid returned home within twenty-four hours. Emma and Watson looked at each other and silently moved closer to the window. They were under cover of darkness now.

Emma heard the name "Amy." Her hand instinctively went to her mouth. "Oh, no," she whispered. "It just can't be—what if she's with Ned?" Emma's voice was shaking. "I'm gonna havta tell—I think."

"Be cool, Em—let's find out what happened first. We can't hear everything from here. I'll go in with you."

They opened the creaky screen door and walked to the dining room carrying an empty plate, two glasses and the half-full pitcher of lemonade. Gram and Aunt Jenna looked worried. Em and Watson stood, waiting for the adults to speak.

"Oh, Em, I'm glad you came in—Kimberly, Amy's mom, called. She thought Amy was in Albany with us. Of course, she isn't. It's thrown her mom into a panic. She's so upset. I told her we'd talk to you and call her back if you had any ideas." Anna caught her breath.

"It might not be such a big deal," Aaron chimed in.

"So, what did her mom say?" Emma pulled a chair to the table. Watson carried their dishware to the kitchen, then came back in and sat down next to her.

"Well, it seems Amy's cell was turned off and her mom needed to reach her today—something about a change in the day her dad was picking her up next week. She tried to reach her all day, and finally called the flower shop hoping to leave a message. I guess, when she got home last night, there was a scribbled note from Amy saying she had ridden to Albany with you and me to go on a camping trip—thought it was a good opportunity to get away and hoped it'd be okay, and she would call in Tuesday. "Kim," Anna said, turning to Jen and Aaron, then back to Em, "figured if she was with you it would be alright. You know, she was surprised, but not worried." Gram was looking expectantly at her.

Aaron asked "Did she mention anything to you? Does she have a boyfriend?" Now they were all looking at her.

Emma felt queasy. She wasn't sure what she wanted to say, or how much. Her mouth felt dry, and the lemonade had been taken to the kitchen.

"Um … Amy and I haven't talked since over a week ago, when I was packing for our trip here. There are a few boys she likes … mostly we all hang together, like at soccer and band. She went to a movie with Carl Brownell a few weeks ago. His father drove them—sat with them, too … "

"She have any problems at home—at school?"

Uncle Aaron was grilling her—in a nice voice. She looked at the flowers on the table. She had promised not to tell.

"Well, I promised Amy I wouldn't tell … she cuts herself sometimes. Mostly it's on her arms where it doesn't show. She can't explain why she does it, but says she likes the way it feels. I think for a while her mom didn't know … Amy's in counseling now. I think she's stopped doing it because she likes to wear t-shirts in the summer. I think she knows its a little sicko. She's a good soccer player … and is smart—her grades don't show it though …"

"Anything else?" Aaron asked.

"Not really." Em scratched her right arm anxiously. Watson kicked her under the table—then she added, "Well, there's something that's probably not relevant … but it's been on my mind … "

Then Emma told them all about Ned. She described how she and Amy were shopping at Berkshire Mall and that he'd bought them both Cokes—and that Amy liked to flirt, even with older guys. She hesitated. Her eyes watered. Plunging on, she told how Amy said Ned was her Facebook friend and they had fun writing notes to each other.

"And another thing—Ned's a photographer and wants to do some fashion shots of Amy because she has good bone structure and is so pretty." Emma looked up. There was a quiet moment.

"And that's it? Anything else?" Uncle Aaron shot out.

"*Jesus Christ!*" exploded Gram. "You're telling me you thought that piece of information wasn't relevant? What were you thinking?"

Gram was pissed, and Em wished she had said something sooner, but who knew Amy would act so stupid—if that even *is* what was happening.

"I'm sorry Gram," she choked. "I just didn't know what to think—and Amy's my friend." Gram was still glowering at her.

Aunt Jenna came to the rescue. "Hold on, folks, we don't even know whether this Ned character is involved or not. It could be something else entirely. Kids pull all sorts of stunts."

"Yeah, no point rushing to have two and two make five," said Aaron. "Maybe Em should have mentioned this stuff earlier and maybe not. Hindsight is a squirrelly critter. So's there any way we can check on this Ned character, see where he is—and who he's with?"

"My friend Miles works for Ned a few days of the week," Anna offered. "The problem is, he doesn't have a phone, though he did mention he was helping Mary Lou out today. She has a phone and I have her number. It's worth a try." Anna bolted up the stairs to get her address book.

Talk about keeping secrets—Gram and Miles must talk a lot, thought Emma. She made a mental note to ask Gram about that—not now, of course.

Anna hurried back downstairs and dialed from her cell. They waited anxiously. Mary Lou picked up on the fourth ring. Anna identified herself, apologizing for any interruption. Mary Lou said Anna was in luck, they'd had a late dinner and Miles was still there—and she knew he'd love to take the call. *Gosh,* thought Anna, *she thinks I'm making a girlfriend call.*

"Hullo—what a pleasure to hear your voice! We were just talking about ya."

Anna quickly turned the conversation to the serious matter at hand. She told him about Em's friend Amy gone missing—and how Ned had sent her e-mail notes and had said he wanted to take photos of her. She said they hoped nothing was going on, but wondered if Ned was working at the store or if Miles had seen Ned with a young girl.

"Holy Christ! Anna, this doesn't sound good. As for Ned, he's on a buying trip. I worked at the store for a few hours today. I expect he'll be back tomorrow. What should I do? I don't have a number for him, since I don't have a phone." He thought a moment. "Maybe his cell number is back at the shop. If you want, I could borrow Mary Lou's car and check." He paused, then added, "Ned may have some unsavory qualities."

Aaron, who was following the drift of the conversation, asked if he could speak with Miles.

"Hi, Miles—Aaron here, Anna's brother-in-law. Sorry to barge in—I'm a semi-retired cop and I'm trying to figure out if I need to bring any police resources to this situation. You know, it's as likely as not that the kid's on a lark and will be home tomorrow. On the other hand, there are some red flags to consider—"

"Look, I don't want to pile on Ned. He may be completely innocent as far as I know. I figure the guy's personal life is none of my business. But, you know I work at his store, right? He travels a lot, and I help out a couple of days a week. Here and there I've had a few odd inquiries about what they call "erotica"—seems like there's been more in the last three months. Just a couple of days ago a sleazy-sounding character called thinking I was Ned and said he was peddling what he called erotica, but what sounded more like porn to me." He was going to mention that Ned had dated Anna's friend Cara, but decided not to.

"Did this guy on the phone give you any specific information?"

"Yeah, but not much—name and phone number—Connecticut area code." Miles thought he might as well divulge all his concerns "But another thing about Ned that I discovered recently and that has me concerned is his computer screensaver—it's a picture of naked girls splashing under a waterfall with a man hiding in bushes watching them. It's kinda artful and not crude, until you notice the guy in the bushes. And it bothered me that the girls seemed pretty young. I suspect he might have a lot more pictures in his files."

"And you haven't checked it out?"

Miles said, "I'm kind of a straight arrow as far as that kind of thing goes, I guess. Snooping around is something I don't do. I saw the screensaver by accident. But, I have access to the store and, under the circumstances, I'd go look for Ned's cell phone number if you'd like."

Aaron hesitated. "Any information about Ned and his whereabouts could be helpful—even if it does nothing but clear him concerning Amy. It's my duty to tell you, however, that in a worst-case scenario you could be putting yourself in danger. Besides phone numbers, things like his dealer's license number and social security number would be good, too. What's his last name? I'm gonna go to the station and run it through our national database."

"He goes by Ned Silver, but a few years ago he told me he'd changed it from Stavanos—said Silver was easier to spell."

They ended the call with Miles agreeing to go to Ned's shop and grab any information available, while Aaron would search for criminal history on Ned. Anna said a quick good-bye to Miles, asking him to be careful.

Wheels were set in motion. Mary Lou looked worried as she handed Miles her car keys.

As Miles drove down Mary Lou's driveway and turned left towards Wells, he thought how inconvenient his hermit lifestyle was in a crisis—no car and no phone. Yep, he was getting more and more out of step—but that was something he could ponder later.

Main Street looked quiet, as usual, as he turned into the alley next to Ned's shop. At the end of the street, he saw that June's Place was still open. Maybe he'd get two muffins on his way back to Mar's. As he stepped out of the car, he noted that there were no lights on upstairs in Ned's apartment and no car out back. That was good. Although he often went to the shop in Ned's absence—at night, too—he felt like an intruder this time as his key turned the lock. The sound of his boots resounded on the wooden stairs.

The best way, he thought, *is to go about this like an ordinary work evening at the shop*—not that he'd normally be there this late. Everything looked as tidy as he'd left it. He quickly copied the number on Ned's dealers license and, as luck would have it, saw the sticky note with the phone number he'd copied from the erotica purveyor stuck to the side of the cash register—right where he'd left it. He rummaged in the desk for something with Ned's Social Security number, but grew anxious when he realized that the papers would look riffled.

Looking at the computer in the back room, he had a bold idea— *Okay, I'm crossing the line here, but I should try this.* The computer hummed to life after he entered the password "boyoboy." He felt his adrenaline rising. *This is as exciting as stealth recon in Nam.* If there was danger, there was no way to avoid it now. The class he'd taken to help Mar with her computer was paying off. He scrolled files and began looking in the "My Pictures" folders. There was lots of raunchy girly stuff. Then he looked in the folder labeled "special mine." *Unbelievable! That bastard!* There were close-ups of girls playing soccer, probably taken with a telephoto lens. A few were of Em and another girl—Amy? Then there were other girls—all young, very young, in seductive poses. It got worse—there were some loathsome shots, the worst examples of child pornography. Ned, or whoever took these pictures, was a serious predator. Miles felt flush with anger.

He knew that this was evidence he needed to take with him. There was a stack of blank CDs. He and Mar had learned to copy—now, if he could only actually manage to do it. His fingers shook as he looked for a copy program. *Where do I put the fucking CD?—Oh, yeah, here on the side. Jesus, I'm an idiot! Okay—I've got it.* He copied "special mine" and a bunch of other folders, stuck the CDs in his pocket and turned off the computer. He hoped to hell he'd done it right.

He turned off the lights and started toward the door. He heard sounds. It was Ned, coming up the stairs.

"Hey man, working kinda late, aren't ya—some problem here at the shop?"

Miles could feel the cords in his neck tighten and his fists clench. "You're one sick dude—I saw the pictures on your computer—"

Ned misinterpreted at first. "Don't blame you for sneaking a peek—some choice stuff there."

Miles lost control. "You piece of shit!—How can you stand yourself?—They're just kids!" He lunged at Ned, swinging wildly.

They tumbled down the stairs into the alley. Miles felt his leg twist as he went down. He was the better fighter, but Ned was surprisingly strong. They were both on the ground. Ned started to get up, but Miles had hold of his shirt collar. Miles got a direct punch at Ned's nose and felt the cartilage crunch. He didn't see what was in Ned's left hand before he felt something crash into his temple, then pain in his ribs. When he came to, his head throbbed and he was bleeding. A brick lay by his head. He looked around. Ned had driven away. He had to get back to Mary Lou's. He patted his pocket. The CDs were still there. He had trouble standing. Once in the car, he hoped he'd stay alert and conscious long enough to drive to Mar's house.

"Oh! My dear, my dear! What in ever! Please lay here on the sofa."

Mar returned with a bag of ice. He couldn't have gotten up even if he'd wanted to. He insisted that Mary Lou bring him the phone. She insisted on calling her doctor friend first.

Anna picked up on the first ring. "We have good news. Amy has returned to her home. We don't have the whole story—well, we don't know anything really. The important thing is, she's safe."

"Look, I think I'd better talk with Aaron. I'm okay—really—but I got in a tussle with Ned. Long story short, I hit my head and I'm feeling sick and dizzy."

He told Aaron about the information he'd found, including the pictures of Em, and who he thought might be Amy at soccer practice. He said there was kid porn in the files and that he'd copied a bunch of folders—also, that Ned had gotten away.

"I hope to Christ I didn't screw up the copies. I'm not exactly high-tech."

Mary Lou opened the door for a young woman, her physician friend. Dr. Nora peered at his bruise and rearranged the ice bag, waiting impatiently for him to end his conversation.

"I dunno, Aaron. I'm not sure I know how to copy and send the files on Mary Lou's computer—not sure I can sit up long enough to try." He leaned back and closed his eyes. Mary Lou quickly gave the details to Nora.

"Aaron, Nora Granger here. I'll copy and send the files, just give me the address—and then I need to tend to my patient."

That done, Nora finally saw to Miles. Mary Lou stayed on the phone with Anna, describing what Miles had told her had happened at the antique shop—and reassuring Anna that she'd keep Miles there overnight unless the doc had another idea.

Anna told her that Aaron had found some possible criminal records for Ned, but that he wouldn't be sure until tomorrow. Mary and Anna agreed to talk again after they'd all had a good night's sleep.

Doctor Granger sighed. "I'm not due at the clinic until Friday, so I'll stay over tonight to keep an eye on Miles—and don't you dare tell the neighbors. I've no intention of making this a habit."

Mary Lou felt relieved, thinking how fortunate they were that Doctor Nora was so young and unencumbered at this stage of her career, except for her lovely cats.

Amy's first story was that she'd wanted to get away for a day or two by herself because she needed some space—and that she didn't like Mom's new boyfriend. She said St. Michael's Church in Lee was open at night and she'd slept there, after hitching a ride with an old lady in a blue BMW. She'd made up the note so her mom wouldn't worry. "Honest, Mom, I'm really sorry."

Em was so relieved that Amy was okay. She sent her a text message, and then decided she'd like to talk to her instead. Initially, Amy told her the sleeping-in-the-church story—it was cold, it was scary, etc. Once she was out of her mother's earshot, however, her story changed. She told Em that she'd stayed at a fancy spa in Lenox with Ned so that he'd have time to take pictures at various times—under different lightings. She laughed and said that Ned had to pretend he was her father.

"Anyway, it was all pretty innocent. But, get this—he says he's madly in love with me *and*, in a few years, we could run away to France or someplace and get married." She whispered, "He actually says he *worships* me. 'Course, he's way too old. It would be nice if he launches my modeling career, though. You promise you won't tell, right?"

"Oh, sure," Em responded, this time knowing she'd tell. "Amy, I hope you won't do this again. You don't know this guy. What if he kidnapped you? Weren't you scared?"

"Yeah, I was a little scared at first. But, it felt really exciting. He was kissing my hands and crying, saying this had never happened to him—begging me to do stuff, which I mostly didn't do. Really, it was kinda cool. You know, Em, I'm more a risk-taker than you, and I don't think I can help it."

"Amy, we're both just kids. That situation with Ned sounds … well, weird. I gotta go now. See you next week. Call when you get a chance—okay?"

Emma could see Watson pulling weeds in the garden from her bedroom window. She didn't feel she needed his advice this time. Nevertheless, she felt like talking to another kid and, after all, he was in on the Amy drama.

"Hey, Watson, need some help weeding?"

"Sure, hoped I'd run into you anyway. Mrs. Curtis says Amy just went away for a day. Guess we might have been letting our imaginations run away, too."

"I wish!" Emma told him about Miles getting beaten up by Ned and about Amy's *real* story. "So, basically, she lied to her mom. And some of what she said worries me. I'm definitely going to tell Gram this time."

"Yeah, this guy sounds pretty creepy. I suspect Mr. Curtis is already investigating him."

They continued weeding around the tomatoes. Watson mentioned that he'd like to play some music with her—he'd seen the violin case on top of the oak chest in the dining room next to Jenna's piano. They decided on next Friday, as she and Gram were leaving Saturday.

"Let's invite Gram and Aunt Jen and Uncle Aaron, too. They'd enjoy some tunes, I'm sure. Well, wish me luck—I'm going in and spilling the beans."

Emma turned and waved from the porch. Watson gave her the thumbs-up sign.

six

FLIGHT PATTERNS

NED and MARGO

Meanwhile, Ned was ensconced safely, if not comfortably, at his old friend Margo's marijuana farm north of Plattsburgh. She'd decided he should stay in the barn until they could be sure his trail wasn't hot. That way, she figured she could plead innocent should he be located there. It was a horse barn with six or eight horses that pawed and snorted all night. He didn't especially like most animals, including horses—unless he was betting on them. And he rarely had a good season at Saratoga.

Margo was a semiretired nurse and had been able to set his nose. For that he was grateful; unfortunately, he seemed to have an allergy either to hay or horses—his nose ran like a son-of-a-bitch, not a pretty sight under the circumstances. Then there was his blue BMW. It was hidden under a pile of brush, at Margo's insistence. It was probably scratched and would become a nest for vermin. She had plans for him to help with the harvest, too, which didn't suit him. Still, he couldn't complain. He got three squares a day—plus Margo was good company.

He'd actually met her in a legitimate context when he worked at an antique shop in Atlanta. She collected old seed catalogues and agricultural ephemera. They dated, smoked a lot of weed—then he almost got busted for endangering a minor. In one of those late-night, hazy, dope-fueled romps, they'd become mutual confessors. In fact, she'd advised him to move far away from Atlanta—one of the reasons he'd landed in Wells.

Margo was born and bred in the northern Adirondacks. Her dad, killed in a construction accident, had originally lived on one of the Native American reservations near Potsdam. Her mom, still in the picture, was of Irish heritage and from a tiny town near the Canadian border. Margo had inherited her dad's Mohawk features—dark hair and high cheekbones. She was a strikingly beautiful woman. She graduated from nursing school as an RN and still did occasional stints at local hospitals. Her mother's family were small-time farmers, and Margo had remained involved in farming. To this day she made sure to keep a booth at the farmers market in town and was known for good corn and heirloom tomatoes, in addition to exotic varieties of beets and squashes.

The thing is, she'd always had a hankering for weed. So, what started as a personal-use crop soon grew into a profit-making illicit business under her knowledgeable care. She also believed that late-stage cancer patients should be given marijuana, and she did so, on a regular basis. Still, she was careful to not let her marijuana business get too big. It allowed her family to have a better life, and that was enough for her. Yeah, she had to pay the occasional bribe, but that was okay. Her big fears were the downstate dealers and the Canadian racketeers—not the law. Some days it worried her enough that she considered giving it up and sticking to legal crops. Most days, however, she was at ease, kicking back and intent on enjoying life.

She dearly hoped her old friend Ned would not be a problem. It sure would be helpful if he could help her harvest some weed. He knew enough to keep his mouth shut, something you couldn't rely on with the Vermont stoners. Besides, she couldn't get him over the border until his nose healed and people stopped looking for him—if they *were* looking. "Caution" was Margo's mantra.

After dark, Margo let Ned in the house. His whining about hay fever was getting on her nerves. She joked about being too old for a roll in the hay anyway. It was a warm evening. They sat on the screened back porch while she rolled a joint, took a toke and passed it to him. The smoke easily dissipated through the screens.

"Man, I'd forgotten how great the good stuff could be." He inhaled and coughed, unable to blow the smoke out through his nose.

"No blow for you these days? Reformed, eh?"

Ned envied the blossoming stream pluming from her nostrils. "Well, ya know, I'm thinking it best to limit my vices." He exhaled. "That ways there's less to keep track of. 'Course, I drink more, but so what?" *Wow!* He was already feeling stoned.

"Look, buddy boy—I've been going easy on you, but we need a heart-to-heart. You were in rough shape when you showed up here. I'm buying at least half of what you're saying, but I need details—all the details. And if I catch you lying—no, if I even *think* you are lying— you're out on your butt. Friend as I am, I'd turn you over in a minute if you put me in danger—clear on that?"

One look in those hard dark eyes was convincing enough. "Jesus, Margo, I swear to God—I don't think I did anything bad. I'll try to explain …" He was definitely feeling buzzed. "There's this girl named Amy. She's kind of fucked-up—but really beautiful." He hesitated, lost in the moment. "I mean, I might of originally thought of taking advantage, her being inexperienced and all. We started sending e-mails. She's one of my Facebook friends. Before you know it, she's telling me her whole life. She's *sooo* gorgeous." He took a deep drag. "I took her to this swanky resort to impress her—to take some photos of her. Tasteful, not really porn, ya know? Then I realized I'm in love with her. That sounds crazy, but it's true. I'd marry her if I could." Ned started bawling. Margo handed him some tissues.

"So, what's the problem? She married?—You married?—The guy who punched you her boyfriend?—You taking dirty pictures to sell?—What's the problem?"

"Mostly, it's that she's too young for me—not really—but her parents would think so … and then, I've been selling some erotica over the past year."

Margo blew another plume. "So, how old is she?"

"Under eighteen." He saw Margo's black eyes narrow. "Okay, okay—I think more like fourteen." Margo's look turned to anger—no, disgust. If he wasn't so stoned, he would have run into the woods.

"Christ almighty!—I'd think you might have learned something by now! Can't you content yourself with the photos?—Or maybe game-playing with adults? You are fucking *nuts!* I don't know if I want you to stay here. You got more to tell me?"

Ned was actually blubbering now. "Maybe I am nuts, but I honestly am in love with Amy. I'll admit it's wrong and I've made some bad mistakes in the past—but this time it's different. I'd do anything if I could just touch her little hand or hear her voice right now." *Weird but true*, he thought.

Margo just looked at him. Ned cautiously wiped his eyes. He had tried his best to tell her everything.

"Well, Ned, the sins of the past cast long shadows, she said, pausing. I doubt you'd stop at her smooth little hand … and, as we like to say in the health professions, you have 'serious mental health issues.' But, you know what? Except for your bizarre sexual inclinations, you're not a bad egg. Maybe I'm just stoned—or getting warped myself." She paused for a moment. "There's something sad and kinda poignant about your situation … and *wrong*, of course. As a friend *and* a health professional, I'm telling you to get into counseling once we get you safely outta here." She paused again. "Can't guarantee it'll fix you, though."

She thought, *the trouble with getting older and more tolerant was you might get too tolerant. Maybe I'm being too soft.* She would watch him like a hawk until he left—for sure.

As for Ned, the predator now felt like prey. He was free for the moment, but that could end in an instant. His brief taste of the entrancing butterfly dancing in her black shorts and burnt-orange halter was torturing him. But, he was *glad* he had taken her pictures in the Chesterwood gardens. At least he had those, and still in his camera, too. And his camera was in his overnight case, which was still in his car. *Well, if you have to make a hasty departure, it was at least some kind of good luck to have luggage already in the car.* It looked like Margo's temper had subsided. *She's plenty good-looking, no doubt about that.*

EMMA

Emma opened the back door cautiously. Gram and Aunt Jenna were sitting on white wicker chairs in the sunroom, sandals off, feet on the coffee table. There was a pitcher of iced tea on the blue-and-white tray between them.

"Come join us, Em."

Emma took her time pouring a glass of tea for herself. Gram was telling Aunt Jenna about her Adirondack photo show last month. Emma took a breath. She figured she might as well interrupt them. She knew that the most important thing was to be clear and accurate. She took a swallow of tea and sat on the yellow-flowered chaise directly across from Gram.

Clearing her throat, she said, "I called Amy today. She lied to her mom. Last night's story about sleeping in the church isn't at all true."

She told them everything she could remember from the conversation—the fancy resort, the photos—even that Ned claimed to be in love with Amy, but Amy just wanted him to help her become a model. Aunt Jenna put her hands to her mouth. Gram's eyes grew dilated. She sat erect, leaning slightly forward. Then the words exploded from her.

"I knew it! I just knew there was something devious and dangerous about the man! I sensed it from the beginning. How dare that piece of scum prey on young girls!" Anna rose and paced the room, knocking her glass to the floor in the process. When she returned from the kitchen with a cloth to wipe up the mess, she was calmer.

"I'm angry, but really not that surprised," she said to Em. "I know it's hard to tell something like that, especially about a friend. You did the exact right thing, Em."

She could see that Em was startled and dismayed by her outburst and held back any further comment. But, damn it, she was fired up and furious about Ned's impropriety. Her radar had been spot-on this time. She'd have to question Cara more, too. But she knew Cara would never have expected this turn of events.

Em was feeling terribly upset. She had never seen Gram this angry. At the same time, however, and for the first time since they'd heard about Amy's disappearance, Em also felt relieved. She didn't try to hold back tears and actually liked being comforted and fussed over by Gram and Aunt Jen. They told her Uncle Aaron was at the station investigating Ned—just in case. What Em had found out was important information, and Aaron needed to know.

When Aaron returned they were still in the sunroom. Anna relayed Em's story about Amy to spare her the anguish of repeating it. Aaron scowled and looked very somber, but not surprised. He told them that the alias, or earlier name, used by Ned showed he'd once been accused, though not convicted, of endangering a minor in Atlanta. And there was definitely pornography on the CD downloaded from Ned's computer. They were trying to tie the pornography to the Connecticut phone number—no luck yet on that. Besides, it was a cell ... and the bad guys knew to routinely discard them, so they couldn't easily be traced. The information given to Em by Amy might mean the local police could pick Ned up for questioning—if they could find him. Also, Amy and her folks would have to cooperate ...

"So they'll throw Ned in jail? What about Amy?" Em was curious about how it all worked.

Uncle Aaron sighed. "It all depends ... It's kinda like a puzzle; sometimes you just can't find all the pieces, or fit them all together. But, my girl, you found one of the most important pieces—definitely a reason for questioning him. 'Course, we got to find him, amongst other things."

To himself, Aaron thought, *it might just have to be good enough that this girl Amy and Em too, are safe from a predator. Maybe we'll get to bust a porn ring, but it's way too early in the game to make predictions.* For the moment, he wanted to simply keep his family safely away from this stuff—and try to get Anna and Em back on the vacation track.

ANNA

Anna was glad to be sunning on the beach with Jenna. They had only two more days of loafing and lobster. Truth be told, she was getting anxious to see Miles. He said he was fine, but that nice Doctor Nora thought he should stay at Mary Lou's for another week.

Emma had decided to go out on the boat and give Aaron a hand again—Anna thought, *Strange what kids think is fun.*

She and Jen continued to circle around the Amy and Ned incident, especially when Em wasn't around. However, without new data their conclusions were stymied—at least for the moment.

Anna had called Kim, Amy's mother, last night and found her chilly and defensive. Perhaps that was to be expected. After all, they'd actually never met. Kim said that Amy was going to stay with her father in Hartford and would probably remain there for the following school year. She said they'd also confiscated Amy's cell and closed her Facebook account.

Anna, Jack and Dee had talked and agreed that Em might best stay in Albany an extra week—until Amy had been packed off to her father—and Em, to Anna's amazement, took this in stride, even welcomed it. She now was focused on visiting the Hancock Shakers and continuing to explore documents in the State Library archives.

ANNA and JENNA

Jenna wondered if Anna had remembered the time Aunt Clara's friend, Joe DeBello, had taken them to Washington Park to take photos.

"I remember him combing my hair and unbuttoning my cardigan. Do you suppose ...?"

"You remember how strict Aunt Clara was—especially about men? Pity the guy who made a pass at *either* of us. So, nuff said." They laughed. They loved to talk about their guardian, Aunt Clara, who was truly of another age—even in her *own* era. They were always fond of her, but her luster glowed richer with time. No doubt, they hadn't found the prim clothes and makeup restrictions endearing back then.

Anna and Jen were so comfortable with each other that they easily drifted back to their own thoughts—or books. Being together on a beach and whiling away a few aimless hours was still one of life's joys.

Anna's thoughts turned to Miles. *I have to admit that I'm anxious to see him. And it's not just concern about his bumps and bruises, either. It seems his friend Mary Lou has that situation under control. No, I like him—and I look forward to being with him. We'll plan some good hikes over the summer ... maybe go to some concerts. And, of course, there's sex. That's a nice thing.*

She turned to her sister and poked her on the arm. "You know, I really like Miles."

"Do tell," Jen smiled, and returned to reading.

Anna rose and walked to the water, letting the cold surf reach her ankles. Her feet left prints in the wet sand along the length of the beach that were erased by the time she returned. *Even ordinary lives, whatever that may mean, sustain many changes in their more routine patterns, one ripple easily erasing another. Blue meeting yellow turns green.*

EMMA and WATSON

Em was her usual sunny self the following evening. She had spent the early part of the day hauling traps with Aaron and was showering off the effects of the salt, sea and fishy boat. She bounced onto the porch golden-haired and smiling. Anna could never quite get over the resilience of youth. *Thank God!*

"Thought I'd finally wear the skirt you bought me, Gram—for the concert. Watson will be here at eight o'clock."

"It looks pretty. I can never resist blue and yellow flowers." She was also going to mention how pretty Em looked—tan, freckled face with sun-bleached golden curls—but didn't. The thought of Em's being attractive was pleasurable, but now also scary.

Em and Watson enjoyed playing music together. They had briefly practiced an interesting arrangement of "Greensleeves" that they played well. But the songs that proved the most fun were the sea shanties. Watson's dad had provided sheet music that Emma could readily follow.

The next morning Watson stopped by to give Em copies of the sheet music. They both agreed to be Facebook friends. Watson gave her an awkward hug, and they laughed.

Em wondered if Tess and Luke would have been Facebook friends if they had lived in today's world.

JENNA and AARON

After Anna and Emma said their good-byes, Jen and Aaron sat on the screened porch with a second cup of coffee. Aaron cleared the dishes and loaded the dishwasher. The house seemed quiet and settled. The gardening kids weren't likely to stop by before afternoon, if then; they'd picked produce for the farmers market late yesterday.

Jen had been reticent to ask more about Aaron's findings on Ned while Emma was still around. She knew how Aaron was when he was investigating someone he felt had likely been up to no good.

"A penny for your thoughts about that Ned character," she said.

"Can't say's I've turned up anything new ... wish I had. One of the problems is jurisdiction. Ned's living—or was—in New York. Amy's from Massachusetts, and the possible porn ring, if the phone number had panned out, is in Connecticut. *If* there was criminal activity across state lines, there would be a federal case, but so far, based on evidence, that'd be a stretch. I've got a trooper friend in New York watching Ned's store, in case he returns. He even searched the place on the QT, which could technically be breaking-and-entering. All he found was garden-variety girlie stuff and old-time erotica that *might* be classified as kiddy porn. Luckily, we have the CD Miles copied with the real dirt. Unfortunately, however, the laptop seems to have disappeared. Ned could be charged with endangering the welfare of a child, *if* we find him. On the other hand, our Amy is less than forthcoming. I suggested the juvie social worker interview her—and, with her parents okay, she did. Amy's pretty crafty, though. Her story changes to suit the circumstances—maybe her mood.

I spoke with Miles, Anna's friend, yesterday. He's racking his brain for any names or clues Ned might have dropped over the years. So far, nothing much—Ned's a slippery fish that jumped the hook and is back swimming with the other fishes—or other sharks. So, do I think this guy did wrong and deserves to be grilled about this kid? You bet. Will we catch him? Hard to say—at the moment." Aaron scowled into his coffee.

Jenna looked thoughtful. "Don't you think in some of these cases it boils down to imperfect people trying to live in an imperfect world?"

"Oh, crap, Jenna! Yes, there's imperfect people—perverts, psychopaths, malicious, mean-spirited, cruel, or just otherwise messed-up. In the trade, they often turn out to be criminals, the reason we need laws." His anger dissipated. He looked apologetically at Jenna. "Look, I'm okay with this particular case, no matter how it goes. We'll do our best to find the guy, and that'll be that."

He was relieved to see Jen brighten. "You know what I think? We should take the day off and drive to Portland—just poke around a bit. Sound good?"

Jenna nodded and smiled.

ANNA

Anna easily found Mary Lou's house. Emma was acting as an able navigator. As they pulled into the narrow driveway, they spotted Miles and, presumably, Mary Lou sitting on Adirondack chairs in the side yard. Anna was somewhat surprised to see that Mary Lou was African-American, as Miles hadn't mentioned that when he'd described her as an elderly, retired librarian. *Then again,* she thought, somewhat chagrined at her own assumptions, *why should he have mentioned that?*

Miles and Mary Lou waved. Miles rose from his chair and walked towards Anna and Em. His face was bruised, and there was a large bandage over his left eye.

"I'm not as pretty as when you left," he joked, giving them both a careful hug—partly because his ribs still ached. He was pleased to see Anna. She was tanned and her hair was a shade lighter. Em was her lovely, energetic self—she began walking around Mary Lou's yard, exclaiming over the plants in the small raised bed.

"My Aunt Jenna is growing these same purple flowers—so pretty. They're supposed to attract butterflies, you know."

Mary Lou smiled indulgently. "Yes, they really *do* attract them. We've been watching a pair of yellow swallowtails and a humming-bird this morning. By the way, Miles tells me you all have been up to some interesting research. He says you're the instigator—true?"

"Did he tell you the whole story? Anyway, we even found new stuff when we visited the Shakers in Maine."

Emma related their findings at Sabbath Day Lake. She had thought to bring some photos of the plain white clapboard buildings, all in good repair, dazzling white against the blue Maine sky. Aaron had taken one of her and Gram at Cape Elizabeth Light, which she passed to Miles.

"You can keep that one. I was gonna send you a postcard, but didn't know the address."

Miles was pleased that the kid had thought about him. He carefully placed the picture in the pocket of his green plaid shirt—an ill-fitting hand-me-down with cowboy lapels that Mar and Dr. Nora had picked up at St. Joseph's thrift shop. He wondered, fleetingly, if he looked goofy—and if he dared impose on Anna to pick up a few items from the cabin. Ideally, he'd like to just go back to the cabin. But Mar and Nora were formidable opposition. Besides, he still hurt. For the first time in a long while, the fact of his mortality gave him pause. He could see that Mar could hardly wait to offer her tidbit of information on Griffin.

She leaned forward. Her small, brown, compact frame looked childlike in the large Adirondack chair, her alert hazel eyes set in an old walnut face rimmed with a cloud of white fluff. She was brimming with interesting news, and she knew it. She softly cleared her throat.

"Don't know as Miles got to mention this—what with all the recent commotion. I'd had this vague memory of a story about someone in old Griffin going to live with the Shakers. Of course, that wouldn't have been so unusual in the late 1900s. Their communities were pretty nice, in that they built neat, sturdy houses and grew their own food. I think single womenfolk might have been drawn to the communities because they provided good food, clothing and shelter—and they wouldn't be hassled by men. Remember, this was way before women got the vote. Single women without means really were in a sorry state. But I digress—old ladies tend to do that," she laughed.

"Ever since Miles mentioned you two being interested in Griffin, I've been trying to recall the story. Then, in talking to my sister Josie— she lives in Florida—we both got to recollecting. Seeming outta nowhere, the names Girard and Gifford popped up. We're both sure it was a Girard, though we disagree whether it was a man or woman. The thing that made the story of any interest to us—remember, we were kids when we heard it—was that the person who joined the Shakers did so because the person they were in love with was already living in a Shaker village. I suppose as teenagers Josie and I loved stories of unrequited romance!"

"Wish the two of us could remember more. When you're young, your thoughts go straight to the future, so the details of the past are hardly interesting. Now that we're old, we wish we'd paid more attention. Josie and I talk every week, so no telling what we might remember if we keep rummaging."

Mary Lou realized that she could say a little more, but she and Josie had agreed that the story as remembered had been long ago embroidered over with their girlish flights of fancy. And as a former librarian, Mary Lou prided herself on sticking with what she was confident were the facts.

Anna and Emma were listening intently and were clearly excited by the story. Emma sat kicking her legs.

"This is like finding—like finding . . . " she started to say.

"Another thread in the raveled tapestry?" offered Mary Lou.

"Um—maybe." Em was thinking. "Yes! Like that. That's it!"

Anna was fully engaged in watching the tableau around her—old Mary Lou's remembrances, Em's youthful exuberance, Miles' kindly connection to it all. She wished she could always feel this way—so entirely present in the moment.

Surely, by next week Miles could go back to his cabin . . . or I could offer to take him for a drive. Em should be home with Jack and Dee by then. Miles interrupted her thoughts.

"Anna, any possibility you and Em might check my cabin? I didn't expect to be gone so long—not even sure I locked the door, not that it much matters .. " he hesitated.

"Don't be silly, of course we'll go. Em and I need to stretch our legs anyway. Besides, that shirt you're wearing isn't really you," she smiled.

He told them where to find the hidden key, if needed, and they set off.

It felt great to be walking on the shaded, worn path. To think, it wasn't so long back that Em and she had gone on their first exploration—and that she'd been apprehensive about the friendly fisherman on that very riverbank. *Who'd have thought?* Actually, it was hard to think at the moment—Em was chattering nonstop about the Girards and the rest. The prevalent songbirds were no competition.

The cabin looked lonely and a bit ramshackle. The door was unlocked, and Anna made a note to lock it before they left. Inside it was neat, except for the brown cereal bowl and green coffee mug in the sink. Anna felt her cheeks grow warm as she entered the bedroom. They stood a moment facing the dresser before she opened a drawer. Even with his permission, it seemed an invasion of privacy.

Em giggled, "Hope we don't find grey jockey shorts. Sometimes Mom has to toss Dad's. She says he must get dressed in the dark."

Anna laughed, thinking of the boy Jack. In the spirit of silliness, she opened the top drawer with a flourish—"Ta-da!"

Everything was folded and orderly. Though there were some shorts, they were blue, green and black—sensible. They decided three changes of undies, three t-shirts, a pair of jeans and one long-sleeved blue chambray would do. They folded them neatly in Anna's day pack. Anna sat on the bed as she did so—feeling a bit like an aging Goldilocks, or was that Red Riding Hood? ... Hmmm...

Em had the idea that they should weed the garden. It didn't look too bad, but it was definitely much improved by the time they'd finished. The tomato plants looked a little dry. They filled the watering can three times at the old-fashioned pump. Em was so intrigued by it that she insisted on doing all the pumping. The cold water was so inviting they each drank from the enamelware cup hanging on a nearby tree. They'd worked up a sweat from their gardening and thought a brief sit was warranted—at least Anna thought so.

"Gram, can I ask you some stuff about Amy?" It was the first time Em mentioned Amy since they'd returned from Maine.

"I'm feeling confused ... Don't get mad at me. I'm wondering about if Ned *is* in love with Amy—and then, say, it turns out she's in love with him—well, wouldn't that mean Ned wasn't bad? There are novels where the younger girl marries an older guy—right? I'm not saying I like Ned. Actually, I think he's creepy. What I'm saying is—is he bad?" Em looked perplexed.

Anna wanted dearly to get this right and not respond with knee-jerk platitudes. She fully understood Em's confusion.

"I understand your thinking, Em. Certainly, love can be mysterious—human relationships are complex. Then, there's the cultural aspect. However—and this is true—adults want to nurture and protect children. They do their best to see that kids are secure and not harmed. This is doubly true for parents. So, when we see that a stranger has attempted to coerce a child, or has caused a kid to lie to her parents—well, we're going to be hard on him. Ned's an adult, and he was dishonest. Make sense?" Anna held her tongue and managed to avoid saying what she really thought—*He's a slimy piece of shit!* She hugged Em. "Oh, Em, it's so hard understanding these things—just trust me on this one."

"Yeah, and then he went and hurt Miles. If he was innocent, he wouldn't have attacked a friend. I always thought he was phony."

Em felt relieved. She'd know what to say if Amy called again. She was still mad that Amy had implied that she, Em, was a cautious nerd—not a risk-taker.

They walked back to the car by way of the stream. They made a quick detour to stop by a small grocery and pick up some items they thought might appeal to Miles and Mary Lou—cold cuts, tomatoes, apple juice, cola and Oreo cookies. It was early afternoon and still sunny.

Upon reflection a few years hence, Em was glad her Gram and others had been protective of her back then.

Though in her case, she had felt repulsed by the idea of Ned as a sexual prospect. You could say she had a natural immunity to his advances. But the words and actions by Gram and the others had raised her level of alertness. She had grown antennae for sensing predators that summer. And her sensors still generally served her well.

Barbara Delaney

MILES and MARY LOU

As Anna pulled away down the driveway, Mary Lou was full of amiable conversation.

"I like her better than I even thought—and that granddaughter is a gem," she exclaimed. "This is definitely someone worth waiting for—have you made plans with her for when you are up and about?" She reached and patted his knee.

"Hmmm . . . I'd havta say yes, and yes, to that. When I walked her to the car, she suggested we plan something for a week from Saturday—with any luck, I'll be less achy and back in my cabin well before then. Which reminds me, don't know what I'd have done without you, Mar. You're a good friend."

"Tell the truth, it's nice having you here, and it's a chance to do for someone else—for a change. You've been carting me here and there and doing chores for a while, you know."

"Yep, and I've been getting many a nice meal. Hey, we're friends." They both laughed at the awkward but heartfelt "thank-you's."

Miles thought, *this is as close to a mother-son relationship as I'll ever have.* He had some guilt about his own mother. His life had been in such turmoil during her final years that he'd neglected her. He supposed he'd been just young enough to think she'd always be there. His friendship with Mary Lou was a gift, really.

"Everything you've been intuiting about me and Anna is true. I seem to almost have a girlfriend. Gotta say—you, me, my counselor buddy at the VA—everybody's mighty surprised." He stopped to think for a moment. "I would say I was happy today—glad to be here with you, Anna and Em. Now, lots of time I'm happy all by myself at the cabin, too—it has its challenges and I'm usually up for it. Being happy with Anna is different than that." He paused again, trying to get it right.

"I've had time to think here. Being with people has challenges I haven't had to consider. For example, say I want to contact someone—well, Anna. No phone, no computer. The same goes for her reaching me. You and me have our routines that mostly work, and I use your phone for appointments and such. When I worked at Ned's, I had use of the phone and the computer—but that's a gone situation. Then, there's the horrible fact that if I'd had a cell phone, Ned might have been caught right away. I guess it was hours that elapsed. All this is bothering me—a lot. I'm feeling … feeling …"

Mary Lou interjected, "Like you're out of step with the times? The world is passing you by?"

"Yeah, I guess. The big problem is, I haven't figured out what to do about it. I like living in the cabin—I'm used to it. It's comfortable and peaceful—got my garden, huntin', fishin'." He sat hunched over, shook his head. "Just don't know."

Mary Lou scraped her chair a little closer. "You know how I hate to give advice, right? Well, here's what I think anyway—change can be good, especially if it's for a good reason. Did you ever think all this could be about *wanting* change?" Her small hand waved an encompassing arch. "Now, I know nothing about your finances—none of my business." She held her hands in a stopping gesture. "But you could always rent an apartment in town—see how you like it—and keep the cabin, too. Try having it both ways. Maybe it's time to come out of your cocoon, so to speak"

Miles wasn't used to being this open, but what the hell.

"Full disclosure, Mar? I could afford an apartment, though it's kind of a foreign concept to me. You know my lifestyle—pretty simple. As it stands, however, I have VA benefits, Social Security and a small inheritance. Actually, my bank account has grown embarrassingly large. Get's any bigger, the tellers are going to call me '*Mr.* Hermit.'"

"So, you've got some things to mull over." Mary Lou sat back and folded her hands on her stomach. She could envision beautiful possibilities under the circumstance. Miles was sure to stretch his wings soon.

Miles rose from his chair and tuned the radio to the classical station Mar loved. He sat down and fell comfortably into his own thoughts. Trajectories had always intrigued him. Who could ever imagine the consequences of even the smallest action? "Hello" could change your life forever.

ANNA

Cara and Stan were being great about taking on more hours at Bella Fiore. First, Anna had stayed a few extra days in Cape Porpoise, and now Em was her charge for the rest of the week. Still, she tried to spend some mornings at the shop.

It was Tuesday. She brought Em with her in the early morning, grabbing pastries and coffee on the go. She made sure to include a chocolate croissant for Cara and an oat bran muffin for Stan—their favorites. She had discouraged Em from going to the library alone, all the while knowing that she was being irrational. Once that protective instinct was activated, it was hard to turn it off. Em had pouted a bit, and then turned Anna's guilty feelings to her advantage. The upshot was that they'd spend Thursday touring the nearby Shaker sites—Albany/Watervliet and Hancock Village.

It was only 7:30 a.m. when Anna unlocked the shop door, enough time to check her mail and sort bills before the crew arrived. Em took the initiative to work in the back room freshening and dead-heading plants.

When Cara and Stan arrived, they made a fuss over Em. They genuinely liked her. Much to Anna's surprise, Em told them she hoped to be a real help today.

"I'm going to work hard to help out. Actually, I've learned a lot about plants. Besides, Gram's going to take me to Shaker Village Thursday. I hate to be a burden by letting work pile up here at the shop." Em continued munching her second apple muffin.

Oh crap, thought Anna, *she sounds just like Dee.* Although clearly she had Cara and Stan buffaloed.

"Oh honey," cooed Cara, "you are such a thoughtful girl." Stan nodded in assent. Nevertheless, good to her word, Em put in a full day's work.

After lunch, Anna had let Em work in the greenhouse with Stan. Cara and she needed to catch up. She didn't want to raise the Ned issue within earshot of Em. Em seemed to have drawn away from the subject, and Anna didn't want to pull her back.

"We'll probably talk more about this next week—when Em goes home. But I swear, I was shocked by that incident with Ned. I'm so sorry, Anna." Cara said. "I'm glad to hear Miles is doing well—must have given him a scare. I just didn't see anything ominous in Ned. Somehow your sense of him was spot-on—mine wasn't. And I think I'm *good* at sizing up guys, too." Cara scowled and shook her head.

Anna could see her remorse and wanted to free Cara of any guilt she might be feeling.

"I think it's easy to miss cues when you're not the likely prey. On the other hand, my radar was up because of Em—it's probably a protective Gram thing."

Cara nodded. "And a lucky thing, too. Ya know, when Amy's mom called the shop looking to speak to you—to contact Amy—Stan and I figured she might have gone off with a boy her age—there was no suspicion of a creep in the picture." She paused. "I did meet Ned in Saratoga for dinner a few times—he's an outrageous flirt. And, okay, I like to flirt. But he didn't wear well—all veneer, if you know what I mean—like one of those old Birdseye maple tables, looks good until you realize the top layer is beginning to peel. He does know a lot about antiques, however. Anyway, I'd had second thoughts, what with Tony in the picture."

Cara felt somewhat absolved by what Anna had said. She touched her lip in thought. "You just never know, do you? Thank God I never had sex with him!" She decided it was best not to mention the phone sex. Also, she never counted it as sex if she didn't have an orgasm.

Anna felt relieved that Cara hadn't pursued a relationship with Ned—not that she thought that she had—but, with Cara, it would not be out of the question. She patted her friend's arm.

"Of course, it's hard to say where this is all going," Anna said. "Ned has disappeared. According to Aaron, the landlord says his rent is paid through September. So he might come back, depending. Apparently Amy is slathering on the whitewash. There is the possibility that any of Ned's acquaintances or friends could be questioned—like you and me. Right now that seems unlikely."

There really wasn't more to say. Anna thought, *human threats are a bit like viruses. When they're active, they command our complete attention. Once quiet, they quickly recede from thought.*

Anna decided that she and Em would drive after work to the Shaker Heritage site near the airport. There was supposedly a hiking trail around the pond, and they could have dinner at one of the restaurants on Wolf Road. Em had invited Cara to join them.

Anna was always amazed at Cara's rapport with Em. *It must be their love of music,* she thought. *As much as I love Cara, however, a role model she's not.* Em was telling Cara all about the "concert" she and Watson had played, and Em offered to make copies of the sea shanties for her.

At first, Em was not too impressed with the old Shaker buildings. All but one were closed to the public; the rest were in need of paint and maintenance. Once they began walking and reading the signs, however, their interest was piqued. The plaques told the story of a once-thriving village that had grown, canned and sold vegetables to sustain itself.

Near the herb garden, a couple who were knowledgeable about Shaker history spoke with them for a while. They learned that Mother Ann, the society's founder, had traveled all the way from England in 1778 to escape persecution and found the sect. The couple went on to tell about Shaker inventions and the attention the sect received from famous people like Nathaniel Hawthorne, Thomas Jefferson and President Cleveland, and how Mother Ann's grave was right here on the premises. They pointed to a small cemetery across the way.

Anna thanked them, and then she, Em and Cara walked in the direction of the cemetery. Mother Ann's stone sat primly amongst rows of identical markers. The three women stood there briefly before walking around the pond.

The pond walk was just what they needed. There were pickerel weed and water lilies afloat. After crossing a narrow footbridge, the path wended through deeper woods full of the green shoots of summer. It felt remote, except for the drone of planes from the airport.

Cara said she'd once visited Hancock Shaker Village and assured Em that she was going to like the demonstrations of crafts and the open, furnished buildings.

"They even have a big garden and live animals. They sell home-made jams and herbs. It's really cool," she said.

Later, sitting on her pretty back porch, Cara thought some more about Ned and his predilection for young girls. She could not shake a niggling feeling of remorse for not having paid attention to cues that he might be a predator. She poured a splash of sauvignon blanc. She remembered him asking if she liked playing sex-game roles—like knee socks and short plaid skirts. She had laughed, saying she hardly had a school girl body. Actually, this kind of silly sex talk didn't faze her. Yet, she wondered why or when she became inured to sexual innuendos.

She remembered when, as a young woman living in Vermont, an older professor had pursued her. It was a casual affair and she felt flattered. One day she'd run into him in Shaw's grocery and cheer-fully waved and walked towards him just as his wife and two kids came around the cereal aisle. He acted embarrassed, like he hardly knew her. She had felt sad and exposed—mortified, really. There had been nothing in her over protected adolescence to prepare her for this. And she knew these scenarios played out time and again for young women … pursued, captured, and hurt. She supposed the game continued, but eventually a woman learned to adroitly parry with her pursuer in order to gain advantage. In spite of herself she smiled, remembering him fucking to *William Tell's Overture*".

She topped her glass of wine, thinking she'd prefer a glass of red, but she'd just whitened her teeth. She resolved, should she get the chance, to be more alert in ferreting out men who might try to prey on girls like Em. She shuddered at the thought of Ned contacting Em.

Anna awoke early Thursday thinking of her conversation with Miles the night before. It sure was convenient for him to have access to a phone. He said he felt clear-headed—no aches over his eye. He sounded great. He was thinking of driving to Albany on Friday—something about forms and paperwork he had to fill out at the VA.

She had told him he'd be welcome for dinner—it was Em's last night. He said he'd call Friday morning to make a plan.

One of Anna's favorite things was to sit in her kitchen in the early morning with the first cup of coffee, cradling the cup and inhaling the fresh aroma. Birdsong and a gentle breeze wafted in through the screened window. Em was still sleeping, which was fine.

The next day Anna drove to Hancock Village with Em as promised.

"What an amazing place!" exclaimed Em. "This *looks* like a real village."

And so it was, in times past. Presently it was a museum with periodic demonstrations illustrating the former industries. This particular Shaker community had been founded in 1790. Shakers had lived there until 1959, when they sold the village with the stipulation that it be operated as a museum.

Olivia, the young, pleasant, round-faced docent, told Em that they'd gotten the name "Shakers" from the free-form dance they incorporated into their worship services. Their basic tenets were productive, industrious labor and the chaste separation of the sexes.

In response to Emma's question, Olivia said, "Yes, indeed, they penned the hymn 'It's a Gift to be Simple.'"

Today there was a weaving demonstration. Anna and Em both got to try their hands at using the wooden shuttle, which Em thought was "way cool."

The day did fly by. It was a perfect grandmother/granddaughter outing. Unfortunately, there was no way they could look at records on such short notice. Olivia said that they'd need to make an appointment to use the research library. She was fascinated by Emma's story about Tess and Luke and the possibility that one of them might have joined the Shakers. Her genuine interest went a ways in soothing Em's disappointment at not being able to use the library.

"This was a real fun day, Gram. Couldn't you almost see how it was to live here? If Tess lived here, I think she would have done weaving—maybe made some cloaks."

"Yep, I could see it."

They visited the gift shop on the way out, buying mostly herbs and jams. Gram gave in to indulgence and bought Em a small, traditional Shaker box. The herbs and jam were for Miles and Mary Lou.

"Gram, you're the best!"

"Uh huh."

When they got back to the house, the light on the answering machine was blinking. It was Miles saying that, yes, he'd take her up on dinner. Laughing, he said Mary Lou told him that ladies liked a day's notice—which was why he hadn't waited 'til tomorrow.

seven

BREAKING FREE

Miles was due to arrive around six o'clock. Em said she was eager to see Miles and got in the spirit of decorating the table for dinner. She decided on a blue and yellow theme. The cloth was from Florence and featured bright yellow lemons on a patterned blue-and-white ground. Em found some yellow candles and opened all the windows in the screened bay window. The long white curtains billowed in the late-afternoon breeze. She thought the blue glasses were fine as long as they were serving lemonade, not milk. She also found some yellow napkins that she'd folded into elaborate fan shapes, which Gram said were a bit much, but in the end agreed *were* decorative and pretty. Em had selected a bunch of flowers from the shop and she arranged them in a cut-glass pitcher on the buffet—blue and white hydrangeas punctuated with spiky purple flowers. She was trying to decide whether to borrow some stems from the arrangement for the table when the door chimed. Em skipped to the door before Anna could walk from the kitchen.

"Oh, good," she said, seeing the flowers in Miles' hands, "yellow delphiniums—perfect." She took them from his hands and ran past Anna to the kitchen.

Miles and Anna barely had time for a quick kiss before Em bounced back with a Delft vase and the flowers, which she set in the middle of the dining table. Miles said the flowers were from Mary Lou's garden. She'd insisted he bring them.

They sat in the airy alcove off the living room for appetizers and drinks—just to settle in and catch up, really.

Anna liked the rose-and-cream décor of this room—summery, she thought. Miles was thinking how nice the Eastlake rocker would look here. He was waiting for the taint of Ned's shop to fade from their memories before he gave it to her.

As usual, Em wanted to talk about Tess and Luke. She provided Miles with more than enough information about the visit to Hancock Village.

"Of course, we didn't really find any new stuff—'cause we couldn't use the library. One thing I've been thinking about is how Hancock had a pharmaceutical business, and if that fits in with Dr. Bleeker going there, like they said in the old newspaper. Remember?"

"Yep, could be," nodded Miles.

Em scrunched her brows. "But how am I ever going to know the truth?" She crossed her arms and sat back. "What if I don't find any more than I already know?"

"Well, no reason to give up yet," said Miles. "Ya know, Em, lotsa times we only get the bits and pieces. Even when we think we got it all, it's only part of the picture. Follow?"

"Sure, but what help is that?—sounds kinda hopeless to me."

"Maybe—but not really … What would you like to have happen to Tess and Luke? If you imagined their story, based on what you know—and more stuff you'll find out—would they fall in love? Move away from each other? Live together in New York City? One or both join the Shakers? Have kids? And on and on … you're free to give them many different lives. Should we try it?"

"You mean, make up stories, like a game? Maybe—but they can't have kids if they're Shakers. Which reminds me—I was going to ask about the 'chaste' thing? What's with that, anyway?"

Anna came to the doorway. "Hey, you two philosophers—dinner's ready."

Em had really made the dining room look pretty, transforming the simple lemon chicken and green salad into a truly festive occasion.

The conversation around the table was relaxed but lively. At Em's request, Miles described his life in the woods and his early life growing up in the town of Saranac Lake. He described it as a beautiful small village nestled in the High Peaks. He said he learned to love the woods while he lived there.

They talked more about Shaker life, especially Shaker women. Miles admitted to being somewhat clueless about them, which caused Anna and Em to laugh. Em thought that some of the Shaker women probably didn't like men or children—maybe they'd been disappointed in love. Anna reminded them that women of that period didn't have a great range of choices. For example, if they were widows, or widows with children, the Shakers at least guaranteed them good food and shelter— things they might not otherwise be able to have. In response to Em's question as to why the Shakers had to remain chaste, Miles ventured that male/female relationships could make life complicated. That gave Anna and Em another good laugh. Although Miles hadn't intentionally been trying to be funny, he saw the humor and laughed along with them.

Anna couldn't help thinking about the delicious sexual tension that must have occurred within the Shaker communities, though she didn't voice that.

Em reminded them of the spiritual aspect of the community—not that piety was especially her strong suit, either.

They brought raspberries with whipped cream and coffee back with them to the living room. Em was keen on playing the "imagine" game that she and Miles had talked about earlier, the idea being that, based upon what they knew, they could speculate on the possible subsequent directions—or trajectories, as Miles would call them—in the lives of Luke and Tess.

"Okay, this is one thing I think," Em began. "Let's suppose Luke and Tess really liked each other, but something happened—like Tess went away to school and wasn't ready to get married. Luke gave up waiting, because he figured she wasn't interested. He married another girl and, when Tess found out, she was crushed and joined the Shakers. Okay, Gram, you make up something." Em was having fun with this.

"Let's see … Remember the letter that mentioned Abigail Bush— the suffragist relative? Supposing Tess joined up with Abigail and

Elizabeth Cady Stanton. It all seemed too radical for Luke, and they broke up. Later, heartbroken, she joined the Shakers." Anna dramatically put her hands to her heart. "And, one time when she was sick her father, Dr. Bleeker, drove over to Hancock to treat her." They turned towards Miles.

"I'm gonna go another direction. Mar says she and her sister remember hearing about someone from Griffin joining the Shakers. Maybe this Luke fella got religion and became a Shaker—or his little heart got broken when Tess turned him down and he joined up. Oh wait!—I've got an even better one. They were both Shakers! He was drawn to it after his first wife died in some kind of tragedy. When Tess went to find him and make amends—see if he was still interested—he was already living in Hancock. She became a Shaker sister just to be near him." Miles sat back smiling, pleased with his story.

Em was tickled with that one. She looked full of mischief. "Guess what happened next? Going with Miles' story, I'm thinking they both stayed a while and then decided to leave so they could get married and live together!"

"Well now," said Miles, "then they could live happily ever after—all's well that ends well."

Em was happy with that. Anna was pleased that Miles and Em were having fun together. Em told them she was going to continue doing research. Miles told her that, with a few more clues, she'd be able to make an accurate hypothesis or two.

After a while longer, Miles checked his watch and said he should be heading north. Anna walked Miles to the door. They made plans for her to help him get settled back in his cabin on Sunday.

Just before dozing off for the night, Anna thought about their early relative, Abigail Bush, and the suffragists. *Not very much was known about her, but plenty had been written about Susan B. Anthony and Elizabeth Cady Stanton. They had all worked so hard and so long for women's right to vote. Anthony and Stanton both died before 1920, when the 19th Amendment granted the right to vote to all U.S. women over the age of twenty-one.*

At some point, having worked for many years without succeeding, were they sustained by the faith that all their efforts in life would continue after they were gone—that they'd paved the way for future women?

In fact, how many generations had fought the currents of opposition before reaching that final destination? Surely, it had taken at least four generations to complete the journey. Her eyelids fluttered and then closed to dream.

1876
GRIFFIN

Luke walked along the road to Wells. He decided to follow one of the deer paths leading to the waterfall. It was midday in September, and all was quiet here but for the sound of rushing water. He wished to carefully study the letter that Tess had sent him. He knew it did not say the words he longed to hear. Nevertheless, he wished to parse the words carefully for signs of hope. He smoothed the creased sheet from its envelope and read:

Dear Luke,

I'm sorry your letters take so long to find me. I left my aunts in Boston early August. At the moment, I'm staying with Cousin Abigail in Rochester, helping Elizabeth and Susan gather materials for a book on the history of women's suffrage. Poor Elizabeth is not so well. She complains of aches and pains, her fingers are stiff with arthritis. Yet, she is full of fire to finish. I spend many hours jotting down her interesting notes. I do think it's to be a very important work. So, I must stay here until we've finished.

I've thought so much about your kind proposal. Believe me, if it were simply a matter of caring for you, I'd be with you in Griffin. Our last time together there made me realize how beautiful love combined with friendship might be. The potential of marriage is very appealing. I feel honored that you have those feelings for me too.

The part I sense you find strange, perhaps incomprehensible, is that I feel duty bound to help my older "sisters" in their mission, because the mission of women's suffrage is for me and all the generations of women that follow. The thought that Belle and I may get to vote in our lifetimes is so tantalizing. I beg that you try to understand my feelings.

I think, under the circumstances, it is probably unfair of me to ask again for more time, yet it seems that that is what I need. So, dear one, you are free to consider other prospects. Since we did not formally announce, there will be no embarrassment in that.

Most Fondly,

Tess

Luke read and reread Tess's letter. He thought, *yes, she may love me. Perhaps if I were to wait, she would someday marry me. On the other hand, it's hard to say how long it might be before women get the vote. Pa thought it likely they never would get it. Even if she would consider it when the blasted book was finished—didn't seem that was gonna happen very quick, either.* Truth is, he didn't care one way or the other if women vote. Sure, he would try to agree with Tess when they talked, but when he was with Pa and the guys he stayed pretty mum, though he saw her points, too.

I never would have let our physical relationship go that far if I didn't assume marriage. I imagined she might feel dishonored without marriage. Apparently, it's not like I thought for her. I wish she were here now so's we could talk. When we hold hands and I look into her clear blue eyes, everything makes sense.

Luke sat sad and brooding, and then started skipping stones in the pool below the falls.

"Hello, Luke. Nice day here by the river, isn't it?" she said.

"Oh—hello, Jessie. Yep, this is one of my favorite places," he said, turning to look her way. Jessie was a former classmate who now worked in the dry goods store.

"You goin' to the church supper tonight?"

"I'm supposing I might." He figured he would. It was a chance to get the latest news. There'd be time enough for him to consider sending another letter to Tess, and what that letter would say.

ANNA and EMMA

Anna and Em both awoke early and decided on a brisk walk around the park before breakfast. It was lovely to be there while the dew was still on the grass. Anna knew she'd miss Em's youthful, exuberant observations. Em asked if she'd be seeing Miles soon. Anna smiled and said it was likely she would. Em nodded, saying she liked Miles and Mary Lou. They enjoyed their morning stroll.

Dee and Jack arrived by 10:00 a.m. Dee hugged Em and was unusually demonstrative. She and Jack stayed for coffee and scones. They all treaded lightly on the Amy situation in deference to Em's feelings.

On the other hand, Em seemed to have moved on. She was more interested in telling her parents about her experiences lobstering with Aaron and their trip to Sabbath Day Lake. When Jack hesitantly mentioned that Amy might stay in Connecticut with her father for the coming school year, Em replied, "I think Amy might like that. She misses her Dad. She'll be safer there, too."

Anna wondered if Em was relieved to not have to worry about her friend's behavior—and the stress of keeping further impossible confidences.

Jack and Dee told Em they were taking her on a surprise family vacation to Yellowstone the following week.

"Cool!" exclaimed Em.

ANNA, MILES, MARY LOU

Sunday displayed a cobalt-blue sky, cloudless—the kind of sky perfect to write a smoky white message on. Anna threw sunglasses in her canvas bag. Along the way she stopped at the food co-op to pick up some grapes, dried fruit and creamy goat cheese as a treat for Mary Lou, hoping she'd guessed right in her choices. It was a good day for helping Miles get settled back in his cabin. Maybe he would like to go grocery shopping on the way. What about Mary Lou?—Should she take them both shopping? Actually, she knew very little about their routines. She plopped an Emmy Lou Harris disk in the car's CD player and listened to the beautiful, whispery, wavering voice—"Here I Am," "Cup of Kindness." Yes,—*we can stumble into grace.*

It was quickly decided that they would all go for groceries. Mary Lou clearly enjoyed the outing. She and Anna exchanged opinions on the freshness and ripeness of melons and bananas, *tsk-tsking* about the sparse produce in the small North Country market.

After they returned from shopping, Mary Lou insisted on providing lunch. She had made a chicken salad and brownies. In addition there were Anna's offerings from the co-op. Mary Lou poured tall glasses of sparkling Saratoga water with lemon, and sat in her large green Adirondack chair.

Miles declared it looked like a party. Mary Lou leaned her small frame back in her chair, hands folded at her waist, glass balanced on the chair arm. "Well, I must say, it does seem festive to be sitting here with the two of you," she said. "Miles, don't you think this is as good a time as any to show Anna your gift?" She smiled in her satisfied way.

Miles wasn't sure that this was the right time. He was still smarting from the turn of events with Ned at the shop and unsure whether he wanted to bring Ned to mind. His bruises had faded, but would he ever erase the stain of complicity he felt for having worked there? He started to object, then thought *what the hell* and brought the diminutive Eastlake rocker from the house and set it on the grass outside next to their chairs.

"Here 'tis," he said without ceremony. "A present for you—thought it would fit with your house, maybe in that rosy room. I … " he hesitated. "I bought it for you sometime back and stored it in Mar's parlor."

Anna was surprised and touched. "I love this chair! You must have seen me admiring it. And you are exactly right—perfect for my rose room." She knew her enthusiasm would go a ways in dispelling the lingering sulfuric cloud of Ned. She hugged Miles hard, leaving them both breathless and a bit embarrassed.

"Ahh … this does my old heart good," said Mary Lou. "A nice present like that rounds out the celebration." She beamed.

Miles wondered if she meant the chair or the hug. Mar was inscrutable on these things.

Miles and Anna took their time walking to the cabin. Anna insisted on carrying the large backpack with the heavier items. Miles could see no point in arguing. Truth be told, Dr. Nora had been firm about his limits.

The cabin showed at its best in the summer light. The warm wood tones blended into the leafy green; the neatly squared, fenced garden was robust with shoots and tendrils.

"I'm surprised it's not overgrown … Oh, you didn't," said Miles.

"We did. Em was adamant about that," Anna laughed. "I havta say, everything is growing well."

After lugging in the provisions and Miles' few clothing items, they went outside to bask in the sun's warmth.

"I've been meaning to say how much I appreciated your way of tackling Em's discouragement about unearthing enough clues—it was ingenious. How did you come up with that imagination thing?"

"True confessions—it's something I used to do when I realized I'd dead-ended on finding Una and my daughter Evie. I spent a lot more time looking for them than I'd let on when I mentioned them to you." He rubbed his hands through his hair, thinking. "You know, when someone disappears like that—young, healthy—and, of course, I was young, too … you're sure they're gonna turn up, maybe even call. After, say, a year goes by, you think to get serious and hire a de-tective, which I did. Then, five, ten, fifteen years go past and you still wonder. Are they alive? Dead?—Killed in a plane crash? Drowned? Leading a secret life? Mostly, I'd think of the bad things that could have happened—reasons they didn't contact me. So, eventually, you give up. But, at the same time, or near abouts, I realized I could just as well imagine them happy and doing okay—and so I did that." He paused again.

"So, do you still do that?" Anna asked.

"Nope, that's all in the past now. I was merely saying how I came to think of doing the imagination game with Em."

"Yes, but there's more technology to finding people now. What if you tried again?"

"The thing is, I don't really want to try again. Una was twenty-two when she left. Evie now would be in her forties. Both complete strang-ers by now—really." *I hate to say Anna's getting on my nerves, but, she's getting on my nerves.*

Anna could see that this was turning into a going-nowhere con-versation and pulled back. She reached for Miles' hand and smiled. "Nice weather we're having."

"Yep, and the past is the future is the past, too," he said squeezing her hand.

There were some monarchs in the garden fluttering from flower to flower, sipping nectar. Anna and Miles watched, idly entertained.

"Mar picked up some books on monarchs for me from the library."

"Yep, I noticed,—they weighted down the pack some. They sure are intriguing little creatures."

"Uh huh … You can borrow the books when I finish. You in any hurry today? Would you be thinking of staying a while?"

"I packed my toothbrush."

"Umm—that's a good thing. You'll havta go easy on my bruised ribs, though."

They laughed easily, having navigated some tricky shoals...

It seems that over a month has passed in a breath, or a flutter.

→←

Anna was especially busy at Bella Fiore for the rest of July and into August. They had a lot of weddings to contend with—moody brides, nervous moms. On more than one occasion Anna heard Stan tell a sniffling bride that pale pink roses were every bit as nice as peach-shaded tea roses and that, besides, this was not exactly on par with life and death. Anna wondered how he got away with it, but was relieved that he did.

Cara adored weddings and advising on bouquets and flower arrangements. They were busy enough the last week in July to hire Brianna's niece to help.

Em sent newsy postcards from Yellowstone and other points west. Jack sent a few too. Between the lines, his cards seemed to say that they were enjoying being a family without the usual work intrusions. Anna felt glad to think that. She knew she'd likely see them Labor Day.

Anna and Miles had been able to develop their own routines of sorts. They made plans together for weekends and occasionally midweek. Sometimes they included Mary Lou. This past Wednesday they'd all gone to a concert in Saratoga—the New York Symphony Orchestra playing Mozart. They loved it.

This coming Friday, Anna and Miles were planning to explore the Saranac Lake area. Miles said camping out would be fun. Anna said there were also some nice B & Bs she'd seen online. When she mentioned the weekend prospects to Cara, Cara had rolled her eyes. Anna sensed that her good friends and work cohorts were pleased that she was seeing Miles even if they gossiped behind her back.

She continued her weekly chats with Jenna, who suggested they all meet in the fall for a weekend in Boston. According to Aaron, Ned seemed to have slipped the line, maybe skipped the country. It was now considered a "cold case." Secretly, Aaron still had feelers out for Ned, should he try any internet shenanigans. *You just never knew when he'd slip-up . . . and perps often did.*

Ned, however, unbeknownst to them, was still lying low north of Plattsburgh and resisting the impulse to contact Amy. Sometimes he thought it might be possible to make contact with her though. He dearly hoped to scoot over the border to Canada soon but, being a resourceful survivor, he was comfortable in his temporary niche with Margo—who knew how to maintain her own advantage. Harvest season was just around the corner.

Amy, being a kid, had put all thoughts of the unfortunate incident between her and Ned behind her. Luckily for her, she was a good and consistent liar—once she figured out the best story. As a matter of fact, she was enjoying living in the 'burbs of Hartford with her father. Since, under the circumstances, she thought it best not to act up, she was actually having fun doing normal kid summer stuff, like swimming and kayaking. She liked the looks of her new school and had met a neighborhood boy who wasn't too nerdy.

The busy bees of summer are humming.

Anna was looking forward to their trip north to the Saranac region, even though she was hesitant about camping. They'd decided to pack the tent—but to keep an open mind in regard to more "civilized" accommodation.

When they arrived in Saranac Lake, Miles asked if she'd mind walking around the town a bit, which seemed agreeable on this fine summer day. He hoped to find some markers of his past.

"You know, Robert Louis Stevenson lived in Saranac Lake for a while. He came here to take the cure. They counted on fresh air and rest to cure TB at the time. Did you ever read *The Strange Case of Dr. Jekyll and Mr. Hyde*?" Miles asked.

"Well, maybe some version or other. The idea of grappling with 'good' and 'evil' is always intriguing." She thought that was most true in the abstract.

On a deeper level they knew that their recent experience with Ned had planted seeds of distrust for their own abilities to judge evil, should it come their way again.

Miles returned his attention to locating his childhood home. "Let's see, I know our house was on Church Street—don't remember the number, though." They continued walking. "It was past this corner. Of course, those new condos weren't here. Yep, it was one of those two white ones, though it was painted yellow at the time. It had been one of the early twentieth-century 'cure cottages' before my family rented it." He pointed to the large sunroom—he was satisfied.

"Does it bring back memories?" Anna said.

"Not so much—the old school more so," he reflected. Miles said he was glad for the chance to explore his old village—and, no, there had been no big revelations; it was just good to see it.

Miles located an agreeable campsite, so they went with that option. They set up camp, pleased that they'd been able to rent a canoe from a small marina upriver. Floating on top of water in boats hadn't been part of Anna's childhood repertoire of recreational activities.

"I think because we grew up in a city with Aunts Clara and Annie, we didn't get to paddle canoes. Well, we rowed boats on Washington Park Lake sometimes," she laughed. "What I'm saying is, I'm not going to be very good at this."

Nevertheless, by the time they debarked from the small launch site and paddled the half mile to their campsite, she felt comfortable in the prow of the canoe. Miles steered from the back.

Noting the location of the campsite, they continued downriver to where an incoming stream broadened to a bay of sorts. They rested and drifted in the still waters, knowing they'd have to paddle against the current back to camp. Anna took some photos.

She loved the feel of floating on the water, and said so. There was something appealing about the graceful pattern of long grasses echoing the current of the water, waving deep in the clear stream under the canoe. They were entertained by a family of ducks and startled a great blue heron, who squawked before flying a broad arc to distant tall trees. A monarch was balanced on purple pickerel weed—certainly not an unusual sight this time of year as they were beginning their seasonal migration south.

The trip back was harder. The current was not fast, but swift enough to push back. Anna thought going with the current was far more pleasurable.

They spent some time swimming and floating after the paddle— very refreshing. The campsite was in a cove, allowing for riding the river current downstream after swimming upstream a ways, and then detouring to the calm waters of the cove below.

Miles built a fire at nightfall. The shadows wavered and flickered. Anna saw two animal eyes glowing beyond the brush. They joked about telling ghost stories. Anna brought up the subject of "Dr. Jekyll and Mr. Hyde" again.

"Could bears or coyotes attack us while we're sleeping?" she asked.

"Not very likely—they're mostly curious. But, that's why we have the metal food canister—and that's why it's stored away from us. Also, that's why we didn't cook anything. Hope you didn't mind the spare fare. I guess I was a little overzealous about the low impact thing."

"I wondered about that—thought you were putting us on diets. I'm already looking forward to breakfast. Good thing the place is nice and you're such good company," she said.

Anna repositioned her back on the log. "The river has caught my fancy," she said. "I've been thinking about all the water images we use in language."

"Such as …?"

"Oh, like "deep thoughts," "ebb," "flow," "awash," "washed up," "taking a spill," "drifting through life," "floating along," "swimmingly—"

"Uh huh—well, we are water, mostly. What is it, 80 or 90 percent? Must always be in our subconscious, ya think? " Miles said. He thought, *Yep, just skins of fluid tethered to rickety frames. It's a wonder so many reach their three score and ten.*

They watched the fire a while. Miles stoked it well before they entered the tent and crawled into sleeping bags.

During the night Anna was awakened by the rustle of tent flaps, and then pelting sounds on top that grew to sheets of rain.

But the stars were out earlier, she thought. *Was this expected?* Miles was awake, too. She could tell by his breathing.

"Let's see," he said, "'torrents of emotion,' 'cloud buster,' 'washout,' 'flood of relief' …

"Miles, what should we do?" She was uneasy in the storm. It was dark. They were isolated.

"Go back to sleep, I guess. Do you want to share my sleeping bag?"

This is cozy, she thought; drifting back to sleep. Will the storm pelt the butterflies to death? It would seem so. Still, she slept.

The rainstorm had passed, and the morning was innocently sunny. They opted to let the tent dry while they went to a diner in town for breakfast. Their clothes were a tad damp, but no matter—it was a warm August day. By the time they paddled the canoe to the boat launch and hiked back to the campsite, they were at midday—time to pack up and leave. They agreed it had been a pretty spot to camp.

"Next time we go away we'll try a B&B," Miles said.

"We'll see," said Anna, noncommittally.

Mary Lou was pleased to get an e-mail from Emma. Apparently, the little reference that she had found in the *Adirondack Herald* archives about the Girard boy going to visit the Hancock Shakers had thrilled Emma. She also sent Emma a link to a Web site called "Monarch Watch." Emma wrote back saying she knew that Mary, Miles and Gram were becoming obsessed with the little butterflies.

Mary Lou thought, *I suppose it must seem that way.* She zipped a note back to the effect that old ladies needed hobbies, too.

Mary Lou found the site fascinating. She was rereading about the process of tagging monarchs when Miles and Anna came to the screen door. She waved them in from her computer desk.

"Come over here. Pull up a chair—you are *not* going to believe this."

The Web site described how you could work with the organization to tag monarch butterflies. They showed you how to do it and supplied the tags.

"By golly! We *are* going to do this! Just imagine—you put the little tags on and send them on their merry way. Later, if someone finds one, they know right where it came from!"

Mar sure seemed animated. "What's this 'we' about?" Miles asked quizzically.

"Come now, you can hardly expect an old woman to run around her yard catching 'em. The thing is, they're already plentiful in the garden this season. It would be a breeze for *you* to do the catching. Anna and I'll do the gluing."

"Well, I suppose after all you done ..." he laughed amiably. *Then again*, he thought, *after all the reading and talk about monarchs that me and Anna have been doing, it is an appealing idea.*

Anna marveled at how tuned in and thoughtful Mary Lou was. "Count me in," she said.

In a matter of days, Miles had helped Mar Lou catch and tag four butterflies. First, they had driven north of Speculator to learn the process and get the tags. A young blond woman, Harriet, with a baby said that she had been tagging for three years now. She was so intense and knowledgeable that they felt less compulsive and silly. Harriet wished them good luck. "There are a few fields of milkweed on the River Road past Lake Pleasant—you can try there in a pinch," she said. She hitched the baby on her hip and waved good-bye.

Come Friday afternoon, when Anna told Cara and Stan that she was leaving early to go catch butterflies, they didn't even try to hide the snickers. Then Cara impulsively hugged Anna, and she and Stan waved as Anna turned to say good-bye at the front door of the shop.

I made good time—lucky to beat the traffic, she thought, pulling into Mary Lou's driveway.

And there they were, heads bent over the garden table looking at— something. They didn't even raise their heads when she approached.

"Jesus, Mar—I'm all thumbs here." Miles looked perplexed. The monarch had looped out of his grasp. Looking up at Anna he smiled and said, "Hi." Mary Lou nodded and smiled, too.

"My old fingers still have the knack," she said. Anna noted Mary Lou's small hands were shapely, though she claimed a touch of arthritis. There was one fluttering monarch left in the net. Miles and Mary Lou coached Anna through tagging it.

"It seems so delicate and fragile—hope I haven't hurt it," she said, watching it falter and then fly.

Since they had released all the butterflies for the moment, they relaxed in the lawn chairs and chatted. It was warm and humid. Miles pulled the chairs into the shade, relieved he had finished the task of watering Mar's garden before the heat of the day.

Mary Lou always picked up the local gossip on her forays to the town library.

"Helene, the librarian, tells me a woman approached Charlie, the landlord of the antique shop building with an eye towards opening the shop or buying the inventory. He said she was a nice-looking, Native American woman from somewhere up north. Course that Ned fella still holds the lease – paid up 'til October, says Helene"

"Well, the town needs businesses on the main street. Hope Charlie gets a taker in the fall—don't think Ned will chance coming back," Miles said. *You can go to the bank on that one.*

After a little more languorous chitchat, Miles and Anna said their good-byes. Mary Lou cheerfully walked them to Anna's car.

The heat was intense. Anna declared that it must be near ninety degrees. It was less than a mile to the cabin, but they were sweating profusely by the time they reached the door. Miles suggested that they take a swim once she had placed her pack inside. They set out on the dirt path to the river with two towels and water bottles.

Anna was reticent to swim nude. Miles thought she was merely being modest, but the truth was that she knew women of a certain age could hardly expect to find their bodies flattered by harsh sunlight. She thought she'd set him straight and tell him just that.

"Yeah, but I don't wear my specs in the water—for that matter, neither do you," he replied. He swam next to her. "You are a nice-looking woman, you know," he said and smiled, "even with my glasses. I've probably never thought to mention that."

"Thanks, but for the record, I wasn't fishing for a compliment. I've gotta say, swimming on this hot day is a brilliant idea."

Anna was freshly amazed at the freedom she felt, languidly kicking and breast-stroking unclothed through the cool waters. It really was 'freeing' being unencumbered by a sodden swimsuit. She supposed the sensation was akin to flying – limbs suspended, hovering gracefully above the rocks and sand.

They stayed in the water for the better part of an hour swimming, floating, sometimes sitting with their backs against the large boulder in the shallows and just talking.

Miles told Anna about Mar's proposal that he stay in her house while she visited her sister Josie in Florida for the winter. Mar said she'd wanted to go for the past two years, but hated leaving her house to the varmints and the elements. The idea was that he'd move in and keep things safe and tidy while she was gone.

"Are you gonna do it?" Anna said.

"I'm seriously considering. I've been promising to paint some of her upstairs rooms. I could do that best while she's away. Then, there's the advantage of having use of a phone and computer—"

"And—?" prodded Anna.

"And, we'll see what we see," said Miles, his brows slightly furrowing.

Eventually, they felt chilled and exited the water. They toweled off and put on shorts and t-shirts, and walked up the path to the cabin, feeling cool and relaxed.

They decided it best to remain inactive because of the heat, and instead brought their books to chairs in the shade. The golden twilight was seeping through the leaves. The backlit greens were in their glory.

"What a beautiful place this is—magical," said Anna. "This reminds me—I've been meaning to tell you about Genoa and the symbol of the griffin. Genoa, Italy, that is."

Genoa and the Liguria coast held personal meaning for Anna, though her reveries most often took her to the Tuscan landscape, which, after all, had been her home.

Miles looked up from his book with interest, one finger holding the page place.

"The griffin is a special symbol in Genoa, kinda magical too" she said. "You can see it carved in the nooks and crannies of buildings everywhere. It's a legendary creature, of course, usually depicted with the body of a lion combined with the head and wings of an eagle. Actually, it's a scary, fierce-looking creature symbolizing divine power, military courage and intelligence."

"So, why did they choose that symbol?" Miles wondered.

"They say the Genovese adopted the griffin as their city's guardian sometime between the end of the Middle Ages and the beginning of the Renaissance. During the expansion of the Republic of Genoa, the image of the griffin spread like wildfire. The mystical beast was placed on the city coat of arms and even flown on ships' flags. It's still on flags." Anna paused.

"It sounds like a protective creature." Miles said. "Kind of a mythical good omen, ya think?"

"Could be." Anna nodded.

"Well, I could see the sense of carving it as a good luck charm around here" he joked. Anna laughed. "Oh, and one more thing—the griffin is also a symbol of the sanctity of marriage, because the myth holds that griffins are monogamous. It's said that the legendary creature's fidelity is so strong that, if a griffin's mate died, he or she would remain alone to forever mourn their lost love. Fascinating, huh?"

"Yep, it is an interesting symbol alright"

"You know, the funny thing is that I've known this since my days in Italy, but the memory just popped into my head a few days ago."

Miles thought about Anna's life in Italy. "Do you ever think of going back there for a visit?"

"Oh, sure—someday fairly soon I should visit Uncle Nunzio." Anna paused. "But you know where I'd really like to go, if I had my druthers?—to that town in Mexico where the monarchs roost and the Mazahua people pray for their arrival. They fill the trees like flowers. Now, *that* would be something to see."

Miles appeared to be thinking, unconsciously rubbing his chin. "The Mazahua think of the Monarchs as embodying the souls of the dead. That's why they offer up prayers." He paused. "You're talking about the Michoacan Valley, right?"

"Unh, huh" Anna said.

"Well then, I think we should go there."

"You do?" Anna's eyebrows rose as she turned towards him, smiling.

"Yep, I'm guessing October would be good. Course I haven't flown in awhile. We'll have to figure out flights and such—then we'll see what we will see."

And so, he thought, a new trajectory was being subtly recalibrated by the imagined orange glow, roosting in the far away oyamel firs of Cozumel.

Finding Griffin, Barbara Delaney's first novel, is set in the Adirondacks, Albany region, and on the New England coast. Though the novel is, of course, fiction, it was inspired by walks in the woods near Griffin— a long since vanished nineteenth century mill town.

Barbara Delaney has previously co-authored three works of nonfiction with Russell Dunn - *Trails with Tales: History Hikes through the Capital Region, Saratoga, Berkshires, Catskills, and Hudson Valley* (Black Dome Press, 2006), *Adirondack Trails with Tales: History Hikes through the Adirondack Park and the Lake George, Lake Champlain & Mohawk Valley Regions* (Black Dome Press, 2009), and *3-D Guide to the Empire State Plaza and its Collection of Large Works of Art* (The Troy Book Makers, 2012). Delaney has written a range of articles for magazines, and also does presentations on a variety of historical subjects for museums, libraries and historical societies.

She is a New York State licensed hiking guide who leads treks through natural areas with a particular emphasis on history. For the past ten years she has conducted history-oriented hikes in the Adirondacks, Catskills and Berkshires.